TOY CHILDREN

I might as well be talking to a cat . . . But the cats are strange here, too. Alvin's kitten isn't getting any bigger. Neither is Alicia's. In fact, I've never seen a grown cat or dog anyplace in Jamay. It makes me wonder if they're just . . . toys.

Maybe all of us are just toys. We're not just children, we're toy people. In fact, *everything* is a toy in Jamay. We got toy Bibles, and a toy library, and a toy school. Nothing is serious. Everything is a plaything.

I guess I'm just a big toy, too.

I got things figured out now. Jamay Lake is a place for a bunch of nutso people and the doctor is watching all of us, and someday he is going to kill us all, or something. That's my theory. Something's really wrong with this place.

I got to get out of here.

HAUTALA'S HORROR—HOLD ON TO YOUR HEAD!

MOONDEATH (1844-4, $3.95/$4.95)
Cooper Falls is a small, quiet New Hampshire town, the kind you'd miss if you blinked an eye. But when darkness falls and the full moon rises, an uneasy feeling filters through the air; an unnerving foreboding that causes the skin to prickle and the body to tense.

NIGHT STONE (3030-4, $4.50/$5.50)
Their new house was a place of darkness and shadows, but with her secret doll, Beth was no longer afraid. For as she stared into the eyes of the wooden doll, she heard it call to her and felt the force of its evil power. And she knew it would tell her what she had to do.

MOON WALKER (2598-X, $4.50/$5.50)
No one in Dyer, Maine ever questioned the strange disappearances that plagued their town. And they never discussed the eerie figures seen harvesting the potato fields by day . . . the slow, lumbering hulks with expressionless features and a blood-chilling deadness behind their eyes.

LITTLE BROTHERS (2276-X, $3.95/$4.95)
It has been five years since Kip saw his mother horribly murdered by a blur of "little brown things." But the "little brothers" are about to emerge once again from their underground lair. Only this time there will be no escape for the young boy who witnessed their last feast!

THE FOREVER CHILDREN

ERIC FLANDERS

ZEBRA BOOKS
KENSINGTON PUBLISHING CORP.

ZEBRA BOOKS

are published by

Kensington Publishing Corp.
475 Park Avenue South
New York, NY 10016

First printing: April, 1992

Printed in the United States of America

"Children's playings are not sports and should be deemed as their most serious actions."

—Montaigne, *Essays.*

William's Voice

I am not a bad boy.

Some people have said that about me, but I never really hurt anyone much. I don't want to hurt anyone.

It's just that people like to make up things about me sometimes. They say things that aren't true about me, because they're jealous of me and what I can do. Because I'm big. And I'm smart. And I know lots of things. Like words. And secrets. And how to twist the words and secrets around when I have to.

So, to be truthful, sometimes I do have to hurt people a little bit, but mostly they're other kids, so it doesn't matter that much.

My name is William. I am only a child. An only child too. My mother says I will always be her only child. She says one child should be sufficient for anyone, and that I am more than enough for her. I ask too many questions and I am way too smart. You see, there's danger in knowing too much and in being too smart.

Like the mothers say, "You're too smart for your own good." Somebody's always saying that to me.

That's supposed to be a moral lesson of some kind, I guess, though it doesn't make much sense to me. How could you be so smart it would be bad for you? Isn't that the point in having a brain? To become as smart as you can?

Sometimes I wonder when I see the way grown-up people act. There are many adults around me who seem to be too *dumb* for their own good. I know I'm smarter than they are, and they know it too. But I can't go against them. Not yet. I'm only a child.

Even though I'm not popular with other kids or the other mothers, my mother seems to like me in her own way.

She likes me as a child, of course, not as a human being. Not as a person. It's hard to describe the way I feel about the way she feels about me. My feelings are not easy to dissect. I don't know how I feel, or think about things.

I mean I don't know how feelings *work*. They seem to be uncontrollable things, sometimes, which can create themselves out of nothing. They come out of nowhere, like when you get really mad at somebody—like some kid who calls you a name, and even if the name doesn't hurt you—you feel like you have to hit him. That's the way feelings work.

My mother treats me like I will never grow up, like I'll always be her child, her "baby."

No, it's different than that. She treats me like I *can't* grow up, or that if I did something awful would happen, and it would make her very unhappy. She doesn't realize I can see in her dull eyes what she's thinking sometimes, and that I can understand it or, at least, I think I do. You see, she doesn't know how well I can think. Or the depth of my thought.

She doesn't even recognize that my brain is just as capable as hers, maybe even more capable, in grasping certain thoughts. She dismisses everything I do or say or think as the actions of a child.

She doesn't know that I really am too smart for my own good. Because she doesn't know how much I've learned in the past few weeks.

She doesn't realize that I know many secrets. I think I even know the Big Secret. I have *observed* things—not just seen—because to observe means also to understand what you see.

At least I think I understand. My world is not made for understanding, but I think I understand anyhow.

8

So I have observed. I have learned and, as a result, I *know*. I am twelve years old and I know things I'm not meant to know, because I have observed things I wasn't supposed to—by being in places where I wasn't supposed to be.

All the mothers are sick. I think maybe everybody who lives here—where I live—is sick, because we all have to get shots or take medicine. I think we are in some kind of leper colony. I read about them in an old encyclopedia at the library—where all the books are old and out-of-date.

Mother should pay closer attention to me, though. Because of what I know. Of course, she doesn't know what I know, because she's too involved with herself and the town.

If she did realize the extent of my knowledge, my awareness, my intelligence, she would tell the doctor about me, or one of the patrol men. She'd tell them without hesitating, even though I am her son, her only son.

Then something would probably happen to me.

I have many choices to consider. I have to be completely serious about my choices too. I won't be able to change them later.

I don't like living in a leper colony. So my choices are really limited.

Should I run away? *Can* I get out of this place? Where can I go?

Will I have to kill someone to get out of here?

I think my mother would let me get away with murder. After all, I am only a child.

PART ONE:

THE NAMELESS CHURCH

"Woe to the land that's governed by a child."

—Shakespeare, *Richard III*, II, iii.

Chapter One

You Can't Get There From Here

Jamay Lake, Indiana,
three months before William knew the secret:

There are many ways of looking at a town. Each way reveals different aspects; each way causes certain ideas to form in the observer's mind. Any way will change the town, because the act of observance itself can effect a certain degree of transformation—especially if what is being observed has escaped notice before. That is the type of reasoning supporting the theories of physicists who put forth the idea that subatomic particles come into existence as a result of being observed.

Perhaps that is true of everything in the world. The tree falling in the forest makes no sound if there is no one around to hear it; a city might not exist—its people might not exist—if there is no one around to see it or its inhabitants. Perhaps the world was not truly round until a great thinker saw it as round in his own perceptions of the universe.

The great question, of course, is always whether the universe has already been created or is continuing to be created, from nanosecond to nanosecond, by the people who live in it and reshape it with their constantly-shifting perceptions as to what the universe should or should not be.

Jamay Lake, a mere particle in the vast presumed-to-exist universe, either existed on its own or it did not, until a certain speculative moment when the *possibility* of it formed in the minds of various people who can be said maybe to have seen it, each in his or her own way. The vantage point of each observer shaped the town, while at the same time generated each individual's particular speculations.

The only problem remaining, and one that cannot be resolved, is whether the observers themselves existed. Fortunately, that problem does not need to be solved to establish the setting of a story—or a book.

Nothing needs to be real; nothing can be established to be absolutely true or untrue. Fairy tales contain as much truth as the most painstakingly researched tomes of history.

It's all relative to the observer.

Thus, Jamay Lake, for the sake of its own existence, had a definite shape, a certain smell, a distinct ambience, because it could be seen in a number of ways—

Consider the possibility the town could just form, just *be* there all at once, on a particular day when someone decided to observe it.

On this day, from the air, Jamay Lake resembled most of the small, rather ordinary-looking towns in the northeastern corner of Indiana. It was yet another of countless nondescript clusters of buildings and small houses set among the many square acres of farmland comprising most of the state. It was located about forty miles from the Ohio border.

Its geography was crisscrossed with narrow paved streets, many of which came to abrupt dead ends. There were bold splashes of orange, red, and yellow dotting the terrain at this time of the year, marking the autumnal display created by the many ancient trees in the town.

By comparison, Jamay Lake was not unlike some of the Amish or Mennonite settlements in that general area, since it had secluded itself from civilization and was as self-sufficient as those communities were, interacting with the outside world primarily to make money or to obtain those goods and services its inhabitants could not manufacture or supply on their own. However, it did not allow tourists to come in and witness its cultural

14

differences. Nor did it sell postcards with pictures of local landmarks. There were no landmarks of note nearby. There were no connections with any of history's great events. No one famous was known to have been born there.

Jamay Lake was not a primitive community dedicated to preserving the past as the Amish and Mennonite settlements were. It had its own modern clinic, a school, a few stores, a police station, and a church. It provided electricity, gas, and a public water supply and sewage system to its citizens. There was even a television station. It was a town unto itself, like a kind of out-of-the-way Disneyland, which, like that theme park, did not observe local state laws because it had its own laws and customs. No one ever called upon the county sheriff or even the state police. The town's own law enforcement sufficed for any trouble that might arise.

If an airborne observer were to swoop down closer to Jamay Lake, he might notice a few features of the town that set it apart from the other small towns in the region. This day, he would see few cars, if any, moving along its streets, not even pickup trucks, which are the vehicle of status in rural and agrarian communities; he would see no buggies such as the Amish would use to get back and forth. He might see a patrol car, but it would most likely be parked and unoccupied.

He would note that only one road ran into the town and no others left it. He would also spy Jamay Lake's most singular feature: a stone wall surrounding the entire town. If he were also so brave as to fly low enough, he would see the wall was topped with tangles of barbed wire, and if he could somehow lean out of his plane and touch that wire, he would find it was electrified. He might then find himself speculating if the wall were there to keep people out or keep people in. He would decide he might not want to know and pull up and fly away from the strange village, perhaps musing that in Indiana, a state in which many types of madness were allowed to develop and fester, a town with a wall around it was not that remarkable.

In any case, the message of the wall would be clear: stay away from this place.

A traveler in a car on the ground would become frustrated by negotiating the maze of back roads, many of them no more than dirt paths, that eventually connected with the single road leading into the town. Only a few people ever reached that point, and they were always lost since no one ever chose to go to Jamay Lake.

Such wayward travelers would ask at the main gate— the only opening in the wall—where they were and be informed they were lost and should go back where they came from. They would be told this by an elderly man whose task was to misdirect anyone who came near. The man resembled a troll and had a troll's disposition. He would make it sound as if their arrival at Jamay Lake was an impossibility, that it was difficult to get there from anywhere else. He would seem to be trying to confound the travelers deliberately, maybe even with malice, and he would make sure his directions took them away from the town. If they happened to get lost in another place, that was their tough luck. A troll didn't care what happened to stray people.

As the ground travelers drove away, they would naturally find themselves forming their own speculations about Jamay Lake, wondering if it was a prison or a bastion of one of the state's extremist groups—or perhaps even a secret government facility. There were several military bases in Indiana, after all, and not all of them were well-known. They might even worry that they had stumbled upon something that they were better off not knowing about and keep looking back over their shoulders, in case anyone might be following them.

They would be haunted by paranoia for several days after their encounter with the town and its gatekeeper. If they were extremely curious, they might later make timid inquiries of friends or acquaintances, perhaps even calling a newspaper office or a government information number, but instead of going to such trouble they would probably prefer to forget all about it. They would remember the troll, shudder, and go about their lives,

16

hoping never to get lost at that place again.

The omnipresent, omnipotent, sometimes omniscient observer who narrates all stories is the only type of person who could explore Jamay Lake's streets fearlessly, since he is only an invisible presence. He could add to the airborne observer's estimation that Jamay Lake did indeed seem very ordinary except for the presence of the wall. And he would investigate the odd characteristics of the town that made the ground travelers nervous.

His first impression would be that Jamay Lake was a town cut out of a children's story book, with quaint, older houses, pleasant tree-lined streets, and many cracked sidewalks, some of which bore the chalk outlines of hopscotch games. As he continued through the town, he would come across many kittens and puppies at play in the front and back yards of the houses. He would see tricycles, bicycles, and other evidence of children.

If he were to go inside any of the houses, he'd probably find many dolls, a surprising variety of them, most of them old-fashioned, though obviously not really old. He would not find dolls for boys, not even toy soldiers or sword and sorcery figures. Nor would he find toy guns.

In his further explorations of a typical house, he would be somewhat confused by the apparent absence of men. He would note the house was decorated strictly for female habitation, the only exception being the children's room, which, if occupied by male children, would be almost too obviously a boy's room, with all the likely paraphernalia a boy's room would have in a movie or stage set, including pennants on the wall, footballs and baseballs, and perhaps a few comic books. The room would seem like a snapshot from an old *Life* magazine, as if it represented a moment arrested in time—not a room where a child actually lived and was nurtured and grew and developed.

Everything in the house would be scrupulously clean, almost antiseptic.

He would file these observations in his mind for later contemplation, then re-embark on his stroll through the town. He would at first marvel at the wonderful clarity of the unpolluted country air, until he breathed it in more deeply and recognized the underlying scent of something burning, or something having been burnt recently, tainting it.

He would ignore the smell and go to examine the wall close-up, scrutinizing it with the eye of a detective, establishing it was as least as old as the rest of the town. He would note the presence of childish graffiti on the wall, and the crude likenesses of local personages drawn thereon, again obviously done by children. He would smile at the faces the children had rendered, perhaps remembering his own minor vandalisms of youth.

He would leave the wall and explore the small commercial area, actually only a single street, Warren Lane, where the clinic, the pharmacy, and a few other small enterprises were located. He might peep through the window of one of these buildings, but he would not see anything particularly interesting or disconcerting. He would wonder, though, why a whole store was devoted to selling dolls in what was such a small community, and why the pharmacy carried so much stock for the care and nutrition of babies.

Making quick mental calculations, the omniscient observer, whose ominiscience would now be somewhat in question, would realize the town had a very small population, two-hundred or even less. He would play with that figure in his mind, and wonder why such a small population needed its own police force.

After he made a complete tour of Jamay Lake, he would conclude it was a town with a secret, a secret big enough that it needed to be contained within a wall. He might even consider staying around to discover the secret, sensing it might make a good story.

He would speculate on the secret, but he would not guess it. He would only wonder where everyone was and ask himself why there were no children playing in the yards or on the sidewalks on what was a beautiful Indian Summer day in a town that evidently had many children among its inhabitants. He would eventually consider the speculations of the ground travelers, knowing how it was

18

still possible, even in the most advanced society, for covert societies to exist. He would rule out certain possibilities, based on his knowledge of the government and the state, but he would still append a very annoying question mark to the name "Jamay Lake" in his mind.

He would want to know more.

He would suppress his curiosity, though, and leave Jamay Lake, perhaps noticing on his way out that there was no cemetery nearby, even though just about every little town in the nation had its cemetery with ancient tombstones on which the names had eroded with age. There was not even an old abandoned graveyard to add a touch of atmosphere and mystery.

Perhaps he would consider the town no more than a curiosity, a strange hamlet in an out-of-the-way place. There were many such towns in the country.

But he would probably decide to explore no further.

He would be too glad to be out of the town, since after spending only a short time there, he would be overwhelmed by the feeling of claustrophobia pervading its environs. He would feel so threatened that he would decide not to write a story about the town, because it would mean having to return. Instead, he would continue homeward, somehow finding his way back along the convoluted roads without getting lost, sit down, and consult an Indiana map to satisfy the last of his curiosity about the strange village.

He would discover the town was not on the map.

Chapter Two

Dawn's Voice

Church is boring today. Of course, it's always boring, but Mom says we have to go, unless we're very sick. We don't get sick very often. I think it's because we drink lots of milk and eat special cookies with vitamins in them.

The minister talks about all these dumb things I don't understand—like "sin" and "redemshin" and "temper-tation." My mom and the other moms get down on their knees and say "Amen" a lot after what the minister says. Kids have to get on their knees too and some say "Amen," but I just pretend to say it, because I don't know what it means.

I don't know why we have to do all of this stuff, because I think it's dumb. It's supposed to be something about talking to God, and we close our eyes real tight, and God is supposed to talk back to us, but He never says anything to me.

Church is not too bad, because I have my doll Shirley with me. She has only one eye. The other one got broken out by one of the mean boys I don't like. He broke another girl's doll too by biting its foot off and spitting it out. His name is Eddie. Some day I'm going to get even with him—when I get bigger.

I put a patch on Shirley's eye and Mom says Shirley looks like a pirate which is some kind of bad man who carries a big knife. Mom showed me a picture of one in an old book. There used to be a lot of pirates who robbed people and stole women. And there were bad people who stole little kids, and they were "gypsies." That was all back in the old days, way before anyone was born.

Some of the boys must think they are pirates, because lots of them have knives, and they play mumblety-peg with them, which is a stupid game. A boy got his toe cut off with a knife playing that game, because he was playing with no shoes on. His name was Pete. Somebody saved his toe and they tried to sew it back on, but it didn't work and his toe rotted.

That's what I heard, anyhow.

Then Pete left town, I guess, because we didn't see him any more. His mom wouldn't say where he went. And nobody else knows either. Maybe his mom didn't like him any more without having all his toes.

Some other kids left town too, and none of them came back, either. I don't know why.

William tried to gross us little kids out by saying Pete's whole body rotted because of his toe and that they had to put him in a trash bag and throw him away.

William thinks we're dumb and will believe anything he says just because he's bigger than us. I know you don't throw people away, even if they're dead.

After the minister—well, I guess he's our minister, but he's also our doctor, and I don't see how he can be both, but Mom says lots of people can be more than one thing at a time—after the minister talks, we have to eat these little pieces of bread that look like somebody sat on them.

Then we have to drink something that's like grape juice only it's icky. The bread is icky too and tastes like it's made out of wood or paper. Mom says God wants us to eat the bread and drink the grape juice, and we don't want to make God mad. Somehow the grape juice is blood and the bread is flesh.

The minister calls it "comoonyin."

Mom says God wants us to do these things because we're "special" people. She says that means all of us, grown-ups and the other children like me too. I wonder why God would get mad at us if we're special, and I asked Mom about that, but she said I shouldn't ask too many questions. She says "enjoy your childhood," which is

21

another thing I don't understand.

I understand "enjoy" okay, but I don't know why I'm supposed to enjoy my childhood. I asked Mom if she enjoyed hers, and she says she doesn't even remember it! Then she won't say anything else about it. She doesn't even have any pictures of when she was a little girl.

Sometimes, Mom gets mad and goes into the kitchen and eats a bunch of orange candy that's shaped like big peanuts. It has some kind of medicine in it, and kids aren't allowed to have it. I tasted some of it once, and it doesn't taste that good anyhow. When Mom eats the candy, she acts better and gets more happy. She also has some yellow pills to take.

I guess I must make her sick, because she takes the pills all the time. The other kids make their moms sick too, which is why they all go to the drugstore for pills. All the moms eat the candy, and most of them take pills too, which they get for free at the drugstore.

At night sometimes I hear Mom crying or making a noise like she is hurt. I got up once and went to Mom's room and she had the covers over her head and was making that hurt noise. I said, "Mom?" and she stopped making the noise and sat up and told me never to come into her room without knocking first.

So I don't do that any more. But I still wonder why she sounds like she's hurting sometimes when she isn't.

I wish I had a brother or sister like some of the other kids, then I wouldn't have to worry about Mom so much. I asked Mom why she doesn't get me a brother or sister, and she said she can't and that I don't need a brother or sister because I have lots of friends, anyhow.

But it's not the same thing. I don't have anybody to talk to at night or play with after dark. Except Shirley. She has a lot to say, but she only says it to me. Sometimes, I think Mom doesn't like Shirley, because she talks so much. I'd like a kitten or puppy, but Mom's "lergic" to animals.

Sometimes in church we sing these old songs called "hims," which are about God and Jesus and the "rocker ages." I know Jesus was God's little boy, and when he

22

grew up he did a lot of things people can't do nowadays. He was like a real magician. The minister said he could walk right on top of water. And he could make dead people come back to life, so they weren't dead any more. I didn't know anyone could do that. But Jesus could. It says so in the Bible.

Jesus was a "special" person too.

Everybody we talk about is special and everybody we know is special. I wish I knew what "special" means. I looked it up in our dictionary and it didn't make any sense the way it's written in there so I asked William if he knew what it means.

William is a big boy who lives in the house down next to where Alicia and Alvin live. Alicia and Alvin are twins, but not alike, because Alicia is a girl and Alvin is a boy. They have different hair colors. They are the same age as me, which is ten.

William is twelve, I think. He's the smartest kid in Jamay, which is short for Jamay Lake. He knows lots of big words, but he doesn't say them around us little kids a lot, because we ask him what they mean, and he says he doesn't have time to explain what they mean, and he says he doesn't have time to explain everything to everybody. And I think that's silly, because everybody has time to do what they want, if they really want to do it. We don't have to go to school *all* the time.

So I kept asking William what "special" meant, and he told me it was a word grown-ups use when they want to act like they love you when they really don't.

I still can't figure that out.

William says nobody loves us, and that's a big lie because Mom loves me, and all moms love all their kids. It's a rule. One of God's rules, and one of Jesus' too, because we sing that him called "Jesus Loves Me" all the time, and the minister says we're all loved by each other.

Sometimes I think William might be crazy, no matter how smart he is.

Yesterday, I was watching William and some other boys, and there was a big fight. William is hard to play with, because he's always so serious about everything

23

and doesn't know how to have fun. I wish he'd go away sometimes, but he's bigger than the rest of us and we can't make him go away. He does what he wants to, and even his mom can't make him go away.

William won't hit a real little kid, but he doesn't like Kevin who is almost as big as he is and maybe just as smart. Kevin called William a dirty word, which I can't say, because Mom told me never to say dirty words. But it was a real bad word.

William got mad and started hitting Kevin. Kevin hit him back. They they both started saying lots of dirty words, some of them I don't even know, except I could tell they were bad words. William is stronger than Kevin, so he hit him real hard and Kevin fell down. Then William picked up a big rock and got on top of Kevin and pretended like he was going to hit Kevin in the face with it.

Kevin looked like he was going to cry, but he wouldn't cry because he's a boy and the other kids would call him a big baby if he did.

I thought William was really going to hit Kevin with the rock, but then his mom came out of the house and stopped him. She grabbed him and pulled him inside.

It's too bad, because I never saw a person get hit with a rock, and I wondered what would happen to Kevin if William did hit him with that rock. Maybe they'll get in another fight again and next time William's mom won't stop it.

I know what happens if you hit a kitty or a puppy with a rock, because I saw Alvin do that once. His kitty bit him and he didn't like it, so he hit it with a big rock. Well, really it was a brick, which is almost as bad. Anyhow, he hit his kitty with the brick and its head mushed up, and blood came out of its ears. It was gross. Then the kitty wouldn't move.

Alicia started crying because she said it was *her* kitty, not Alvin's, and then Alvin cried too, because he knew the kitty was dead. So they took the kitty and put it in a hole in their back yard. Alvin put one of those toy Bibles in with it, the little Bibles they give us to read. Of course, no kid reads them, because the printing is too little and the words are hard to understand, but the minister says the Bible is something God made, so it's like having a piece of God with you all the time, if you carry it around like you're supposed to.

I don't know if Alvin ever got a new toy Bible. He was probably afraid to tell the minister what happened to the one he had before.

Alvin covered up the kitty and he and his sister were sad for a whole day. Then his mom got him a new kitty, or I guess it was for Alicia, because she was right—it was her kitty Alvin hit. The new kitty was a different color. It was kind of yellow with stripes, and the old one was gray and white.

So I wonder if William hit Kevin with that rock if he would mush up and stop moving and blood would come out of his ears. I'd like to see that. I don't like Kevin very much because he's always pinching me and making fun of me for being a girl. He does that to all the girls, even the big ones.

I tell Kevin I'm special just like him, and he just laughs and says girls can't be special.

William is going to hit him real hard some day. I just know it. I hope I'm there when it happens.

Everybody gets to stand up now, and we sing a couple of hims, and that means church is almost over. I know because the minister is getting up in his little box and opening his big Bible, the one that has all those pictures in it, and is going to give his last talk to us.

He says something about how moms are special and kids are special and it's the same old stuff he always says. But at least he doesn't talk very long.

Then he closes his big Bible and smiles and everybody gets up, and we wait till the minister goes and stands by the door, so we can talk to him on our way out of the church.

Today is a nice day, so we're going to have a picnic behind the church. Picnics are fun.

Shirley likes them a lot.

Chapter Three

Upon This Rock...

It was mid-morning on a Sunday, and the streets of Jamay Lake were uninhabited by people. Aside from the small animals scampering and playing in people's yards, the wind seemed to be the only thing stirring, causing multi-colored swarms of leaves to sweep through the town as they were gently torn from the trees' yielding branches.

Everyone except those who were bedridden by illness was attending church at the far eastern edge of town.

The church had no name. It was a tall, rather imposing white frame structure with a limestone foundation, perhaps a hundred years old, capable of holding all the town's present population. There was no sign out front with a clever religious motto. There was no lettering or decoration on the outside. Only the well-kept shrubbery attested to any reverence for the building and what it represented to its residents: not a church so much as a sanctuary, a place to be reborn mentally, and spiritually, if possible, but most of all a place to gather and reaffirm the basic tenets of belief that was the structure upon which the entire mind-set of the community was founded.

Inside the Nameless Church there was no cross above the altar. The old stained-glass windows depicting religious tableaux had been removed and replaced with rose-tinted standard, square-cut panes. There were no pictures on the walls, not even a velvet Jesus. The pews were hard oak, polished by decades of parishioners shifting their sermon-deadened butts on their surface. The ceiling was high and held aloft by a matrix of thick, solid hardwood beams. The main features that identified the interior as a church were the organ behind the pulpit and the presence of a man in a dark suit standing in the pulpit itself, preaching.

The man was not a minister, though he preached a fundamentalist brand of gospel that was an amalgam of many faiths. Still, the congregation regarded him as a minister as he stood there, and they took his words seriously.

The man whose current pretense was minister to an oddly unbalanced flock—all women and children—was in his early sixties, with hair that was still predominantly black. He was just under six feet tall, thin and deceptively frail-looking, though his arms and hands were very strong—as any child who had ever tried to resist him could affirm. His face was oblong, with a small chin in the center of which was a mole that had recently turned dark, so that it resembled a misplaced beauty mark from a distance. His skin was pale; his gray eyes watery; his nose a crooked chunk of gristle set slightly off-center in his face, for it had been broken twice. His eyebrows were bushy and almost met in the center, failing to do so by scant centimeters. His lips were thin, surrounded by purse-string wrinkles, and invariably dry. Overall, he was an ugly man, who was growing uglier with age, but his appearance had not deterred him from achieving any of his life's ambitions so far.

The man's name was Warren Hubert Barry, M.D.

When Warren opened his mouth, revealing a striking, perfectly natrual-looking set of dentures, he spoke with a surprisingly rich bass voice that always startled people the first time they heard it. It seemed too deep and resonant to come from such a slight man.

Today his sermon started out with the basics: sin, redemption, and temptation, underscored with a couple of practiced anecdotes about how sin had felled many a righteous person. Then he shifted from that rather

27

ominous note to one of joy in the knowing that God loved each and every one of them, even the greatest sinner among them.

Communion came next, then the singing of a few old-fashioned hymns, which Warren had chosen despite the sexist and militarist implications of some of the words. His congregation needed to cling to the older ways of believing, because that was what helped them to cope with the many troubles with which their lives had burdened them. For most of them, their roots were in the former ways of belief, and they needed reinforcement that this was the proper way by which to conduct themselves.

After the hymns, Warren opened his Bible, barely glancing at it, because he was not going to use it as his text. Instead, he closed by speaking on a favorite theme, that of how special the children were. This concept formed the basis of his gospel, and he had decided he couldn't address its importance too often, especially since he had noticed lately some of his flock were beginning to waver in their acceptance of that credo.

It wasn't totally their fault. He couldn't expect all of them to be as strong as he, or his wife Sondra, was. He couldn't expect them to be sustained solely by the dreams—that is, by *his* dream. He had to give them a foundation on which to build their faith, a rock upon which to build their church.

Jesus had Peter; Warren had only himself and the dream.

That's why he had planned the picnic today. It was because he felt the women needed more social activity, such as a special event to reaffirm the promise of the dream.

The picnic would serve a second purpose as well; it would give him the opportunity to observe the people who had entrusted themselves to his leadership from a clinical standpoint, to watch for signs of stress and suppressed sexuality. He had to be very critical now—for the dream was beginning to erode in a way he had never anticipated—and he had as yet to formulate a strategy to check its erosion.

He said his final words, blessed the congregation, acknowledged their chorus of Amens and closed the big Bible, signalling the end of the service.

Then Warren stood by the door to interact with his people as they passed out of the church. He smiled at each one of them, hugged some of them, and kissed the babies.

Just like a politician, he thought to himself. Yet he wasn't the first person to mix religion with politics—and propaganda. It had become part of the American way of life.

Chapter Four

William's Voice

I hate these stupid picnics. I hate "fellowship" as old Dr. Barry calls it when he's pretending to be the minister. It means having to be friendly with people you don't really like. It's a phony thing. I don't like anybody here, except Dawn and Alvin and Alicia, because they're little kids who don't mess with me. They're about the only kids who don't make me nervous.

There's something strange about this picnic. For one thing, it seems to me like there aren't as many of us children here. Last time, at the end of August, I'm sure there were more. There *should* be—unless they're all sick.

But *all* the mothers are here. The only adult missing is Barry's wife. She's been out of circulation for a while, sick or something, I guess. Nobody will talk about where she is or what's wrong with her. Maybe nobody knows.

I wish I knew how many children there are supposed to be. It's my own fault for not keeping track. And there's nobody I can ask, because I can't trust anybody, not even my mother.

I know Pete's gone, though. Totally gone. Disappeared. And nobody will talk about it. Nobody will talk about anything except what they feel like talking about, and they don't talk about feelings, either. Not their real ones, anyway.

There sure are a lot of screaming babies, though. Too many. Why don't they leave those babies at home?

I know some of the other children are like me. I mean they're not very happy here. They're not happy with being "special" or with much of anything that goes on here. I wish I could talk to them about things and maybe about what we should do, but nobody likes me that much, either.

They're afraid of me, I think.

I can tell the other *boys* don't like the whole deal, even if they won't say so. We're all thinking the same thing—why do we have to do all these stupid things? Why can't we just run around on Sunday and play or at least just watch TV?

We sure don't learn anything at church. There's not even a Sunday school. I wouldn't like Sunday school much, either, but it would be better than listening to Barry.

I asked my mother this morning why we don't ever go anywhere else, and she gave me the same old answer—that we can't afford to go anywhere on the money she makes as a clerk at the doll store. I ask her why she doesn't work somewhere else where they pay more money, but she says it's because she's not capable of getting another job, and besides we should be thankful for what we have.

I like that. Be thankful.

For what we have.

What do we have, anyhow?

My mother says we have happiness and a nice house to live in and that's paid for by the doctor. I ask her why the doctor gives us a house and she just ignores me. I found out, though, that everyone lives in their houses for nothing. It doesn't make much sense.

It's like the doctor is keeping us as pets, or something.

Our television only gets three channels. One channel is for the mothers and it's mostly old movies and soap operas. The other two channels are nothing but cartoons and old kiddie shows in black-and-white, and some dumb old movies for kids, like *Bambi* and old Westerns. I mean that's *all* they have on them—we don't even get any news. Dumb. I guess it's better than no television at all—

31

and better than church.

And we can't have radios. We can have tape players, but the only tapes we can legally get are at the Jamay General Store, and they're mostly old stuff. I heard someone say they were going to sneak some new music into town, but I haven't found out yet if that's really going to happen. I know it's possible, though, because Pete—before he disappeared—showed me this little comic book he had with dirty pictures in it, people having sex and doing other nasty things. He kept it in his toy Bible. I wonder if his mother still has that Bible. I'd like to see those pictures again.

I asked Pete how he got that comic book, and he said it was sneaked in by somebody, but he wouldn't tell me who. I wish Pete's toe hadn't rotted him. He was a good guy. They didn't even do anything to the other kid who cut his toe off—I guess because it was an accident.

I just noticed the patrol men are here—all six of them—Barry's cops. That's what they really are. They're strange. They all got that look in their eyes, like the mothers usually get—like their brain is on another planet or something. They don't seem to be looking at anything, but they're *watching* us all the time. You can be sure of that.

I'd like to give them something to watch. I have some matches. Maybe I'll think of something.

The best thing about this picnic is dessert. There's lots of pie and cake, and orange peanut candy, which all the mothers like. In fact, it's just for the mothers, and we kids aren't supposed to eat it, but I swiped a piece once. It had a real bitter taste, sort of like alcohol with pepper in it and lots of sugar to try to cover up the other stuff.

Old man Barry is acting strange today too. He's watching everyone, though he's trying to pretend he's not. He's also keeping his eye on one of those patrol guys.

You see, that guy was at the last picnic, and his eyes weren't burnt-out-looking like they were supposed to be, and he tried to cop a feel off one of the mothers. She screamed and I thought everyone was going to pee their pants right there. Barry went half-crazy. He got the other

32

patrol men to take the guy down to the clinic. Next time I saw him, his eyes were like marbles—nothing in them at all. I wonder if Barry fried his brain somehow. He's a real zombie, today, so Barry doesn't have to worry. That guy is *not* going to touch any more mothers' boobs.

Dr. Barry doesn't eat much. He never does at picnics, or even at the birthday parties. I guess that's why he's so skinny. He's stronger than he looks, though. When he gives you a shot, you can't get away, and now, because of something or other, all us kids over ten have to get shots every month. They hurt too.

I heard Dr. Barry and his wife had to hold old Kevin down to give him his last shot, because Kevin is a big pussy. I think old Barry likes to see us squirm. Me, I just let them poke me, and don't let on how much it hurts.

I won't let them make me cry.

Chapter Five

Women Who Like to Watch

Everyone was watching William. At least that's how he felt as he hovered around the edge of the churchyard, standing among the smaller children who were already playing games.

His mother's eyes were locked on him; he could feel their penetrating gaze shifting warily with his every movement. Warren Barry was paying unnecessarily close attention to William as well, and since Barry was observing the boy's every movement, the patrol men kept him in their sight too.

William frowned at them. The combined power of so many eyes on him made his skin feel crawly; it was like they expected him to explode.

Why only him? he wondered. Kevin was known to get into trouble. So did some of the other kids, even the girls. Why did they have to pick on him in particular?

Did they think by watching him so closely they would stop him? Stop him from what?

What did they expect of him?

Then, as suddenly as the wind shifted, everyone looked away from William, and the picnic continued.

William huddled under a tree, allowing a long sigh of relief to escape from his lungs. He understood how deliberate their actions had been, and that made him angry.

He decided he ought to give them something to watch.

34

*   *   *

When the wind changed direction, one of the patrol
men relaxed, as he realized the doctor's attention was
turned elsewhere. He had been tensed up for the last
hour or so, channeling all his energies in appearing to be
a zombie.

He couldn't let the doctor know that the drugs he had
administered were not having the desired effect—at least
not consistently. Today, for example, he had only to look
at a woman to become semi-aroused. He had to dwell on
visions of ugliness and pain to prevent his condition from
becoming obvious. So he thought about some of the
things he had seen at the clinic.

The patrol man's name was Paul Daniels. He was
thirty-nine, stood six-foot-one, and possessed a well-
developed, trim and muscular body. His hair was close-
cropped and prematurely gray. His face was square, his
forehead low, his eyes dark brown; he wore a neatly-
clipped moustache which was mostly gray, but streaked
with reddish-brown strands that recalled the color his
hair had been only a couple of years ago. He wore the
standard Jamay Lake Patrol uniform: light beige with
dark crimson stripes along the outside seams of the
trousers, complemented by a brown trooper hat and
black boots. Patrol men had access to weapons, but
carried none in the normal course of duty, except for a
short billy club in a loop on their belts.

Some of the men carried more lethal weapons hidden
on their persons. Dave Stillwell had a small .38 strapped
on his left calf; Bob Gale had a switchblade; and Paul
himself carried a short-barrelled .22 automatic tucked
inside his shirt behind his belt.

Paul was the only patrol man who had formerly been a
prison guard. He had spent eight years in that capacity at
Michigan City, until he could no longer endure the stress
and the daily imminent possibility of being killed or
maimed by one of the inmates.

He had been divorced twice, had a lot of child support

35

to pay, and felt, at age thirty-nine, he was on a treadmill in Hell, doomed forever to run in place, getting nowhere.

Then he had answered the blind ad in a local newspaper which solicited the services of "a man experienced in law enforcement, to work in a special minimum-risk environment."

He didn't expect much when he answered the ad by mail, but a week later, he was called by Warren Barry. He had to go through psychological testing and two or three interviews before he got the job, not to mention the most thorough physical he had ever undergone, but he was accepted.

At first, he couldn't believe how lucky he was to have found the job. It was so easy, and it had a great advantage over his previous position. In Jamay Lake he had, for all legal purposes, just disappeared. No more child support to pay. No more bill collectors hounding him. He was hiding out there—like everyone else in town, he supposed.

The good doctor gave him everything—a place to live, food, and sanctuary; all he had to do was protect and serve this out-of-the-way community the doctor had established. He didn't even mind taking the solemn (but rather silly, he thought) oath of secrecy, which if broken, would result in something drastic happening to him.

The only thing the doctor had forgotten about in his absurd little colony of women and children was sexual urges, which didn't go away.

Paul was the one who had grabbed a handful of breast one day, because he just couldn't resist. As a result, all the guards were being forced to take drugs to suppress the effects of their hormones.

They just weren't working for Paul.

The smell of the old churchyard grill filled the air. It was made of bricks and its interior now glowed with over thirty pounds of red-hot charcoal. Bonita, the organ player, started arranging hot dogs and hamburgers on the grill. She was a chubby woman who always volunteered for any kind of cooking duty; it gave her a chance to sample the food and have extra helpings before the meal even started.

The yard was filled with long picnic tables to accommodate forty-odd women with their children and infants. Each woman had contributed a dish to the picnic, so there was quite a spread on the long serving table next to the grill. About half the contributions were various desserts. At each end of the table was a large bowl filled with the orange, peanut-shaped candy only the women were allowed to have.

There was a small gazebo in the churchyard too. Inside, a music system was set up, playing rather forgettable instrumental tunes, mostly voiceless renditions of old standards, changing occasionally to a tune by the Beatles, or Simon and Garfunkle. The volume was low; the music was meant to be soothing and unobtrusive, so its subliminal messages would be more effective.

Satisfied that the picnic was going to proceed well, Warren circulated among the women, some of whom were already sitting down with appetizers, others standing off in little groups chattering. He exchanged pleasantries with most of them, making mental notes concerning his estimation of their well-being and general attitudes.

On the whole, they seemed to be having a good time; most of them were apparently happy as ever. Of course, so far, only a few of them had lost children. He had yet to decide what to do about that problem. He had contrived to keep the slight decline in population a secret.

It was yet another thing he hadn't considered in structuring the society of his dreams.

William watched as Dawn and a group of smaller children played Ring-Around-The-Rosy, London Bridge, and other mindless children's games. He quickly became bored and wandered over to the serving table to check out the spread. He was very hungry, since he'd had no breakfast, and his stomach was starting to growl. But they couldn't eat until the hot dogs and hamburgers were ready. He stole a handful of corn chips and grabbed a cup of punch to take the edge of his hunger off, then strolled back to the farthest corner of the churchyard, which was also the inside northeast corner of the wall.

He stood there a few moments, not really thinking about anything as he munched the corn chips and drank his punch. Then he noticed how the wind had gathered a great pile of leaves in the corner.

He smiled to himself, then walked away quickly, in case someone saw him and guessed his plan.

Sally Henderson and a group of other women had formed their own elite clique, based primarily on the fact that their children were six-to ten-years-old, which, they had all agreed, was the ideal age range for children—not too young to require constant attention and not so old as to present discipline problems—and undeniably cute.

The women had congregated at a table in the southwest corner of the churchyard, far enough away from the rest that they could talk about the other women without being overheard. By now, with the music and all the noise the children made, they didn't need to worry that much, but they still felt more secure by keeping a distance from the others.

Sally was thirty-three, a brunette with a slim figure. She had an odd scar under her left eye, which only her closest friends knew was the result of a severe beating by her former husband. "That stupid Wanda," she said, her hazelnut eyes shifting back and forth, "she has to clean loaded diapers all day long."

"All those stupid ones do," a woman named Myrna joined in. "How anyone can want to have an infant—well, all the time—I just can't understand it."

All the women at the table—indeed, every woman at

38

the picnic—were wearing ankle-length, light blue dresses with ruffled collars and sleeves, the ordained uniform for Sunday. Other days they would wear what they wanted.

"They're stupid, just like you said," Sally replied. "They might as well have kittens, the way they treat their children—like pets. I don't know why Dr. Barry puts up with them. Their little brats are always wailing too."

"Well," Myrna said wisely, "they wouldn't cry if their mothers would use the formula the doctor gives them. You know, some of those women are still actually breast-feeding!"

"Hmmph!" Carla, a black woman, interjected. "That's just plain nasty to have a baby chewing on your tits for three or four years."

"You're right," Sally said, flinching slightly at Carla's crude language. "They're just like cows. I got my Dawn off the breast and on formula just as soon as possible. Formula's better for them. And, in the long run, breast-feeding does make your breasts droop."

"Don't I know it," Harriet, the oldest woman of the group at forty-three, put in. "I wish I'd never done it."

The conversation would have continued along the same vein for the duration of the entire picnic if Brenda Stowe, mother of Pete, the child who had never come back from the clinic after his toe was cut off, hadn't approached the table. She was a tall, young blonde, under thirty, who had been in Jamay Lake less than a year, during which time she had made few friends.

She was carrying a bundle wrapped in a pink blanket close to her. "Hi," she said timorously, blushing at the same time; she was well-aware she didn't belong to their clique—and never would, but she seemed compelled to share something with them.

"Hi," Sally replied, her face registering obvious irritation at being interrupted. But when she looked up and saw Brenda with a bundle, her curiosity quickly replaced her disapproval. "What do you have in your arms, Brenda?"

"My baby," she said simply. "Dr. Barry couldn't save

my Pete, so he gave me a baby."

Carla snorted. "That's just what you need, a baby. We were just talking about how awful . . ."

"Shush," Myrna said. "Where'd Dr. Barry get you a baby?"

"I don't know. I guess someone didn't want her. I'm calling her Donna Marie. Isn't that a pretty name?"

"She's awful quiet," Sally observed.

"That's because she's such a good baby. She never fusses. And I just love breast-feeding her."

"Nasty," Carla spat.

Sally glared at the black woman. "Could we see her?"

Brenda's face turned ashen. "No. You'll breathe on her and give her something. Then she'll die, just like Pete."

"Just show us her face."

"No, no, no!" Suddenly, Brenda turned around and dashed across the churchyard, almost breaking into a run.

The women at the table exchanged curious glances. "I didn't know you could get a baby like that," Sally said at last.

The other women kept their thoughts to themselves.

The feasting had begun. Sharon Wesley insisted her son William sit across from her at the table. He agreed readily enough, and that made Sharon suspicious. The boy must be up to something.

For one thing, his eyes didn't have that dull gleam of weary discontent they normally evidenced. In fact, his eyes were bright; his face was almost jovial as he ate heartily. She was secretly glad to see him eat—he had been a picky eater recently, driving her to distraction with strange cravings for food that was difficult to prepare, then taking only small morsels of it.

Maybe, she realized, he was just testing her. Children of his age did that a lot. They tested their parents; they tested *all* adults to see what their limits were. Maybe William's discontent was nothing more than a typical

40

condition of youth.

She wished her son would behave. He was such a nice-looking boy. He had dark blond hair and dark blue eyes, and his face was a pleasant triangle with a fairly strong chin. His hands were graceful, slightly bigger versions of her own hands, and she had hopes he might be artistic, though all her attempts to get him interested in art had failed. He seemed to want to do nothing but watch television, listen to music, and occasionally read a book that wasn't required for a class.

Sharon sighed and munched on a piece of orange peanut candy. Its bitterness was as odious as ever, but the aftereffect she desired would be a blessing, making it easier to cope. She washed away some of the taste with a gulp of punch.

She ran her hand through her own hair, which was naturally a shade lighter than William's and continued to watch her son eat. He had said nothing since sitting down with her, and she, despite all her yearning to help him one way or another, had been unable to think of anything to say to him.

They had a lot to talk about together, but Sharon was unwilling to open up the sores their conversation always produced. The theme was always the same: William had been getting into too much trouble lately. Like when he almost killed that other boy, Kevin. Or when he had stolen a candy bar from the general store. Or when he simply just wouldn't mind her.

William had gotten too big, just as Kevin had. He was an inch taller than his mother, and he resembled a man just enough to have a physically-threatening presence.

Now Sharon wasn't sure what to do with the twelve-year-old. He was unruly as a teenager and a potential delinquent. He had begun to ask too many questions. He was dangerously unhappy.

It was her fault too. She should have told the doctor to stop him earlier.

William had two helpings of every type of food he

41

liked, then finished the meal with a piece of chocolate cake and a slab of lemon meringue pie. Then he excused himself, saying he was going to play with the little kids.

Sharon merely nodded. The orange candy was beginning to numb her preoccupation with the problems her son represented. That was okay with him. By the end of the picnic most of the women would be numbed out, and that would make it easier for him to do as he planned.

William went over to the playground area. Dawn was on the swing, and Alvin was pushing her higher and higher while she squealed with pleasure. She was clutching her doll under one arm, gripping the swing chain tightly with her free hand. It seemed she might fly out of the swing on every upward pass, but she managed to hold on.

William smiled wanly. He remembered a moment when he was about five or six and he still had a father. There was a day back then when his father had taken him to a park and it seemed he let him play on the swings all day.

He grimaced and blinked away the memory. He was too big for that sort of fun now. And he had no father.

After a few seconds, Dawn had Alvin stop her. The two younger children went up to William, both smiling.

"I ate a lot of cake and ice cream," Dawn said.

"Me too," Alvin said.

"That's great," William said dispassionately.

"Why don't you play with us?" Dawn asked.

"I'm too big."

"No you're not."

"I don't like kids' games."

"He's just an old poophead," Dawn said to her doll, "isn't he, Shirley?"

William stared at the eye-patched doll and winced. "Why don't you get a new doll—one with two eyes?"

"It wouldn't be the same as Shirley."

"They're already teaching you to be a mother," William said sarcastically.

Dawn tilted her head; the sarcasm was lost on her, though she sensed his tone of voice was judgmental.

42

"What's wrong with that?"

"Never mind."

"Look!" Alvin said, holding up the back of his left hand. "Freckles! I got freckles."

Dawn turned and grabbed the boy's hand, peering at the little brown spots closely. "You never had freckles before."

"That's nothing," William said. "The sun causes freckles."

"Oh," Alvin said, crestfallen by William's deflating the magic of his discovery. "I thought it was because I'm special."

William didn't bother to examine Alvin's hand. He spun around abruptly, glanced over his shoulder to see if anyone was following his movements and made his way to the corner of the wall.

Now that most of the feasting was over, the women were slowly starting to gather up their children. It was nearly three o'clock and the little ones especially were beginning to show signs of fatigue.

Brenda Stowe had stationed herself in the gazebo, where she had sat unnoticed throughout the picnic. She had never joined a group; she hadn't even eaten anything. Warren had not come over to talk to her, probably because he had no need. She was obviously a contented, fulfilled woman, holding her baby while she nursed it.

Sally Henderson saw her there now, though. She approached the gazebo, intent on seeing the new baby. Despite all her protestations about infants, she secretly wondered how she might get a baby herself.

She certainly couldn't acquire one the usual way.

Warren stood talking to the patrol men, giving them assignments for the rest of the day. Before he had finished giving his orders, the smell of burning leaves singed his nostrils.

Then he felt something hot touch his ear. He swatted at it and turned to see burning leaves blowing through the churchyard. Worse, the corner of the yard was on fire—a large pile of leaves was aflame, and they had touched off the dry grass. The airborne flaming leaves had settled on the paper plates in the trash drum, setting them afire, and the flames from that were rising high in the air. Then something inside the drum, perhaps an aerosol can, exploded and the trash drum toppled over, spilling burning rubbish everywhere. The wind helped spread the fire, carrying bits of the flaming trash throughout the yard.

Warren caught sight of various catastrophes—each one a quick snapshot in his vision:

The hem of one woman's dress was on fire.

A child's doll was burning.

A picnic table was smoking.

Billows of dark black smoke filled the entire churchyard. People could be heard choking on it. Women were yelling and screaming. Babies were crying. Children were running around without any sense of direction.

Warren ordered one of the patrol men to get the hose. The others he dispersed through the crowd to try to reestablish order and help anyone who needed it.

Warren shouted at them not to panic, to be calm and orderly.

No one was listening.

Just before the fire broke out, Sally had joined Brenda in the gazebo. She had approached carefully, murmuring how much she wanted to see the baby.

Brenda allowed her to sit down next to her.

Sally sat, glanced over at Brenda, and gasped.

She had the top of her dress unbuttoned and the right cup of her bra folded down. She was pushing one of her nipples into the mouth of a life-size baby doll.

Milk was dribbling down its plastic lips.

*   *   *

44

William had run around to the front of the church as soon as he was certain the leaves would ignite. Now he watched the pandemonium that he had caused.

He wanted to laugh at them, to curse them and proclaim that he, William, had created this great disaster.

But now, as he heard the screams and crying, it no longer seemed like fun.

Chapter Six

Various Voices

Dawn:

There was a fire at the picnic. A big fire. I don't know where it came from, but there was a lot of smoke and one of the patrol men got a big fire hose and was making everything wet, but it took a long time to get the fire out.

Before that happened, I couldn't see any of the other kids, but I could hear them yelling for their moms. I couldn't find my mom, either, at first, so I yelled "Mom!" That was silly, because everybody was yelling the same thing, so nobody could find their moms. All the moms were yelling their kids' names too. So nobody could find anybody.

Everybody was acting crazy.

I was afraid I was going to burn up, because the grass was burning, and I could feel hot air all around me, like a real hot day in summer, only worse. I didn't cry, though, because that wouldn't do any good. I just got scared.

I was worried about Alvin, but then I got his hand, and he got his sister's hand, and we started running to the church, which wasn't on fire. We got up on the back steps and stayed up there. Alicia was coughing real bad. Alvin tried to open the back door of the church, but it was locked. All we could do was just wait and watch everybody act crazy.

Finally, they got the fire put out, and the wind blew away most of the smoke and I found my mom, and Alvin and Alicia found their mom. My mom picked me up and

46

gave me a big hug.

That was strange, because she hardly ever picks me up or hugs me. She had big tears in her eyes, and I don't know if it was because of the smoke or because she was afraid. She carried me away from the church. I waved to Alvin and Alicia, but I don't think they saw me.

I think some kids got hurt and maybe a couple of moms too. The patrol men came and took some people away to the clinic. A real little girl I know, Mecca, who's only six, was crying a lot because her doll got burned up.

I saved Shirley, though. She has a little black on her face from the smoke, but mom says it will come off with soap. She lost her eye patch, so I'll have to make her a new one.

Kevin:
I will kick William's ass. That's what I'll do. I'm tired of that smart-ass wise guy.

I saw him set the fire. He thinks nobody saw him, but I did, because I'm always watching him. And I saw how he ran away before it got out of control—so the little creep wouldn't get hurt himself.

That louse tried to kill me the other day. He was going to hit me with a rock, and I couldn't get him off me. His mother thinks she saved me, but I would've got him off me somehow.

So I have to get even with him. I will too. Not just for what he did to me, either. I'll get even for the fire too. I'll get even for everybody that way.

But I won't squeal on him. I'll tell everybody what he did after I do my stuff. If I told first, he'd probably just get away with it. They'd lock him up for a while, or maybe send him away—like Pete—and I wouldn't have a chance to kick his ass like I need to do.

I'm going to do it real soon too.

Alvin:
Funny thing today was I saw these freckles on my hand

47

I never saw before. I don't have red hair like some of the other kids, so I didn't think I'd ever have freckles, but now I remember seeing freckles on kids who don't have red hair.

William said the sun causes freckles anyhow, so it's no big deal, I guess. Of course, William acts like nothing is a big deal to him. William is okay, but he's just not fun to be around with.

We had a fire after the picnic and I almost got burned up alive. Alicia and me both would've been burned up if Dawn didn't help us get away. Dawn is our best friend. She took us to the church, but we couldn't get in. They got the fire put out, though, so it didn't matter.

For a while, I was afraid mom might get burned, but she was okay. After the smoke was gone she found me and Alicia and took us home. Alicia kept coughing and coughing and said she swallowed a whole bunch of smoke. So mom had to take her to the clinic. They were gone a couple of hours. When they got back, Mom said the clinic had a lot of people in it because of the fire, and they had to stand around and wait a long time. Now Alicia is better and she's playing with her kitty in the back yard.

I asked mom if anybody got burned up, and she said she didn't want to talk about it. She said that if they find out somebody set that fire deliberately they will get real mad about it and punish them.

I'm glad I didn't do it!

Eddie:
We had some fun today, all right. A fire. All the mothers were peeing in their pants over it. Honest-to-God. I mean, it was something else. I watched the fire get bigger and bigger, and it was really something.

I ain't stupid, though. When it got too close to me, I ran out of there. I didn't even stop for my mother. She found me later anyhow. I'm not sure she was that glad to see I was all right, because lately she's been treating me mean and yelling at me all the time. She says I'm a troublemaker.

I don't give a damn, I guess.

It was funny seeing everybody running every which way. Then the patrol men got into the middle of it and kind of spoiled things by putting out the fire too soon. I kind of hoped it would catch the church on fire too, but we ain't that lucky. If the church burned down, we wouldn't have to go there any more. I sure wouldn't miss it. That old man Barry bores me silly. I bet he bores the mothers too, but they won't say so. They're all bummed out on that happy candy, anyhow, most of the time.

Too bad about the church. When I think about it, I guess it wouldn't make no difference if it did burn down, because Barry would probably make us go to church at the school or something. He thinks this church crap is really important.

Hell, I'd still like to see that church burn down. Just so it wouldn't be there no more. Just so we wouldn't even have to look at it.

I wish we'd have another fire. It was the most fun I had in a long time.

Alicia:

It was awful. I breathed in a lot of smoke and it burned the inside of my lungs. I couldn't stop coughing and mom had to take me to the clinic.

The clinic was full of people. It was real noisy. There were kids and babies crying and moms yelling and lots of kids coughing like me. And some kids and moms had burns on them. One mom had this terrible burn on her leg, where her dress got on fire. Her skin was burned off—and you could see this pink stuff on her leg where the skin looked like it was raw meat. She was crying about it, and it was real weird to see a grown-up crying like that. I felt like I was going to throw up when I saw her leg, but I swallowed hard and didn't.

The doctor and his nurses were having a lot of trouble trying to take care of everybody, so Mom and me had to wait a long time. She kept getting me drinks of water, but that didn't help the inside of my lungs.

49

I heard a grown-up woman scream too. I watched her go in one of those little rooms with her baby, but when she came out, she didn't have it. That's when she was screaming. I figured out it was because her baby got burned up or maybe it was smoke in his lungs, which could kill you.

I kept wishing the doctor would get to me real soon so the smoke in my lungs wouldn't make me dead. Mom said I'd be okay. She said to relax. She told me not to look at everything and I'd be okay, and she gave me an old magazine to read. The cover was torn off, but it was a ladies' magazine. I could tell because of all the pictures for lipsticks and pantyhose and other things women need. I tried to keep looking at the magazine, but it wasn't very interesting. It didn't even have any cartoons in it. The funniest thing was this picture of a fat woman in her underwear. I giggled when I saw that, but it made my lungs hurt. So I put the magazine down and just closed my eyes.

I think I went to sleep for a while. Mom had to shake me, and then we went into one of the little rooms. It smelled real bad in there. It smelled like something burning and like alcohol and like throw-up.

When the doctor saw me, he looked real scary. I never saw his face that close before. He's really old. He let me breathe out of a machine which was full of oxygen, and then he gave me some pills. He talked to Mom a little, and used some words I didn't understand, then we left.

I feel better now. When I get home, I'm going to play with my kitty. I'm glad she didn't go to the picnic with us.

Mecca:
My doll got burned up today. I cried and cried but Mama says I can't get a new one till tomorrow, because a doll ain't very much when there are lots of people hurt. And the doll store ain't open on Sunday.

"People come first," Mama says.

I still have my doll. She's dead now. She's kind of melted, like some chocolate ice cream, and you can't even tell it's her face anymore. Her name was Tammy. She was the best doll I ever had.

I guess I'll have a funeral for Tammy. That's what the other kids do when a kitty or puppy gets hurt so bad it's dead. Maybe mama will help me with the funeral.

When I get my new doll, I'm going to name it Tammy too, because that's a pretty name.

William:

I hope nobody died. I saw one mother whose dress was burning, but I think they took care of her. I didn't know the fire would get that big.

If somebody did die, what can I do about it now? The thought of it doesn't seem to bother me as much as I thought it would. If I had killed Kevin, I don't think that would've bothered me much, either. When I get mad, I don't think about the consequences.

I don't know if anyone suspects me.

Mother wouldn't talk to me when we got home because she was too upset. Maybe it was just because of the fire and not me. If she suspected me at all, she'd probably say something.

I hope she goes to bed early tonight. I got to get out of the house.

I feel like everything's closing in on me.

Chapter Seven

Highs And Lows

Sally Henderson was frantic, near hysteria, by the time she reached her house, but not entirely from the effort of carrying her daughter Dawn from the church. Some other cause was pumping adrenaline through her, something she could not quite identify, although it was affecting her in a strangely familiar way.

"All you all right?" she asked Dawn, finally setting her down inside the door.

"Yes, Mom," Dawn answered, "but Shirley's not."

Sally ignored her own sensations, bent down and examined the doll. It had soot on its face and its damaged eye was exposed—that always gave her a creepy feeling—but it was otherwise intact. "That black stuff'll come off if you give her a bath," she said. "That was caused by the smoke. You have some on your own face and I guess I do too."

"Yes, Mom."

"So I guess we *all* need a bath."

"Okay."

"You go first. I have to get this dress off."

"Okay," Dawn repeated and started up the stairs to the second floor. They lived in a small, two-story house with the bedrooms and bath upstairs. Downstairs were the living room, dining room, and the kitchen. Theirs was similar to almost every other house in town, differing only in layout. No one had need of anything bigger; even

Dr. Barry lived in a modest dwelling.

"Let me know when you're done," Sally called after her daughter. Not waiting for a reply, she went into the kitchen to splash water on her face and rub her skin to remove the first layer of soot and dirt.

As she leaned over the sink, she realized she was trembling. Another surge of adrenaline was rippling through her body. She tried to ignore the feeling and began to unbutton her smudged dress with unsteady fingers. She popped the last button off, and let the dress slide to the floor. Its movement over her slip made a cold chill go through her. She pulled the slip up over her head and tossed it down, then splashed more cold water on her face and neck.

Another surge; another chill. "Get hold of yourself," she whispered. "Everything's okay."

But it wasn't okay. The chills and trembling couldn't be vanquished by words. She shook her head, took a dishcloth, wet it and wiped under her arms, rubbing over her shoulders and partially down her back, then moving it back around front to her flat stomach. She paused over her navel, and the tiny scar from her tubal ligation— where the doctor had accidentally made his incision too wide—seemed to stand out—branding her as if she were a neutered animal.

It was so final. The doctor had told her that before the surgery, of course; he had talked to her at length, warning her that it was unlikely the operation could ever be reversed, especially the way he did it—by removing at least an inch of Fallopian tube on each side and cauterizing the ends.

She had said, yes, she understood; it was what she wanted. She did not want any more children. She was content with Dawn. At that time, after three years of brutalizing at the hands of her husband, the thought of letting a man get even close to her—let alone impregnate her—was enough to make her decision not to bear any more children absolute.

But Dawn was ten now. Ten. No longer a cuddly little

53

bundle, not even a cute toddler; no, she was now a small human being. And, despite how Sally carried on with the others in her clique, she hadn't really minded the infant stage of her child. There was so much to compensate for the dirty diapers, the stink, the burping up, and the constant attention a baby required.

The doctors could perform operations on the body, making it incapable of motherhood, but they could not easily alter the basic instincts with which every woman was endowed. They could not stave off the flow of hormones.

They could try, however, with psychology and drugs.

Sally took a deep breath and dropped the damp cloth in the sink. She closed her eyes and clinched her fists, trying to block out her thoughts.

Another spasm shook her; she opened her eyes and turned around, fighting back tears. She looked up and saw the jar of orange candy sitting on top of the refrigerator. She started to reach for it then jerked her hand back.

At that moment she realized what was happening to her. The adrenaline flow caused by the excitement of the fire had washed away the effects of the drug in the candy. She was like a drunk who suddenly became sober when something traumatic happened.

She was having withdrawal symptoms!

No, she told herself. That was impossible. Dr. Barry had said the drug had no such effects. It was a totally safe drug, non-habit-forming, with no aftershocks of withdrawal. Its sole purpose was to smooth out the day-to-day existence for the women who lived in Jamay Lake. It was necessary for the continued success of the community.

Sally now realized it had an effect the doctor had not explained; it also suppressed her sexual feelings and the maternal longings that sometimes accompanied them. She was experiencing in total what she usually only felt briefly—on rare occasions—late at night, when she awoke to normalcy out of her drug-induced sleep.

Those episodes always terrified her, quickly becoming

waking nightmares in which she desired a man. But by morning, when she had time to digest her first dose of medicine, she usually forgot those distracting sessions with her self—with her *true* self, with the Sally that dwelled within the comfortably deceiving cloud of the doctor's sweet high.

Dawn had even witnessed her condition once, having overheard her insensible moaning. Sally had felt great embarrassment then, and had shooed her daughter away almost cruelly.

She realized that the feeling she now had had begun when she saw Brenda with the doll baby. That was the first jolt to her numbed awareness. It reminded her—as if she had somehow forgotten—where babies came from.

Then came the fire, and the complete purging of the drug from her system as she spent those long moments searching for Dawn among the crazed mob of women and children. As she heard her own pulse pounding in her temples during those tense moments, the sweet high was being cleansed from her body.

Now Sally *was* Sally, a normal woman, not like all the others. Or was she?

How many of the others were experiencing the same kind of confrontation with self at this moment? How many of the others had nightmares of awareness? Were they all as hardened against men as they said?

Such questions were too overwhelming to contemplate. She refused to face them.

She was sweating now, and her hormones were rushing in to join the adrenaline. She felt like she was suffocating. Her bra and panties were sticking to her skin, seeming almost to burn her.

"I'm done, Mom!" Dawn called down the stairs, shattering the intensity of the moment.

Yet Sally could not answer. She had to do something. She felt like running through the streets naked, or grabbing the first thing that even resembled a male and . . .

"Mom?"

No! Her daughter came first; and her allegiance to the common cause demanded she overcome these feelings. Sally stretched her hands out for the jar and pulled it down so quickly she almost dropped it. She fumbled the lid open and stuffed several pieces of the candy into her mouth, swallowing them only half-chewed.

She just couldn't allow herself to feel like a woman. It was useless, impossible.

It was, in the context of the little world Jamay Lake represented, even shameful.

The clinic was the largest building in Jamay Lake, four stories high, covering a complete city block in the northwest corner of town. It was an old, severe-looking brick building that had, at one time, been part of a military prep school, the other main building of which was now the town's elementary school.

The emergency room, outpatient treatment facilities, and main offices were on the first floor. The second and third floors were mostly wards and small private rooms. The fourth floor had similar rooms and an intensive care unit; it was presently closed off to everyone but Dr. Warren Barry and two of his most trusted nurses.

That's where the dying children were.

Warren was exhausted. It was now after dark, almost seven o'clock, and he had finally finished with the emergency patients, the last being a small boy who had a trivial first degree burn on his right elbow.

It was over.

For the first time since he had established Jamay Lake, Warren wished he had another physician on his staff. But he had never needed one before. Such a catastrophe as today's fire had been another thing he failed to foresee.

He was fairly certain, though, that he would have great difficulty finding a like-minded doctor to join him very easily. It could take months to seek out such a person, and Warren was getting too old to waste months on anything. It had been difficult enough to find nurses who

56

could be trusted, but doctors, who as a group tended to be so reactionary and cautious, would not willingly admit to agreeing with any part of Warren's theories. They were not great risk-takers, especially in an age when malpractice suits had become so common. And the younger ones—those who might be swayed by an older doctor's experience and status—were more concerned with becoming wealthy than his generation had been. Only a few of them even went into research; it was hard to afford a Volvo when working in a laboratory for a drug company.

Also for the first time, Warren wondered what would happen to Jamay Lake if he died. He was past sixty; anything could take him. Every year was another tick on the clock of mortality. He had hoped Sondra would take over, but now she couldn't, and he didn't think any of his nurses had the desire, or the fortitude necessary to maintaining an experiment on such a grand scale. Would his dream fall apart with his passing?

There was no reason to dwell on that tonight. He couldn't waste time on speculations; he had too much reality to deal with. Such as the reality of two corpses in the cold room down the hall, the fatalities from the fire. One was an infant; the other was a woman—a young, strong woman—who shouldn't have died at all. She had suffered only minor burns, but the shock of the disaster had caused her heart to stop.

Perhaps her heart had been weak in the first place, perhaps due to a condition that had developed since her last physical. He would have to perform an autopsy, a prospect he dreaded. And he might have to inform her relatives, if she had any. Her two boys, one four, the other six, were staying with another woman who had only an infant to care for. What would he say to the dead woman's children? What would he do with the children themselves?

It was amazing how complicated life could become so quickly. Its normal flow could be interrupted and transformed in an instant.

He turned out the lights in the small examining room and stepped out into the hall. The night nurse, a woman of fifty or so who normally had a cheerful disposition, sat behind the admitting desk, a grim weariness on her features. She was having to do a double shift because of the fire. Warren nodded at her and she nodded back, then bent down to work on a book of crosswords. Other nurses were doing double duty as well, tending to the burn victims in the rooms on the second and third floors.

He made a mental note to send out for more supplies in the morning, then turned and proceeded down the hall. He stopped at the elevator and pressed the "Up" button. Creaking and groaning, the elevator descended slowly and the doors opened with a metallic echo. Warren stepped in, inserted his key in the access lock for the fourth floor, and leaned back in the corner as the doors rattled shut and the car seemed to drag him up to his destination.

The fourth floor was staffed with a patrol man and two nurses who virtually lived there. They were people he could trust with any secret; he could confess murder to them and they would tell no one. He needed that trust from them until he could come to a decision regarding the fourth floor. The situation here was yet another time bomb in the gradually disintegrating scheme of things.

The people who worked up here were also under a great deal of pressure, partially due to the covert nature of the assignment, but primarily because of the patients.

Warren had come to check on these patients, knowing to expect no progress, knowing he would come away feeling helpless and forlorn, knowing he would direct his feelings of frustration against himself, battering himself with self-loathing. But he felt he owed it to these truly "special" patients to visit them personally at least three times a week.

Deborah Conners, R.N. stood at the nurse's station, watching him get off the elevator. She was forty-one, a mother herself, and a great believer in what Warren was doing. But she was also as dismayed as he was by the

58

condition of the patients on this floor; her face always reflected a myriad of unasked questions—which she would never put to Warren, out of respect for him.

Warren had, as yet, no answers and didn't expect any soon. Something had simply gone awry. It was another mistake.

Deborah accompanied him on his rounds. He stopped at the first room and looked in on the eight-year-old boy lying in there in semi-darkness. The boy's eyes were rheumy; his hair was thin; the veins beneath his white skin seemed to stand out in relief.

As the doctor approached the bed, the boy's tiny, frail hand reached out to him, trembling with palsy.

Warren touched the boy's hand and tried to smile.

By nine-thirty, Sharon had said good-night to her son, admonished him not to stay up too late watching television, and crawled into bed, falling asleep almost immediately.

William stared at the TV another half hour, listening for sounds of his mother stirring. After he was fairly certain she was asleep, he crept to the back of the house and peeped in the door of Sally's bedroom, and, hearing her snoring, was convinced she was unconscious for the night.

She'd eaten a lot of happy candy that evening after serving a hastily-concocted meal of leftovers.

William ducked into the kitchen and drank a quick glass of chocolate milk, then put on a light denim jacket and a corduroy cap before slipping out the back door.

Outside, in the brisk night air, William's nose twitched at the lingering scent of burned grass and leaves. He ignored the smell, and the accompanying associations of guilt, and crossed a few back yards as he made his way to the next street over. He encountered only a puppy in any of the yards, a beagle who yelped at him twice, then wiggled away around to the front of its house.

Though it was relatively early, most of the houses were

dark. People in Jamay Lake habitually retired no later than ten-thirty; most of them were in bed much earlier. There wasn't that much to do at night—not just on Sunday—but on any night of the week.

Of course, no children were allowed out after dark unless they were accompanied by their mothers.

William was taking a chance, then; but he had done it often enough before, and he knew which routes to take to avoid running into a patrol man. He always chose streets where he could duck into an alley or in between houses if he sensed anyone approaching, either in a patrol car or on foot.

He made it all the way to Warren Lane without being seen by anyone. Now all he had to do was get to the clinic.

Sally awoke abruptly. She sat up in the darkness, straining her eyes for signs of movement. She switched on the bedside lamp and saw nothing. She shivered, though she was wearing flannel pajamas and had her electric blanket on high.

She had that uncomfortable feeling again, the sense of self that had made her afternoon hell until the drugs kicked in. She was certain she had eaten enough of the candy to blank her personality out for a week.

But her body was fighting back. Something inside her wanted out, and it refused to be driven away by the mere application of peppery-tasting candy.

There was another thing bothering her too; her memory of a detail that had been temporarily blotted out in the hysterical moments following the fire—the milk coming from Brenda's breast. She glimpsed it only briefly, but her intuition told her it was real. Did Dr. Barry have shots for that?

Possibly.

She reached for the jar on the bedside table and took out a piece of candy. She chewed on it absent-mindedly as she rose from the bed and walked slowly across the room.

She stood by the window and looked out, glancing

through the branches of a barren tree in the front yard down at the street. She lifted the window open to let in a little air, then knelt by it and kept staring down.

She heard footsteps coming from the sidewalk as someone approached. In a few seconds a person came into view, one of the patrol men.

He stopped and looked up in her direction.

She pulled back a little, recognizing Paul Daniels, who had caused such a stir a few weeks back by daring to fondle one of the mothers.

Sally couldn't remember now who it was he had touched. Now she couldn't help imagining what it must have felt like—to have a man's hand on her flesh. She leaned forward again to see if Paul was still there.

He was. He smiled nastily, gave her a mock salute, then continued walking, making his rounds of the town.

Sally shuddered. Had he read what she was feeling on her face? Would he try something with *her*? Was that such a terrible possibility?

She turned out the light and crept back into bed, uncertain about her own feelings.

Before she slept again, she recalled Brenda and idly wondered if she could get a doll like the one she had. Then she imagined pressing its cold plastic lips against her breast and shuddered.

It was a disgusting fantasy, after all.

William hid in the entrance of the free pharmacy which was on the corner opposite the front of the clinic. He was hunkered down in the shadows and certain no one could see him unless they came right up on him.

He waited a half hour or so like that, until he felt cramped and had to move. Then he came out of the doorway and ran across the street to the clinic. He considered going into the main entrance of the clinic but, since it was so well-lit, he knew somebody must be inside, probably a nurse. The doctor might still be there for all he knew, and he certainly did not want to run into him.

He'd come this far, however; he was determined to reach his goal. He decided to go around the building to the other end. He edged his way to the corner and slid around to the back side of the clinic where it was very dark, the only light coming from a few windows in the upper stories. William made his way to the other end rather quickly, turned the corner, and found the back entrance up a short flight of stairs next to a loading dock. His heart beating rapidly now, he took the stairs in two leaps and pressed against the back door.

It came open with so little effort that William almost fell on the floor. He regained his footing and eased the door shut quietly.

The dark corridor stretched ahead of him. To his right was the elevator. To his left was a door.

He knew he didn't want to take a chance with the elevator, so he tried the door, found it also unlocked and darted in.

It was a small room with four long metal tables in it, illuminated by a single lamp on a desk in the corner. There was just enough light for William to see the forms of a baby and a woman lying on two of the tables, both covered by white sheets.

Without really thinking about it, William went up to the baby and pulled back the sheet.

He didn't expect its eyes to be open.

He jerked the sheet back over the infant's face and jumped back, banging his head against an overhead fixture and upsetting a tray of surgical utensils on the ledge of a cabinet. Their clattering on the floor was like thunder.

His eyes wide, his heart pounding, William rushed from the room and was out the back door, running down the street.

He kept running until his lungs ached. Then he stopped, hunched over and started throwing up.

When he was finished, he resumed walking at a slow pace, massaging his stomach as he moved. The sight of the dead infant was no longer foremost in his thoughts.

He didn't even pause to consider that he was responsible for its being dead.

Foremost in his mind now was the excitement of having gained entry to the clinic so easily. Knowing that it was virtually open to anyone, he planned to return.

Very soon.

Chapter Eight

The Troll's Faux Pas

The churchyard continued to emit the smell of burned grass and wood for a few days, the wind carrying the stench throughout the town, beyond the wall, and into the surrounding countryside.

The charred swing set, the picnic tables and their wooden seats, and anything else that wasn't reduced entirely to ashes had been gathered to one corner of the yard, where later Warren planned to examine them and salvage anything he could. Perhaps, he thought, some paint would restore a few items to useable condition. Inside, he doubted he could really save anything, but he tried to remain optimistic in spite of it all. His faith in the town had been as damaged by the fire as much as anything physical had, perhaps even more.

The fire represented failure—the failure both of foresight and oversight, and Warren dreaded continuing to come to terms with the many ways in which he had failed. He had gambled on a higher degree of perfection in his universe than was possible when dealing with real-life situations. He had put his faith in the ideal of his plan without considering all the potential pitfalls. He thought he had provided for any emergency, any exigency or problem that might arise.

And now he was paying for his myopic idealism.

He was thankful the fire had been contained rather quickly, but what if it had spread to the church? What if the wind had carried it to one of the houses as well? The whole community could have been consumed by fire before additional help could be summoned from the closest town, and the intrusion of outsiders could be as threatening as the fire itself. Perhaps Jamay Lake was too isolated.

Yet its continued existence was dependent on isolation.

It was very fortunate there had been only two fatalities. The majority of the burn patients had been released in two days. The few that remained would recover soon, and none of the survivors would have to lose a limb or anything horrid like that. His worst medical concern was that one woman might need a skin graft, but he wasn't certain yet it would be necessary, and that was minor compared to his other problems.

He had two bodies to worry about, the baby's and that of the young mother. He fretted over her death beyond his normal empathy, because it represented a medical enigma he could not solve. The autopsy he performed on her revealed no particular reason for her to die. There wasn't any smoke in her lungs, and her heart had been strong. She apparently had died from extreme shock— yet that made little sense to him. The fire had not been that threatening, and her children had not suffered any burns at all. Her clothes bore almost no traces of her having even been close to a fire.

It was almost as if she had chosen to die.

Warren shuddered. Had she disliked her life for some reason he didn't know about? Did she have psychological problems? From what he knew of her, she wasn't a person to brood or fret, yet she had given up her life so easily. Even the most despondent person would usually fight to live.

What if there were other women like her—women who might die at the slightest shock? Could that be another unforeseen flaw in his scheme?

Warren wasn't sure he wanted to know. He had to deal with hard facts now; he couldn't allow himself to dwell on the abstract.

Such as the fact that the woman's children were now

65

without a mother. He had yet to inform them of their new status and had to decide whether to put them under the care of one of the other mothers, or check the files to see if any relatives existed who would serve as suitable foster parents.

That second option entailed the risk of interacting with the outside world, and unless the children's relatives were idiots they would have many questions. There would be inquiries and investigations, and he could permit neither. Not unless he was ready to give up on his dream altogether, and he had not reached that point yet, because it would mean having to dismantle his society.

He did not intend to do that. He would make his scheme continue to work, however flawed it had become. He merely had to exercise more control and become a better supervisor.

But there were other facts he had to confront.

There was the matter of the deceased baby. There were no problems with determining the cause of its death—smoke inhalation. But the mother presented another problem. She had another child, a two-year-old, but that wasn't the same as a baby. The mothers who cared for babies were a special breed, in some ways his favorites, because they proved the underlying thesis of his society better than any of the others.

Without her baby, the mother might become unmanageable, just as Brenda had when she learned Pete had died of blood poisoning due to gangrene. Her reaction was partially his fault, he knew, for suggesting she had been less than a solicitous mother in not bringing the child in to him sooner—when antibiotics might have saved him. He should have known better. These women were more delicate than normal women in the outside word. He had taught them—hammered them with the idea, actually—that they were "special" people—which by implication meant they achieved a kind of perfection. And they believed it. To question that perfection made any such woman's psychic balance very fragile and vulnerable.

66

In Brenda's case she had simply snapped. She had become angry at first, but then her eyes became dull, and she started mumbling incoherently, finally becoming a child herself. Perhaps that was her only way of compensating for the loss of her son—by somehow becoming him.

Warren couldn't let her wander around the community in that state. Nor did he want to confine her. One of the nurses suggested the doll—the plastic baby, the child surrogate.

Warren had sedated her heavily and placed the realistic doll in her arms. When she awoke, the nurse told her she had given birth. Brenda had readily acceded to the compulsion of the fantasy. It was sustained by tranquilizers and her unwillingness to accept childlessness.

Maybe this other mother could be persuaded to accept a doll—for a while. Or, maybe, he could get another *real* baby for her somehow. There were ways. He knew how to make the necessary connections. There were many unwanted babies in the outside world.

Too many.

Finally, to top off his worries, he had to dispose of the two bodies. He kept putting it off, but he would have to do it soon, no matter how distasteful it was. He had disposed of bodies before—of dire necessity and without undue inquiry—but eventually he might have to account for the disappearance of the bodies to the community.

He couldn't expect to hide the truths that festered behind the doors of the clinic forever.

The continuity of the west wall of the town was broken by a tall two-piece, wrought iron gate, wide enough to allow two large trucks to pass in either direction at the same time. Over the gate was a high stone arch on which hung a much-weathered bronze sign that said, "Cummins Military Academy."

The gate could be opened only by remote control from inside the sentry station at the right side. In that station usually sat the troll who watched over the town's only entrance, Mr. Maxwell Karp, a former career army man who had seen action with the Green Berets in Vietnam. He was dressed in the uniform of the patrol men, with insignia on his sleeves designating a high rank— bestowed upon him by the doctor. He carried a Smith & Wesson .357 Magnum in his holster, and a German assault rifle at his side, with a 20-round magazine. These weapons compensated for the physical limitations a troll had to endure.

Max had not always been a troll. He had assumed this guise when his left leg was shattered by an anti-personnel grenade, a U.S. Army issue weapon, directed at him by his own men because they hated him. The leg was saved only by the highest surgical skill, but it was twisted, most of the nerve endings were dead, and it was almost two inches shorter than his right leg. As a result, Max had to walk-drag himself along, his worthless leg elevated by means of a specially-designed platform shoe.

Despite the attempt on his life, Max did not reflect on his fate and undergo a personality change; if anything, he had become meaner, his disposition worsening almost daily as he lay in the hospital and, in the times between which the pain-deadening drugs had worn off, brooded on how much he hated the men who had crippled him. Had he not been discharged—with full benefits—he would eventually have qualified for an inglorious Section 8 farewell to the military.

He had been quietly going crazy for some time before his injury, but, due to the peculiar atmosphere and sometimes capricious way the military was run, his mad- ness was not that obvious to his superiors. What were potentially odious personality quirks in the outside world often made for good officer material in the service. A man had to be truly, unequivocably around the bend, frothing at the mouth, dangerous, and hysterical, before he was considered a threat to the way the military machine ran.

Max's long bouts of brooding and dwelling on his condition had rearranged his features permanently into the grimace of a perpetually disgruntled man, who could no more relax his face than could a statue. His nose was puffy from too much drinking; his cheeks were florid. His entire face was covered with wrinkles and his eyebrows bristled with white hairs mixed among the black. His teeth were yellowish and nicotine-stained. His hair was completely white, though he was still under fifty, and his head was too large for his body. He hunched over when he hobbled along, adding to the overall posture a troll must affect to retain his status as one of the lesser types in the real-life monster echelon. Like all monsters and living deformities, he was much stronger than he appeared, though he was rarely called upon to use his strength.

As he sat in the booth by the gate, he would grumble to himself most of the day, rehashing the old days, remembering the men who had tried to kill him, none of whom had ever been caught or tried. He also grumbled about his ex-wife, Carmen, who had divorced him shortly after he came home from the war, claiming as grounds "mental cruelty" and "inability to satisfy her sexual needs."

Max did not want the whole world to know he could not get a hard-on, so he had let Carmen have everything if she would remove the part about his "inability" from all records. She agreed, since everything included a large house, two cars, and a substantial amount of property and investments.

Max's sexual dysfunction was the result of another injury he had suffered; a fragment of the grenade had lodged itself in his prostate gland, mandating its removal, and his left testicle had also managed to get in the way, so it was gone too. A troll with no sexual appetite was unusual, but Max's disposition more than made up for that deficiency.

Warren knew he was taking a chance by hiring a man with such a sour, perhaps even manic-depressive state-of-mind, but he also recognized in Max an unwavering sense of duty, inculcated in him after eighteen years in the service of his country. Max would do whatever his commanding officer told him—even if it meant forfeiting

69

his own life. The psychological tests also indicated that he could keep a secret.

His physical deformities, especially his permanently-grimaced countenance, were an asset in his post at Jamay Lake. His presence was intended to discourage any stranger who approached, and it generally worked very efficiently.

Jamay Lake was an orderly world, a world that appealed to Max because it was run with military efficiency. He held a grand position in the scheme of things as the main gatekeeper—the day man—and his rank, as Warren let him believe, made him the superior of all the patrol men, though they paid little attention to him. He still believed that if a crisis situation ever arose at the gate, they would do as he told them, because the gate was *his*.

Part of the order of things in Jamay Lake was that no one could come through the gate without an authorized pass. These were issued to delivery men, patrol men and, occasionally, special visitors. Max would allow no one to come through the gate without the necessary pass. The *only* exception was Warren.

Max boasted that "Jesus Christ his very own self" could not get through his gate without a pass.

Wednesday afternoon, Max proved he was not just bragging.

Max barely heard the State Police car pull up to the gate and stop, nor did he pay any attention. He was thinking of 'Nam and the "sonuvabitches" who'd crippled him. He still had daydreams of revenge, tracking down each of the men in his former squad, blowing his nuts off and breaking both legs . . .

He heard a rap on the bullet-proof window.

"You!" a voice barked with practiced authority.

Max turned his oversized troll head to regard the visitor. He saw a tall young man, under thirty, leaning against the shack, gazing at Max with curiosity, and perhaps mistrust. He glanced past the man at his patrol vehicle, which was sitting a few feet from the gate, its engine running. He noted the trooper was apparently alone.

Max pulled himself up, balanced himself on his good leg and unlocked the door to come out, leaving his rifle behind while casually unsnapping the flap to his holster.

"What do you want?" he snarled in his best gravelly troll voice.

"I'm here to investigate a fire. We've had reports of smoke coming from this area."

"Fire's out. We got the situation under control."

"I'd like to see for myself." He stepped back and looked at the sign above the gate. "'Cummins Military Academy'? That's been closed down for years, since I was a kid."

"This here's a town. We don't like visitors."

"If it's a town, why do you have that sign up there? What's the name of the town?"

"Jamay Lake, if it's any of your business."

"Never heard of it. 'Jamay.' What does that mean?"

"I don't know. I just keep watch at the gate. Nothing we do here concerns you."

"I just want to investigate the alleged fire."

"Do you have a gate pass?"

The trooper tapped his badge. "I don't need a pass."

Max cocked his head at an angle, squinting at the badge in a way that told its wearer it didn't impress him. But since he was an officer of the law, he could, presumably, bully his way through the gate. Then Max smiled inwardly and asked, "You got a warrant?"

The trooper sighed; this was supposed to be a routine call. "What kind of place is this? You know how hard it is to get back in here? I spent all day yesterday just trying to find it. Now, just let me in so I can make my report and that'll be that."

"I asked you if you had a gate pass or a warrant."

"No. And I told you . . ."

"If you got no warrant, then you can't come in."

"Look, old man, I . . ."

"I'm not an old man."

71

The trooper almost went for his own sidearm. Then he reconsidered. Without a warrant, he had no legal right to demand access to the town; nor was there just cause for just barging in. The only evidence that remained of the fire was the smell of burning wood in the air—and that was almost gone.

This old man, this crippled monstrosity they had guarding the place, intimidated him on a gut level. He had a sidearm too, and a uniform. A squabble with the man could get potentially nasty.

"I'll get a warrant," the trooper said at last. He walked slowly back to his car.

Max returned to his station, reached in and picked up the assault rifle. He turned around, pivoting on his platform shoe like a ballerina.

The trooper leaned into his car and pulled out the hand mike.

Max was remembering things. Something in his leg twitched. A synapse in his brain crackled.

"This is . . ." the trooper began, his hand resting lightly on his sidearm.

Max had the rifle up and squeezed off two rounds before the trooper could identify himself. Both rounds passed through the trooper's skull, leaving particularly large exit holes. His body toppled over.

Max approached the trooper's body and nudged it with his good foot, while pointing his rifle at the ravaged face.

"You better be dead, you sonuvabitch."

The car radio crackled, "Come in? Identify yourself. Come in?" Max turned around, grabbed the mike dangling over the edge of the car window and jerked it out.

He looked down at the prone corpse of the trooper. "Must think you're Jesus H. Christ or something. Nobody gets by my post without a pass. You hear that? NOBODY!"

Something stirred in the back of his mind. He had done his duty; no one could fault him for that. Hadn't Warren told him to stop anyone who threatened to come through the gate? Hadn't Warren implicitly given him the

72

authority to shoot any intruders on sight?

Yet this didn't seem entirely right. Warren didn't like things to get complicated, and a dead man was generally considered a complication. A dead man with a badge qualified as a *real* complication.

Max finally decided it was not his problem; he was only an officer performing his duties. He returned to his station and put in a call to Warren.

"We got a little problem out here," he said when the doctor came on the line.

Chapter Nine

Alvin's Voice

I think I'm getting sick.

The other day, I was combing my hair and a bunch of it pulled out of my head. It was all over the comb and in the sink in the bathroom. Then I felt like I was going to throw up or something, but I didn't. I just got this real bad taste on my tongue, like something sour or like an aspirin when you don't swallow it right and it melts in your throat and burns. Then my belly started hurting real bad.

I yelled for Mom, and she came in and saw the hair, and I told her about my belly-ache, and she said I might have to go to the clinic. I didn't want to do that. She said, okay, I didn't have to go right away. Maybe I just have a cold or "stomach flu" which is like a bad cold that gets in your belly.

Mom told me to go lay down for a while, so I did. I fell asleep for about half an hour. When I got up, I felt a little better.

My belly didn't hurt any more, so Mom let me have some chocolate cookies and a big glass of milk. That felt good for a few minutes, then my belly ached again, but I didn't tell Mom about it, because I wanted to go outside and play with my sister Alicia and our friend, Dawn.

I asked Dawn once why she was named that, and she said her mom told her it was because she was born at dawn which is when the sun comes up, and that she thought it was a pretty name too. Me and Alicia were born in the daytime, so I guess if we had Dawn's mom, we'd be named Today and This Afternoon or something. I guess that's kind of a joke. I guess there might be people with names like that, even maybe Sunset or Midnight. I heard of a girl named Summer. I think we used to know an old lady who had the name Spring, but that was before we came to Jamay. That was a couple of years or something, so I don't remember it all going back that far.

My belly kept aching, but I went out and played with the girls, anyhow. We played around with the kitties, and threw a ball back and forth. Then I felt dizzy, but I didn't want the girls to know that, because they might think I was a sissy or something, so I told them I was tired of playing with dumb old girls and wanted to go watch TV.

I went inside and turned on the TV and laid down in front of it on the floor. I watched *Bambi* again. It's on all the time. It's like a real long cartoon. When nobody else is around, I cry when I see it, because of when Bambi's mother gets shot. The funny thing is the end where Bambi gets grown up and has a different voice and falls in love with another deer. I didn't know animals fell in love, but they must, or they wouldn't put it in a movie, even a cartoon one that is drawn by lots of people.

I don't understand it, but that's how they make cartoons. They draw hundreds of pictures and put them together and it makes a cartoon. I saw how they did it on the *Woody Woodpecker Show*, where this old man, who is Woody's daddy, told all about it. Then I found out Woody's voice is really a woman's. Cartoons aren't real, so they have to use people's voices for the characters. Real animals can't talk except with meowing and barking, and it's not in words. Bugs Bunny talks—which is really strange, because rabbits don't make any noise at all that I ever heard.

I haven't seen a rabbit in a long time. The only wild animals I've seen are some squirrels and chipmunks who live in people's yards. Once, I got a chipmunk to come up real close to me, and I gave it some of my cookie, but it didn't like it, I guess, because it wouldn't eat it.

When *Bambi* was over, I was kind of crying again, but

it was all right. Not even Mom saw me.

Bambi grew up, and I wonder why I don't see any grown-up boys around here, except for the patrol men, who are real old, a couple of them even forty years old! Nobody else is as old as the doctor, though. He's over fifty. I saw some really old people in a movie once—maybe like a hundred or something. They were like grandmas and grandpas. I think I have a grandpa and grandma, but they never come to visit us. Nobody comes to visit us.

The only boy I know who looks kind of like he's growing up is William. He's pretty big, but he's still not grown up all the way. So is Kevin Hamilton. William and Kevin don't like each other. They always say bad words to each other and then sometimes they get in a fight.

I think it's mostly Kevin's fault, because he's mean. His mother is an Italian person. She's real big. She has a bad temper and when Kevin gets in trouble, she hits him with a stick. She calls it her "switch." I think Kevin smokes cigarettes. Nobody's supposed to smoke in Jamay; it's against the rules.

Kevin and William had a big fight about a picture Kevin had. It was a picture of a naked lady. I tried to see it, but Kevin hid it from everybody. The only naked lady I ever saw was Mom when she gets out of the bathtub. She has red hair on her head and *down there*. I saw Alicia get out of the bathtub and she doesn't have any hair down there at all. I wonder if it fell out. I don't have any either, but it didn't fall out, because I *never* had any. I don't know if I'm supposed to have hair down there or not. Maybe it's only grown-ups.

That reminds me. More of my hair came out, and my freckles are getting browner. I'm getting more freckles all the time. And I'm tired lots of the time. Mom says I should rest. She says I might be coming down with something. So I was right, I probably am getting sick.

I wonder if it's because of the fire. I asked Mom, but she said no. Fire doesn't make your hair fall out. It burns it off, but that's only if you get too close to it. She says I might have some "childhood disease," which is something only kids can get, like chicken pox.

When you get sick, you have to go see Dr. Barry at the clinic. I don't like to go there, but I've been there before.

Sometimes he has one of the nurse ladies take blood out of your arm. They do it with a big thing that looks like what they give you a shot with, except the needle is bigger and they pull up on that handle-thing and blood goes up through the needle and fills the tube. Then they put your blood in a bottle and they take it away, and you never see it again. They say they're going to "test" it.

I asked William if he knows what they do with the blood, and he says they give it to the patrol men to drink. He says they test it first to see if it tastes okay. He says the patrol men are really vampires.

I think he made that up. Nobody would drink blood, except people like Dracula. William says Dracula was a real person who liked to eat children. I think William tries to scare us because we're littler than he is, and he thinks we'll believe anything he says. You ought to hear what he says about how babies are made! I *know* he made that stuff up.

Besides, if the patrol men were vampires, they couldn't be out in the daytime. Everybody knows that. I saw a couple of movies about Dracula, and he has to stay in his coffin all day so the sun won't burn him up. Then he has to get up at night and go eat blood. He always eats women. He never eats kids. I don't think he does. But he's not a real person. He's pretending to be Dracula for the movie. In real life, he doesn't even have those pointy teeth.

I don't like to think about Dracula. People eating blood—even if it's a big pretend movie—that's really awful.

I don't feel very good. I think I am getting sick for sure. It's not very cold outside or in the house, but I feel cold all the time. I wish we had a fireplace like some of the houses do. I stand over the heat register and let the furnace warm my legs, but I'm still cold. I got weighed this morning and Mom says I've lost five pounds.

She says I definitely have to go to the clinic and see the doctor. I guess you're not allowed to lose pounds. It must

77

be a rule they didn't tell me about before.

I looked in the mirror this morning and I didn't look like me any more. I looked like one of those ugly men in the story books—like one of those gnomes. At least *I* think so. My skin looks awful and so does my hair, and my freckles are real brown now. I'm a gnome. Maybe that's where gnomes come from—they're little kids that're sick.

Then I threw up. I didn't even eat anything yet and I threw up this green stuff that tasted awful, worse than aspirin. It was like snot or something.

I told Mom what happened in the bathroom and how I thought I looked like a gnome, and she got a scary look in her eyes. She stared at me a long time, and she probably thinks I look like a gnome too. Maybe I am a gnome. That would be funny.

She started crying and hugged me. Then she said she's going to take me to the clinic today. She says we can't wait any more.

I hope they don't poke me with that big needle and take a bunch of my blood out.

Chapter Ten

Hormones

Brenda Stowe manipulated her nipples vigorously, first the right then the left, but the milk simply no longer flowed. She could see the openings in the ends were closing up, and the naturally pinkish color was returning to the aureoles, further indicating lactation was ceasing.

It was too bad. She loved breast-feeding Donna Marie, her new baby, even though the baby did spit much of the milk back out. Most of the women with babies breast-fed their children. It was part of the fulfillment of motherhood, after all. Now Brenda's body was cheating her out of that joy.

She recalled how she had breast-fed Pete, her son, when he was an infant. She had never dried up then, and her son had grown very strong. She had him on the breast a year and a half, until he had too many teeth, and it hurt to nurse him.

Profoundly disappointed, she pulled her bra straps up over her shoulders. Now she would have to get formula for her new child, the baby she had magically delivered after her son Pete had—she hated to use the dreaded word, even in her thoughts—died. Just like that. All because of a silly children's game. The doctor said things happened that way sometimes. What was supposed to be a minor injury became fatal for no apparent reason. Sometimes there were strange germs around. It didn't really make much sense, but the doctor did his best to explain it to her. Pete had been such a strong boy, so healthy otherwise. Why did he have to get into that stupid game in the first place?

Brenda chastised herself; she shouldn't be thinking about Pete, especially since she had a baby to care for. New life replaced the old, or something like that.

But she couldn't help thinking about Pete sometimes. That's why the doctor had given her the yellow pills, which were better than the candy for making a person feel less worried. The pills made it so she wouldn't have to worry about anything bad. She went to the bathroom and took the vial of pills out of the cabinet and swallowed a couple of them with a glass of water, before she got in a really deep depression.

In a few moments, she knew she would feel much better. She returned to the bedroom and slid on a pink dress, which made her feel more like a mother. She smiled at her reflection in the mirror; she *did* have that unmistakable maternal glow that came with a new baby. If only her breasts were full of milk for the child, she would be totally fulfilled.

She would go to the free pharmacy soon and get Donna Marie some formula. Maybe she should go to the clinic too, and tell the doctor how quickly her milk had gone. Maybe he could do something about it. Maybe he had a shot that would make it come back and she could nurse again.

She turned away from the mirror abruptly. She thought she heard the baby crying.

Dawn was playing with Alicia outside. It was a chilly day, so they both wore light jackets over their tops. Dawn was wearing black jeans, and Alicia had on her pink jeans. Her favorite color was pink.

Alicia seemed listless today and a little sad.

"What's wrong?" Dawn asked, picking up Alicia's kitten Gildie and holding it. The small animal responded with an apparently grateful purr. "You're not any fun today."

"Alvin's sick."

"He is?"

"Yeah. Mom had to take him to the clinic yesterday. And she didn't bring him back home."

"Oh, that's awful. Did he die?"

"No," Alicia said, as if the question was silly. "He was just sick."

"Now you're all alone."

"Except for Gildie and Muffin." Muffin belonged to Alvin. Alicia was holding it and rubbing its ears.

Dawn let the other kitten down and picked up her doll which bore a new eye patch that matched its blue dress. "Shirley could stay with you, if you like."

"No. I have a doll."

"I know," Dawn said, brightening, "maybe I could come and stay with you. You think it would be okay with your mom?"

"I don't know. I'll ask her. What about your mom?"

"She'll probably let me. I think she wants to be by herself sometimes anyhow. She seems kind of weird nowadays. I don't know what's wrong with her. Does your mom act like that?"

"Like what?"

"Like she doesn't want you around?"

"I don't think so." Alicia picked up the other kitten and held both small cats in her arms. Muffin swatted Gildie and bit her on the ear. Gildie retaliated with a hiss and a threatening paw with claws open to strike. Alicia grew disgusted with their behavior and let the animals down in the yellowed grass of the yard. The two cats chased each other around the yard, then disappeared behind Alicia's house. Normally, she would have gone after them, but she didn't feel like making the effort. "She always acts the same, except when Alvin got sick. Now she acts sad."

"I think my mom doesn't like me any more. She yells at me a lot, and she gets mad if I come in her bedroom without knocking. It used to be only at night, but now it's all the time."

81

"Did you do something bad?"

"No, I don't think so."

"Maybe your mom's getting sick too. Like Alvin."

For the last week or so, Sally had been dressing like a whore. At least that was the effect she was trying to achieve, consciously or unconsciously. She had taken some of her older clothes out of storage, the ones she used to wear before coming to Jamay Lake, and was now strutting around in tight slacks and blouses with deep necklines or bulky knit sweaters that emphasized the thrust of her breasts. She had even found a pair of black high heels which she polished and wore as well.

She knew the other mothers were probably talking about her behind her back, because such attire was frowned upon in the community, but she didn't care because it made her feel good to look more like a "woman" and not just a mother.

She also spent a great deal of time in front of the mirror applying unusual amounts of makeup, especially under her left eye, taking great pains to hide the scar as best she could. Every time she touched it she recalled how it had been inflicted. Her former husband was a brutal man, and he had hit her often, usually with an open hand. On one occasion, however, he hit her with his fist, and his signet ring had slashed her face; it was a nasty cut that hadn't heeled well and had left a ragged crescent-shaped scar.

Remembering that, she would wonder what was compelling her to "advertise" when men had always been so bad for her.

She kept telling herself it was okay to advertise, since she wasn't really selling anything. She was just going through a phase and if it made her feel better, what harm could it do?

She liked wearing thick red lipstick and heavy eyeshadow. She liked false eyelashes and blush on her cheeks. She was only thirty-three; there was no law that said she had to look dowdy all the time.

When she finished with her "whore face," she always sat back and examined her image in the mirror imperiously, then winked. The effect she had created, she decided, was quite devastating. If only there were a man around who could appreciate that wink. If only there were a man who deserved her favors! She'd show the other women she wasn't a plain old motherly type then. They'd be jealous of her.

Despite her current tendency towards sexuality, she kept eating her candy, supplemented with a yellow pill every now and then—which were always available at the free pharmacy for women with problems—but neither provided quite the results they were supposed to or that she wished for. Ever since the fire, the drugs had barely taken the edge off her renewed awareness of self. Dressing up and making up her face provided more quietude than anything.

Nothing could totally calm her unspoken yearnings, and they gnawed at her constantly, always on the edge of her sensibilities. As a result she was very touchy, and it seemed Dawn was beginning to get on her nerves lately. She still loved her daughter, of course, but she wished she could have a little vacation from her, so she could sort out her feelings and thoughts without having a ten-year-old nearbly alway ready to ask irritating questions.

She didn't like the answers she felt compelled to give, whether they were lies or truth.

William was contemplating the nature of life and death. Life was something everyone wanted, so they made a big deal about dying. Yet when somebody really died, people didn't all act the same. Some people seemed relieved. Others cried and carried on forever. William knew he would not die for a long time, so it seemed stupid to worry about it one way or the other.

Of course, that didn't keep him from being a little uncomfortable around dead people, like the ones he'd seen in the clinic. He wasn't exactly scared of them, but

83

the fact they *had* been alive and now were not was creepy. It was like a big trick God played on people. Now you live, then you die. How's that for a game?

Pretty good game, William admitted. Of course, the hard part was that nobody knew the rules after you were dead. You were on your own. That's why you were supposed to be "good" and worship God and all of that, so when you died, God would put you in heaven.

William wondered if he had already broken too many rules. God, *if* there was one—the notion of there not being a God was an idea William had only recently discovered—would certainly not be pleased with a boy who had deliberately started a fire and killed two people in the process, one a baby.

They really made a big deal when a baby died. For some reason, that irritated William. He hadn't figured it all out yet, but it seemed things were not exactly fair. Babies and little kids got better treatment than big kids all the way around. For one thing, here in Jamay, they didn't have to take shots like big kids did. They didn't have to go into the clinic once a month and have old Dr. Barry jab them with a needle. And no matter how often it had happened, you just did not get used to a needle going in you.

It was like when you got older, your mother didn't like you as much as she used to. Like, well, she wanted you to be a "cute little kid" all your life.

It just wasn't fair.

William was walking along the sidewalk with no particular destination in mind. He saw Alicia and Dawn playing and stopped to talk with them. He personally didn't mind little kids that much, even if they were treated better than he was. It wasn't their fault. He even truly liked Dawn, who seemed to look up to him like an older brother, and that made him feel good, though he would never admit as much to anyone.

"What's going on?" he asked the girls.

"Nothing," Alicia said.

"When you getting a new doll?" he asked Dawn critically.

"Never. Shirley is the best doll there is."

"She's only got one eye."

"That's okay. She's a pirate."

"Who told you that?"

"Nobody," she bluffed. "But she can be a pirate if I want her to."

"I guess she looks like a pirate, except pirates didn't wear dresses."

"Girl pirates did."

William started to say there were no girl pirates, but decided it wasn't worth upsetting Dawn.

"Where's your brother?" he said to Alicia.

She hesitated a few seconds. "In the clinic."

"What for?"

"He's just sick."

"That's too bad." Then, without thinking of the effect it would have on the boy's sister, he said, "When kids go to the clinic they don't come back. You ever notice that?"

Alicia glared at him. "They do too. When he gets well, he'll come back."

William then did something that was rare for him. He said, "I'm sorry."

Alicia didn't appear convinced.

"I didn't mean it. Of course he'll come back."

As he walked away, he had a strange queasy feeling in the pit of his stomach. He knew, with an unusual certainty, that he would never see Alvin playing in the yard again.

He doubted anyone would see Alvin any more—not alive.

Dawn talked to her mother; Alicia talked to her mother. Sally talked to Myrna. Dawn was going to be allowed to stay overnight—maybe two or three nights—to keep Alicia company while Alvin was away. Myrna welcomed the idea of having a playmate to keep Alicia happy and help keep her mind off her brother being in

85

the hospital.

Sally needed a respite from motherhood.

Dawn packed a box full of clothes for herself, as well as two outfits for Shirley.

"You're not going over there to live," Sally said to her when she came down the stairs lugging the box.

"I have to have all this stuff."

"But you can come over here any time and . . ."

"I *need* this stuff, Mom."

"Okay, dear," Sally said, putting a box of cookies on top of her daughter's clothes. "Here are your cookies—just so you'll have enough. Now don't you give Mrs. Lawson any trouble, and do whatever she asks. And watch your table manners."

"I'll be good."

"That's all I ask," Sally said, running her fingers through her daughter's light brown hair. Then she accompanied the girl to her friend's house.

When she returned, she felt suddenly very free.

Perhaps too free.

Brenda had brought home a carton of formula and nursing bottles for her baby.

She also had a new bottle of pills, orange ones this time, which were supposed to be stronger. She didn't get the chance to see the doctor, because he was so busy, but his nurse told him about her problems and then brought her the new prescription.

She would have to call the doctor later and ask about her milk drying up.

She was still a little confused about what happened at the free pharmacy. When she asked for formula, the woman behind the counter—Harriet was her name, she thought—asked her if she was sure she wanted it. Brenda didn't understand why another woman would ask her that. After all, Harriet knew she had a baby at home, and it must be obvious her milk was drying up, and that's why she needed formula.

86

The woman gave her the formula, but with a look in her eyes that made Brenda very uncomfortable.

She would miss nursing, especially the side-effect of her womb seeming to draw up into itself, and the overall warmth produced in her abdomen. But, perhaps, Nature was telling her it was time to put Donna Marie on the bottle—get her growing towards toddlerhood, making her less dependent.

She hoped Donna Marie would grow up to be a well-behaved child who would make her proud to be her mother.

As the sun was setting, Brenda mixed a bottle of formula and took it up to Pete's former room, which she'd had made over to a nursery. The doctor had sent one of the patrol men to help her. He had even painted the woodwork pink.

The doctor was such a very nice person. He did everything for the mothers in Jamay Lake. He let them want for almost nothing—well, not anything that they needed, anyhow. Maybe their lives weren't fancy, but they lived comfortably, and in an atmosphere of decency and morality. That was important for raising children.

She stood in the doorway of the nursery, barely able to make out the crib in the gloom caused by the sun's setting. She listened for sounds from the infant, the cooing and gurgling noises a baby makes that are so electrifying to a mother on a deep, instinctual level.

But Donna Marie was awfully quiet.

Concerned, Brenda switched on the overhead light. The baby was in the crib. She was only sleeping, Brenda assured herself.

She approached the crib, halted at its side, tested the temperature of the formula on her wrist, then reached down to place the bottle into her child's mouth.

Donna Marie wasn't responding. She was totally still. *Crib death!* flashed through her mind.

Brenda set the bottle aside and scooped up her baby. She held it out in front of her watching intently for signs of life.

With a shock, she realized this was *not* her baby at all!
It was a doll, a thing with a plastic head and body.
Someone had stolen her baby and cruelly left this doll behind.

What kind of monster would do such a thing?

The answer was simple. It was one of the other mothers, a jealous woman who had no infant of her own. One of them had sneaked into her house and taken her baby.

Brenda's face flushed with rage. She slammed the baby doll against the wall; its head split and cotton spilled out. She kicked the doll until it was a mangle of plastic and cotton filling.

She'd get the bitch who did this to her!

Brenda went downstairs, grabbed a coat, and went out into the darkening night, her face an intense mask of revenge.

As the evening wore on, Sally contemplated her freedom. She could do absolutely as she pleased with Dawn over at the Lawson house, and she didn't even have to feel guilty, because her daughter was in a safe place.

So she had stripped off all her clothes and now sat naked in the living room, her legs propped up on the coffee table, while she sipped a glass of cola. She felt wonderfully wicked sitting in the nude with no questioning eyes scanning her body.

It was the ultimate freedom.

Maybe she ought to move to a nudist camp and run around naked all day long. Play tennis with her breasts bouncing up and down. Watch other naked women and naked men cavort in the sun. Go skinny dipping. Let it all hang out—and flop around.

The vision soured then; most nudist camps were closed down in the wave of the new conservatism that had festered in the country since old Ronnie's administration.

At one time there had been a camp in Indiana, farther

north, a difficult place to find, but she knew it had been there. She remembered reading about it—it seemed like eons ago—and wondered, as most people did, if anything *sexual* ever happened among the nudists.

It made no difference. It was all a grand fantasy, anyhow. She couldn't really run around with a bunch of naked strangers. She would probably be self-conscious as hell. It just seemed like a neat idea in her present state.

But there was nothing wrong about having fantasies. She closed her eyes and let her mind wander. As usual, her memories drifted back to times spent with men— before, during, and after her marriage. The electric moments spent in bedrooms were foremost in those memories—the times when she actually had orgasms and felt satisfied afterwards. She had even responded reasonably well to her husband's sexual desires, though she could count on one hand the number of times she had an orgasm with *him,* and those were only when she desperately needed the sex for herself, not just to please her mate.

She tried to imagine a man on top of her now, recalling the scent of sex, the entangling of male and female musk, the raging of hormones that could make it an almost magical act.

She trembled. She shouldn't be thinking these things. Even though she was alone and Dawn was safely away, her reveries were beginning to shame her. She needed to put some controls over herself.

Besides, she was getting chilly; her nipples were erect from being cold, not from sexual arousal. She reluctantly covered herself with a light flannel robe and went out to the kitchen for some candy. Nibble a few bites of that, take a couple of pills, she thought, and she'd be okay. The sexual longings would be numbed—or at least controllable, which was all she could hope for nowadays. She might have to ask the doctor if he had anything stronger in his pharmacy. Maybe she was growing immune to the effects of the candy and pills.

Maybe she needed to take much more.

She had a piece of candy up to her lips, when she realized she didn't want to numb herself. She wanted to feel completely, to let her senses take over, to allow her instincts full reign. She replaced the candy in the jar and went up to her room.

She walked across the room languidly, imagining she was a sex goddess in an old movie, or a dreamy heroine in a romance novel, and lifted up the window. She sat on the floor next to the window and took deep breaths of the fall breeze coming in.

There seemed to be a scent of cinnamon in the air— probably someone making cookies or rolls somewhere.

She heard whistling. She peeked out the window and down the street and recognized one of the patrol men.

It was Paul.

William was half way down the street when he heard a patrol man approaching. He ducked behind a tree across from the Henderson house and crouched low.

He heard a woman's voice coming from the house. The patrol man stopped and said something, but William couldn't understand it. Then the patrol man went into the house.

William edged around the tree cautiously and stared over at the house. He stood there several minutes, and the patrol man did not come out.

This might get interesting, he thought.

Thinking fast, Sally had called from the window, "Sir! You, the patrol man . . ."

"Paul Daniels," the patrol man answered. "What can I do for you?"

"I heard a strange noise downstairs. Could you check it out for me? I just know I left the front door unlocked."

"Certainly, m'am."

Paul entered the house. Sally eyed him closely, noting the rhythm and flex of his muscular body as he strode up

90

her walk to the front door and entered, flashlight in hand.

She waited a few minutes, then came to the top of the stairs.

Paul had turned on every light in every room on the lower level of the house. "Nothing down here," he said.

Sally descended the stairs slowly. She still wore only the robe, and it was barely closed in front. She was conscious of her skin being exposed and goose bumps erupted on her arms and legs. Then she felt herself blushing, but she made no effort to cover up whatever Paul might be seeing.

Nor did Paul avert his eyes.

When she reached the bottom of the stairs, she said, "Are you sure I'm safe?"

"Of course, you're safe."

Sally tried to remember how to flirt without being too obvious. Seducing was one thing; attempting to *get* seduced was a different art altogether.

"Is there anything else?" Paul asked, his eyes steadily working their way up and down her barely-draped body.

Sally's flesh warmed even more under his gaze. "No, I guess not," she replied, an edge of panic in her voice.

"Maybe it was your—don't you have a daughter?"

"Yes, but she's staying overnight . . ." She suddenly pulled the folds of her robe together. She was aware of her own scent; Paul would be aware too, unless he was inhuman, or he was as numbed by drugs as the other men were.

Yet if that were true, she realized, his eyes wouldn't be so intense. He wouldn't be able to make her squirm inside as she now was.

"Then she couldn't have made the noise." He stroked his moustache thoughtfully. "I can check around outside if you like."

"No. It was probably nothing. I'm not used to being alone in the house. I'm just being silly."

"All right," he said. "If you need me . . ."

It suddenly occurred to Sally she was being foolish. She was free. She could do as she pleased.

91

"Don't go," she whispered huskily. "Please."

William thought the patrol man was staying in the Henderson house a long time. Much too long for a routine call, if that's what it was.

Then he noticed the light go on in a window upstairs. He got up on his tiptoes, as if that might give him the height he needed to see into the window, but he could make out only slanted shadows through the branches of the tree in the front of the house. He started to forget about the whole thing, then realized he could climb the tree he'd been hiding behind. He jumped up a few inches, grabbed hold of a limb and swung his nimble body up and over. He made his way up through the tree until he was almost directly across from the window.

He steadied himself on a large limb and focused on the window. He could see Sally Henderson take off her robe, except she didn't just take it off; she let it slide to the floor. She had nothing on beneath the robe, not even underwear.

God, if he only had some binoculars!

Next he saw the patrol man, naked to the waist, approach Sally, starting to let down his pants.

Just as it was getting very interesting indeed, the lights went out.

Sally couldn't have asked for a better lover. He was manly, yet gentle; quick when he should be and slow when she needed him to be slow. His pace and timing were perfect, and Sally had her first orgasm almost as soon as he mounted her. He didn't come right then, though. He had incredible control and made her have two or three orgasms before he even got going himself.

He muttered dirty words to her under his breath, and Sally surprised herself by loving the way he talked to her. Everything he said or did magnified the passion.

This is what I wanted, she thought as he rolled his pelvis

92

against hers with each thrust. *This is what I wanted, not a silly doll, like Brenda has. This is what I need!*

Paul finally exploded in her, and kept thrusting long after he was spent—until she finally stopped shuddering with orgasm.

Then he kissed her and lay next to her a long time, luxuriating with her in the afterglow. Finally, he suggested a way to bring him back to life.

Sally resurrected him twice that evening.

William could faintly hear moaning and maybe the sound of the bed rattling, but he couldn't see Mrs. Henderson and the patrol man, and that frustrated the hell out of him. After a few minutes, he climbed back down through the branches of the tree, scratching his arms a couple of times on the bark, and landed softly on the ground.

At least he had seen enough that he knew Mrs. Henderson was screwing that patrol man. Maybe next time they'd leave the lights on, if there was a next time.

He wondered if other mothers were doing this kind of thing. He might be missing out on a lot of action. He'd have to be more observant in the future. Even the little he had seen was better than anything he ever saw on television, and certainly more entertaining.

He brushed himself off, preparing to go on with his nightly prowling. Just as he was straightening up, he felt a cold hand on his shoulder and jumped like he'd been goosed.

He turned and saw Brenda Stowe. The moon had risen in the sky, providing dim illumination, and William could see Brenda's face clearly.

It was scary. Her hair was all messed up, resembling a fright wig. Her grim expression made him think of a ghost.

"Have you seen my baby?" she asked in a hollow voice that scared him even more.

William gulped. "No."

93

"Someone stole her."

"Not me. I wouldn't want your baby."

She stared at him. For a moment William thought she was going to hit him, but her eyes flickered and she looked away, down the street. "If you find out who took my baby, you tell me."

"Sure," William said.

Brenda walked on. As her figure receded down the street, William decided he would return home.

There were too many strange things happening tonight, and, brave as he was, he wasn't up to dealing with them all at once.

Besides, if he stayed out, he might get blamed for something.

Chapter Eleven

Suspicions

Sharon Wesley's job at the doll store was officially that of a clerk, although she also worked with the other women in the back making the dolls. Four women worked in the store in addition to Sharon. The dolls were provided free to anyone in the community, so the establishment was not really a retail outlet. Its storefront was more for show than function; it gave Warren Lane the look of a normal small town main thoroughfare.

The manufacture of dolls also had another purpose—to provide extra income for the community. They were among the town's exports to the outside world, and they were shipped to gift shops, upper class toy stores, and department stores throughout the nation. Most of them were exquisitely detailed, with hand-painted embellishments, appealing to the tastes of collectors rather than children. The realistic baby dolls, however, were among the best-selling items exported.

Dolls made for the community's children tended to be simpler—rag dolls or plastic dolls with soft stuffing, for girls such as Dawn to carry around with them all the time.

The dolls, like any other commodity the town produced, bore labels that said, "Made in U.S.A. National, Indiana." The doctor had picked the name "National" after reading an article about a mythical town called "National" in a magazine. It was a choice that appealed to his whimsy, and it added an extra layer of

95

security. People searching for National, Indiana would never find it. Sales and contacts were made through a shipping office in Fort Wayne, which was less than fifty miles away. Any returned merchandise was sent to the Fort Wayne address, as was all mail connected with the various enterprises. All money collected was kept in a Fort Wayne bank, which Warren visited every month or so to monitor the accounts.

It was a warm Indian summer day. In the back of the shop, the women had a fan blowing over them, since it wasn't hot enough to run the air conditioning and would be wasteful. They worked at a leisurely pace. Their production rate was not scrutinized as long as it was reasonable. The doctor had them working not only to help provide income to run things, but also to keep the women occupied and help sustain the illusion of normality he thought was essential to their well-being and contentment.

A buzzer sounded, signalling the entrance of a "customer" in the store area. Sharon arose from her work station, where she had been painting features on the porcelain head of a collector's doll—a copy of a Victorian original.

Sharon came out to greet Carla Schuel, one of the three black women in Jamay Lake. She was also the most educated representative of her race, though she didn't always display her intelligence, and she worked two or three days a week in the library. Carla had her daughter, Mecca, with her. Carla was wearing a purple polka-dotted knee-length dress, and Mecca was outfitted in a yellow blouse and green miniature overalls.

Mecca was much lighter-skinned than her mother, leading many to speculate her father had been white. No one in Jamay Lake had the temerity to ask Carla, though. She was the type of person who wanted to know everything about everyone else but revealed nothing of herself. Also, she might get angry as she had a short fuse and her moods were mercurial.

"Good morning, Carla," Sharon said. "What can I do for you?"

"This child has been pestering me for days to get her a new doll, so I took off from the library to come get her one."

Mecca was in the corner, already examining the medium-sized baby dolls. She apparently couldn't make up her mind whether to select a black doll or a white one. There were no dolls with skin like her own.

"Her other doll got burned in the fire," Carla explained. "That was a nasty business."

"That's too bad," Sharon said carefully.

"You know, that was an awful thing, that fire. Two people died because of that fire, a woman and a baby." Carla arched her eyebrows as if getting ready to make an important announcement. "Some people say it was deliberate."

"What do you mean?"

"I mean they say someone *set* that fire on purpose— one of the kids. You know any kid that would do that?" Carla's gaze was definitely accusatory.

"No," Sharon said curtly, angry at Carla's insinuation. "I can't imagine any of our children doing anything like that."

"I can." Carla's nostrils flared; she seemed on the verge of bursting into anger, but one could never be sure. "That Kevin Hamilton would do it. He's the meanest little brat I ever saw. He cusses and gets into fights all the time. Dr. Barry ought to move him and his fat-ass mama out of this town. You know how those Italians are."

Sharon tried to maintain a placid pose. She didn't like to gossip. "I didn't think they were Italian."

"Who you kidding? Harriet's got hair blacker than mine, and she didn't get that fat from eating American food. It's all that spaghetti and lasagna they eat. I think they have it for breakfast."

"I don't think it's right to talk about—well, about ethnic groups," Sharon said bravely.

"You don't, huh? I guess nobody goes around talking about us 'persons of color,' when we're not around, either."

"I don't."

"Crap! I know better, and you know better. It's always niggers and wops and spics, when our backs are turned."

"I'm not that way."

Carla snorted, her temper temporarily defused. "I never said you were, did I?"

"No, but . . ."

Mecca had made a selection. She brought over a small black girl doll and showed it to her mother.

"I want this one, Mama."

Carla looked down. "That's fine, honey."

"I'm going to call her 'Tammy,' just like my old doll."

Sharon put a credit transaction through the cash register. All it did was remove a unit from inventory, since no money was involved. She handed Carla a slip, the purpose of which was to maintain the illusion of buying and selling.

Carla stuck the slip in her purse. She leaned forward, her voice dropping to a whisper. "There are things going on around here," she said. "Things that aren't supposed to be going on."

"Whatever do you mean?"

"I mean some people are falling from grace, if you understand what I mean. There's some nasty things going on from what I hear. You keep your ears open, you'll hear too. And, there's a lot more sickness going around than anybody knows about. One of those Lawson twins, the boy, he's gone to the clinic with something awful."

"Like what?" Sharon found herself curious in spite of herself.

"I don't know. I only hear rumors."

"You can't put much stock in rumors."

"There's always a little truth in everything you hear," Carla said, taking Mecca by the hand. "You remember that. No matter how outrageous it sounds, there's *something* behind it."

William came into the store. Carla regarded him with undisguised scorn, then turned to leave. "You remember what I said, Sharon. The time's coming when things are going to change. Big time." She strutted out with

98

her child.

Sharon's mouth was open, but she was speechless. Carla had shocked her with her gossip; she believed the community remained basically stable despite a few problems—none of which was insurmountable. All towns had problems; at least Jamay Lake didn't have crime. A person could go to bed at night and leave the front door unlocked without fear. The town was secure. She shouldn't listen to Carla's ravings. Everyone knew the woman liked to stir things up; she was always trying to make things out to be worse than they really were, and her insinuations weren't worthy of serious consideration.

She looked up at her son and Carla's words about a child setting the fire abruptly returned her mind. William was—probably—"mean" enough to do such a thing. But was he intelligent enough to do it without being caught?

"Why are you looking at me like that?" William protested after several seconds of his mother's steady gaze.

Sharon caught herself and forced her face to relax. "I'm sorry. Carla upset me."

"Is that because she's black?"

"No. You know better than that."

Prejudice was forbidden in the scheme of life in Jamay Lake. The good doctor had preached against it many times in his role as pastor of the Nameless Church, though realistically Sharon knew there would always be prejudice in some people's hearts.

William seemed to be in one of his irritating moods—where he asserted his presence and expected some kind of reaction. He took a pen knife from his pocket and casually cleaned his nails while talking with his mother.

"What do you want?" she said at last.

"Nothing much. I just wondered what we're going to have for dinner tonight."

"I don't know," Sharon said. "Since when do you care?"

"I was just thinking about it."

99

Sharon took a deep breath. She had to see what William would say. "You know what Carla said?"

"Should I?"

"She says there's a rumor going on that a child started the fire at the church . . ."

William stopped scraping his nails. "A kid?" he asked casually.

"She thinks Kevin may have done it."

William could see his mother didn't totally accept that, but wanted to believe it. It was a good idea now that William thought about it, and it wouldn't hurt to help it grow from rumor to truth. "He might do something like that. He's not a very good kid. He's always bugging people and getting into trouble."

"Do you think if a child set the fire, he ought to be punished?"

William noted an undue emphasis on "he" in his mother's question.

"I don't know. Wouldn't it depend on why he set the fire?"

"You mean to tell me you think there could be a good reason for arson?"

"For a kid like Kevin, there might be," William said. "He's half crazy. Crazy people think up stuff like that."

"Kevin isn't crazy. He's just—disturbed."

William reflected on that a moment. Kevin was a disturbed kid which meant he should be disturbed more often in his estimation. There were possibilities in that concept as well. Maybe he himself was disturbed too, disturbed by everything around him. By his mother's definition, then, he also was crazy.

"If he's disturbed, then I guess he shouldn't be punished for setting the fire," William said, almost smiling. "We should lock him up or something. Have the doctor operate on his brain and make him undisturbed."

Sharon was growing weary of this conversation which obviously was headed nowhere; it was just another dead-end word game in which William would ultimately triumph.

"Well, you know, two people died because of that fire.

100

One of them a baby."

William looked into his mother's eyes. "That's what I don't understand sometimes. Why is a baby more special than any other kid? What difference does it make if a baby died?"

"Because a baby is helpless and innocent . . ."

"So they don't deserve to die?"

"Nobody deserves to die!"

"Why not? Shouldn't bad people be punished? Shouldn't people who set fires be punished, even if they're disturbed? Especially if they kill *babies?*"

"Stop that!" Sharon said, raising her voice. "Stop that right now!"

"What?"

"Arguing, playing with words, making it sound like everything's so—I don't know—so messed up, when it really isn't. Things are just right. Things are the way they should be here in Jamay Lake. You don't need to question any of it."

"I'm not a stupid little kid. You can't give me a doll and make me happy."

"What does make you happy?"

"I don't know."

"Do you think the world owes you happiness?"

"I don't know what the world owes me. I don't even know what the world is. I only know this isn't the real world. People don't live like this. That's why . . ." He started to blurt out how he'd seen the patrol man and Sally Henderson together, then thought better of it. It was a secret that might be put to better use than blabbing it to his mother.

"Why what?"

"Why things happen, I guess. Like fires. Like Alvin getting sick. Like, you know, when things go wrong and nobody can fix them."

"Doctor Barry is watching over us. He'll take care of all our problems. He'll give Alvin excellent care."

"Sure he will," William said, exiting. "He's just as good as Jesus Christ."

"Come back here, young man!" Sharon screamed at

101

the door. "You can't talk like that. You can't! You . . ."

Sharon sat down and began to cry, not so much because of William's behavior as because she felt she was reponsible for how he was.

She was his mother; she was a participant in what he had become and what he might become.

But the mother part of her still refused to think he was essentially bad; Sharon believed there was no such thing as a truly bad child.

William was supposed to be going to the library. He had lately discovered that the old *National Geographics* often featured half-naked native women, and he was working his way through the bound volumes, noting which issues carried the best pictures of bare breasts. When he reached the library, however, and saw Carla at the front desk, he decided not to go in. Carla had evidently put some ideas into his mother's head, and that meant she might be watching him. He'd wait a couple of days. The native breasts wouldn't go anywhere.

He turned the corner and walked casually towards home. On the way he passed the Henderson house and wondered if old Mrs. Henderson had stayed up all night screwing that patrol man. Kevin once said that women got "hornier" than men and that they all wanted "it." At the time, a couple of years ago, William himself had been quite naive about things sexual, possessing only a limited curiosity about male and female functions. He was barely aware of the differences. It was only after an intense period of self-education, which was difficult in a town where most printed materials were from the fifties, that he finally figured out what "horny" and "it" were.

As it did to most children, "it" seemed a hideous prospect to him at first, but as he grew bigger and started experiencing pre-adolescent random erections, the idea of "it" became more enticing. Now, sometimes, he even thought he might like to try "it" himself.

Bored, he eventually wound up at home, where he passed a few minutes making a snack and eating it in front

102

of the television. *Bambi* was on again, and it made him sick. He changed to another channel and watched part of a Western—an ancient black-and-white movie shot in the thirties with a very young John Wayne in it. It was so bad it barely held his interest. He switched the TV off, finished his snack and wandered upstairs. He was going into his room to take a nap when he looked up at the end of the hall and noted the access to the attic. It was as if he had never seen it before.

He couldn't remember ever going into the attic, though he knew his mother had a few things stored up there.

She wouldn't be home for a couple of hours.

William brought the step-stool up from the kitchen and climbed up on it. He could reach the panel covering the access quite easily. He pushed it aside and gripped the sides of the square opening and pulled himself up into the attic.

The attic was hot and musty and smelled stale. There was also the odor of old newspapers and mothballs in the air.

There was a bare bulb fixture overhead with a chain which William pulled. Now he could see an old black trunk in the corner, shelving on which lay stacks of old clothes, and several boxes filled with various kinds of junk and keep-sakes.

He went over and sat down, then pulled up a box to examine. He found photos of himself as a young child and many pictures of his mother.

There were also pictures of his father, Brian Wesley. The color had faded on most of the photos, so it was difficult to figure out the color of his father's hair or eyes. He was taller than his mother, though. Probably over six feet.

William tried to remember the last time he had seen his father, but there was only a blur in the space where that memory should be. He realized he had very ambiguous feelings about his father; he had never learned either to love or to hate him.

His mother always talked as if Brian were dead, though

103

she never actually said that. His mother and father were divorced, he knew for sure; he could recall the separation clearly enough, but after that things got fuzzy. And things from the past became more vague the longer he lived in Jamay Lake.

He set the box aside and pulled another one forward. It was filled with old letters, some of them with postmarks going back fifteen years. He recognized his mother's handwriting on most of them. Then he found an unopened letter with a typewritten address. It had been forwarded to a box number in Fort Wayne, and then delivered at last to the addressee, his mother. Its postmark was only a couple of months old.

But the most intriguing thing about the letter was the return address.

It had come from his father.

Chapter Twelve

Warren's Newest Problems

When Warren learned Max had killed a state trooper, his first impulse was to turn Max over the authorities, accept his own measure of blame in the incident, and face the consequences. Then he would be compelled to tear down his mini-society, and perhaps be confronted with even more consequences.

But, after considering the total picture, he realized he couldn't do any of those things. The women and children for whom he was responsible were not disposable. He couldn't simply just jerk them out of their environment. He was sworn and bound to care for them.

What was one life compared to theirs?

That was always the old argument, he realized—when people wanted to worm out of doing the right thing. What was one compared to many? It was used by generals and presidents to justify their blunders; by war criminals to justify their mass murders; by scientists and doctors who wanted to avoid being blamed for the latest nuclear or biological accident.

Yet, in this instance, Warren felt he had no other choice but to resort to that convenient way out, even though it was fundamentally a cowardly, specious form of reasoning. His convictions were being put to the supreme test, not only by this unanticipated event, but by the multiplying number of other incidents eroding the way his ideal society was supposed to function.

He had the trooper's body brought to the clinic

through the back door that same night by two of his most trusted patrol men—men to whom he had to explain nothing. One of them parked the trooper's car in the clinic garage temporarily until Warren decided what to do with it.

He thanked his men and went into the room just inside the back doors. He switched on the light, and the trooper's shattered face made him cringe; there was no need to perform an autopsy on him. No mystery about his death.

Warren sat and contemplated the inert form of the trooper for a long time. What should he do with the man's remains? Should he punish Max for this misdeed? Max would say he was only protecting the community, following orders like the efficient soldier he was. To Max, who had embraced the ideal behind the society, anyone outside the society was an enemy. Max himself might say, "What is one life compared to many?"

I vas only following orders, Mein Herr!

Max didn't say either of those things, however. When Warren asked him why he had shot the man, he had replied, "He didn't have a gate pass."

Simple. Soldierly. Efficient. Unassailable logic there.

Warren covered the body with a sheet and left. He went home for the night to be with his wife, Sondra. He would solve this particular problem only after a good night's sleep—which was rare for him lately—so he resorted to sleeping pills to provide some semblance of sleep.

The next day he had embraced all the old arguments and succeeded in convincing himself that Jamay Lake *was* more important than the killing of a single man—an incident which, given the conditions and the situation, might even be considered an accident.

Why consider it otherwise? What good would it do to bring it out in the open?

Yes, the man had been a human being, a living soul. He might have a family. Maybe even children. But they would be cared for.

People disappeared all the time, leaving loved ones

106

behind. He was in a dangerous line of work, after all, being a police officer for the state. He could've been shot anytime when pulling over a speeder or a drunk on the highway. His life was always on the line.

Warren battered himself no further with the moral issues involved. He had too many other things to attend to. That night, after a long, wearisome day, he forced himself to dispose of the trooper's body by himself.

He wheeled the dead trooper on a cart down to the basement, where only minutes before he had turned on the gas jets to the crematorium, which resembled a blast furnace. It was larger than a regular furnace and generated tremendous heat, which was needed to reduce a human body, bones and all, to a handful of ashes.

He opened the crematorium door to a raging blaze that seemed like it might suck him in, as if it might be a portal to Hell itself.

That would be a fitting way to go, he mused. To be burned as he had burned others. As he burned everyone that had died so far since Jamay Lake was established.

Only a few nights before he had placed a baby's body in the fire, followed by the mother who had died as a result of shock from the church fire. He had decided not to inform any relatives. It was too risky.

It seemed like everything was a high risk nowadays.

He remembered the first body he had given to the flame—that of Peter Stowe—the boy who had his toe cut off in a child's game. He had died from blood poisoning and other complications due to gangrene. Warren had done everything possible to save his life.

But the boy died.

Many people still died despite all the miraculous drugs and equipment doctors had available to them in this modern age.

The night Pete's body was consumed in the crematorium, Warren had cried. Pete was the first fatality.

Now he was the first of many.

And there might be many more to follow.

Warren's mind was clouded with the pain of it. Yet who else could be trusted to perform such an unpleasant task? Who else would want to be an accomplice in his growing list of transgressions?

He hoped there *was* a loving God who understood a man and judged him as much by his intentions as by his deeds—and the necessity of them.

As soon as Warren was certain the trooper's body was burning well and would be reduced to ashes, he shut the door to the crematorium. Instead of leaving, he sat down on a nearby metal folding chair and stared at the glow coming from the fireproof window of the death furnace.

His intentions were good, he kept telling himself. He wasn't a Nazi scientist performing outrageous experiments; he wasn't a mad scientist, either. Everything he was doing was directed towards a goal that he sincerely believed would benefit mankind in the end.

There was probably no single beneficial discovery or event that didn't have some bad attached to it. After all, medical research often demanded the sacrifice of hundreds of living animals. People had unanticipated allergies to medicines that were supposed to save their lives, but killed them instead. It had happened so many times: old people getting flu shots died from the shots; people were allergic to antibiotics and died when given them; people died from the shock of anesthesia on the operating table, before the surgeon applied his scalpel.

He wasn't experimenting with animals, of course, but the object was the same: to save life, to improve life, to help mankind. There had to be sacrifice involved; there would be unexpected fatalities. He should have factored that into his original plans. As a physician he should have known better.

He had morals. He wasn't a monster. He did what he could to compensate for people's losses.

After he burned the baby and the woman, hadn't he taken special pains to place the woman's children with another mother—who welcomed them into her home? Had he not helped the mother of the baby to cope? Did he not promise to find her a baby?

Yes. Yes, and again, yes.

108

But now he was cremating a man whose only crime against the community was to find it.

Life and death were absurd. People were conceived under absurd conditions, on couches, in the backs of cars, during orgies, but it made no difference to the babies; life began with a silly act. So it was a kind of balance of nature that death should also be as absurd. You just happened to be in the wrong place and run into a half-crazed troll like Max Karp, and you're dead. You lose your toe and get blood poisoning. You *see* a fire and drop dead. It was stupid, unrelentingly crazy, the way people died.

It was whimsical sometimes.

Having sorted out his thoughts, Warren left the basement. He had consoled himself to a degree. He could get on with the business of taking care of his people.

The next day, the trooper's pistol and ammo were taken out into the country and buried in the woods; his car was deposited in the nearest river, its trunk full of sand bags and its interior packed with concrete blocks, where it quickly sank out of sight.

Max was allowed to go on being the sentry at the gate, but Warren cautioned him to call first if he encountered such a situation again.

Warren filed the entire incident in the back of his mind with all the other worries he had, praying that nothing more would come of it.

Two days later, Warren was confronted with another case for the fourth floor, a boy named Alvin Lawson. He examined the boy while his mother stood by impatiently.

Alvin was supposed to be ten. He now had the body and general appearance of a man in his seventies. He was balding, his skin had become thin and frail, and he was covered with age spots.

He had contracted one of the strangest childhood diseases in the world—Hutchinson-Gilford syndrome, also known as progeria or premature senility syndrome, which turned young children into miniature old people, by accelerating the aging process at a much increased rate.

Pictures of victims of the disease were a favorite shocker on supermarket tabloid covers, with headlines screaming: "EIGHT YEARS OLD, BUT LOOKS LIKE EIGHTY."

The disease was extremely rare in the general population.

At least it used to be rare. In Jamay Lake, it was becoming a quite frequent occurrence. And the form of it was insidious; its onset quick, the development of symptoms faster than when the disease occurred among other children.

"What's wrong with him, Doctor?" Myrna Lawson asked after Warren completed his cursory examination. No tests were needed. The diagnosis was obvious and he was examining the boy merely to please his mother.

"He needs special care," Warren replied non-committally.

"But what is it?"

"He has a virus, a particularly afflictive form that causes the hair to fall out and leeches color out of the skin."

"What about those spots?"

"Another effect of the virus. Similar to measles." He kept his face turned away from Myrna, knowing it would be more difficult to continue lying if he had to look into her eyes.

"Can you cure it?"

"We have a treatment for it," he said, avoiding a direct answer, though there was no known cure for the disease, which also brought on early death. "But Alvin will have to remain in the clinic."

"Can I have my kitten?" The boy's voice was wavering, like that of a doddering old man.

"I'm sorry, son, but we can't allow pets in the clinic. They have too many germs."

"When can I visit Alvin?"

"I'm sorry, Mrs. Lawson. He's in a contagion phase

110

right now. It's best to keep him isolated at least a week or two. You don't want this passed on to yourself—or to the boy's sister."

"Oh, my God," Myrna gasped. "Do you think she has it too?"

"If she has none of his symptoms, it's possible she won't succumb. I think you may have brought Alvin in just in time."

Alvin looked at his mother with pleading eyes.

"Alvin," she said, "people get ill. You could have chicken pox, or a bad cold, or flu and have to come into the clinic. You don't have to be afraid. The doctor and his kind nurses will look after you."

"I don't want to be by myself."

"You won't be," Warren assured him. "My staff will keep you company. They're all very fond of children. You'll get very special treatment."

Alvin managed a weak smile. "I *am* special, then."

"Of course you are," Warren said, patting the boy on the shoulder. "You're one of the most special children in town now, so we will take very good care of you."

The doctor made a couple of notes on his clipboard pad, then turned away brusquely. "One of my nurses will be in momentarily to take Alvin to his room. You can stay with him till then, Mrs. Lawson. Later on, you can bring some of his toys or favorite books over. He won't need any clothes."

"Can I touch him?"

"Of course. Just don't let him breathe on you." Saying that, Warren went out into the hall.

He felt dizzy. The effort of telling so many lies was wearing on hm, although by now he thought he should be very adept at deceit.

He assured himself his deceptions were necessary. The truth would only hurt the child's mother more.

At least she had another child.

Sondra Barry had been bed-ridden for over six weeks. She was ill not from a disease, but from a self-inflicted

111

experiment. She had volunteered herself as a subject to help her husband without his knowledge. The result was that she had apparently poisoned herself and was slowly dying.

She had taken the drug meant for the children—the drug they received in cookies, candy, and baby formula, and—for the older children—via injections. Warren had yet to develop a drug, an antidote, to counteract the effects of this drug. He knew he would need such a drug some day, but he hadn't anticipated he would need it so soon. And he never thought an adult would take the children's drug.

But his wife, a doctor herself, theorizing on her own that the drug might stop the effects of aging, might, indeed, even bring about a reversal of the aging process, had given herself a series of injections over a period of four weeks.

She had felt nothing at first. Then one day, she experienced a constricting pain in her chest and had fallen over. Warren had thought it was a heart attack, but her heart was strong. He ran some tests and discovered the presence of the drug in her blood.

She confessed to having experimented on herself.

Warren could hardly criticize her, not when he was experimenting with a whole community. She had shown unusual courage in a way. But if she had consulted with him first, he could have told her the drug was no youth serum. Indeed, its effect on adults was always to speed up the aging process.

Sondra was wasting away, aging by the minute it sometimes seemed. The drug had settled into her bone marrow and nothing Warren had tried so far had made any difference. He could only make her comfortable while the two of them waited out the inevitable.

She still had her mental faculties. Warren discussed things with her. One of the things that attracted him to her in the first place was her incisive intelligence. She had helped him to form the community; her strength and his purpose worked well together, because she believed in his ideal as well. She had been driven to correct the same

112

wrongs he had, once she accepted his methods and agreed to share the risks.

Warren had not placed Sondra in the clinic. He cared for her at home where he could be closer to her. Her condition did not require constant monitoring, after all. She would just get worse, and that was all there was to it.

Warren came home and went into the back bedroom where Sondra lay. The room was kept in semi-darkness, because Warren could barely endure looking at his wife.

She was in her late fifties. Before the self-experiment, she had possessed pleasantly silver hair, and her gray-green eyes had a lively sparkle in them that kept Warren going during the toughest of times as he struggled to establish Jamay Lake. Her figure was that of a mature woman, but not obese. She had been very attractive.

Now, in the rare moments when Warren looked at her face, he saw that of an ancient human being, someone who had imminent death etched in her features.

"Are you awake, Sondra?" He sat down quietly next to her on a chair by the bed.

She responded with a weak "Yes, dear."

"Is it all right if I talk to you?"

"Of course, dear."

"If you begin to tire, let me know. All you have to do is listen. I have no one else to share these things with."

She nodded almost imperceptibly.

"I think I'm going mad," he began in a low voice, measuring each word. "I want everything to be okay, to become stable, but things are not okay. I don't know when or exactly how it happened, but our plan—our treasured ideal—is dissolving around me. People are dying. Children are dying. If there is no way I can help you—then I can't help them, either. There's no way to reverse the effects." He deliberately held back the incident with the state trooper; that was an onus he chose to bear alone.

"Keep trying, dear," she whispered. "I have faith in your . . ." She hesitated, searching for a word. ". . . abilities."

"Thank you, Sondra." He patted her hand. Her flesh

113

was cold to the touch. The veins in her arm were prominent, bulging. She could be ninety from the look of her. "I *will* keep trying, but so many things demand my time now. I fear I will find a cure for you and the children—only too late."

"It doesn't matter. I'm responsible, not you."

"I have to bear some of the responsibility. It was I who created the drug in the first place."

"But I . . ."

"Let's not go over it again." He sighed. "What's done is done. But I wish I could change things before they get totally beyond my control."

"Be patient, dear."

"I'll try." He looked at his watch. It was almost midnight. "Would it disturb you too much if I slept with you tonight?"

"Of course not."

"I need the touch of your closeness." He undressed slowly, went around to the other side of the bed and carefully crawled in under the blankets. He slid next to his wife slowly and let himself be comforted by what little warmth remained in her frail body.

He fell asleep within seconds.

The next morning, Warren arose early, his mental clock rousing him before seven. He fixed breakfast for himself and for Sondra. The last week or so, he had to help her eat. It was time for him to assign a nurse to watch over her, but he couldn't really afford to take one from the clinic at the moment. Maybe he could assign one of the mothers to take care of her, helping her eat and tending to her basic needs. She merely needed a little personal assistance, not medical care per se.

He gave his wife an injection of vitamin A, which seemed to make her feel better, and two tranquilizer tablets, which would take the edge off her awareness. She wasn't really in pain; her condition kept her in a perpetual twilight, where rest didn't come easily. Her active mind, her great intelligence, would drive her crazy

114

from inactivity if she weren't sedated most of the time.

At eight o'clock, Warren left the house and walked two blocks over to the clinic.

One of the nurses, Deborah Conners, was waiting to see him. She was very upset and distraught.

Someone had stolen her baby.

Chapter Thirteen

Night Wanderings

The Jamay Lake school was a staid institution that served primarily to keep the children from getting "wrong" ideas. Among such ideas was the concept that they needed to learn much more than what the eighth grade provided. Education higher than that was not offered. Within the context of a traditional curriculum including such subjects as basic math, English, art, music, science, social studies, and history, the students were also subtly instructed in population control theory, ecology, and a non-denominational brand of Christianity to reinforce the ideas the Nameless Church espoused. The joys of childhood and its magic, as well as the concept of being "special," were among the Christian philosophies that were presented under the guise of a general education.

Older children were required to go to school only three days a week. Warren's ultimate plan was to take each child out of school altogether when the child had attained a certain, suitable level of knowledge. Then he would observe how the society functioned when the children were out of school permanently. Would they treat their time as if it were an endless summer vacation? Or would they become problems to their mothers and to the society as a whole?

William's age meant he had only to attend school three days a week; the other two days William was expected to do independent study at the library. But he and the other children in his advanced stage rarely used their days off for study; instead, they pretty much did what they pleased.

After all, the library grew very dull after a few visits. There were no recent magazines or newspapers available there. No books printed after 1964. Records were available to take home, but they consisted primarily of classical music, swing, and early rock 'n' roll—music that appealed more to the adults than to the children. Video tapes were available as well, but, predictably, they were either educational or of films made before 1960, the vast majority being films that were intended for children.

In some books, whole portions were blacked out with indelible markers to prevent the children from being exposed to "undesirable" ideas. Sex education was almost impossible to obtain; it was deemed unnecessary.

The only publications of recent origin were the local newsletter and texts of speeches and sermons by Warren. If it weren't for the *National Geographic* William probably would never visit the library at all.

Carla Schuel, who worked at the library on Tuesdays and Thursdays, had given up trying to keep track of children who did not report for independent study. She had decided on her own it was not such a big deal after all, especially since the older children were usually unruly and troublesome when they did show up.

The all-pervading message of the educational system and the library materials available was that being a child was all anyone needed, that childhood in itself somehow guaranteed a state of bliss and happiness. The children were supposed to appreciate that and revel in the wonder of it all.

It was supposed to be enough.

William was not only bored by the library, but by school as well. He found the instruction repetitive, dull, and uninspired. He had a natural desire to learn, but the curriculum in Jamay Lake was laughably easy for him. The teachers were generally condescending and, in his view, had warped personalities; they were, after all, mothers and, as a result, they offered no alternative or controversial views to stimulate the type of mind William had.

He was not alone in his boredom. He had lately observed that many of the children—in all the grades—were becoming bored. The only excitement was at recess when fights would invariably break out. But these mini-spectacles did not hold the children's interest very long.

Sports were not encouraged. One of the patrol men had tried to get a softball team going, but discovered there were not enough children of the proper age or size to compose two teams. He could not get the children interested in playing baseball, football, or basketball even for the sheer fun of it. Faced with physical challenges, most of the children became restless and whiny. They wanted sports to be easy—as everything else was.

William had also noticed there were more and more empty seats in the classrooms. He wondered if anyone would pay much attention if he stopped coming to school altogether.

So he didn't go in on Friday. As far as he knew, there were no immediate consequences to pay for his truancy. No one came looking for him; no one paid attention to his being out on the street wandering around when he should be in school.

Maybe he wouldn't ever go back.

Friday night, after William learned from Alicia that Alvin was still in the clinic, he decided to pay his little friend a visit. He knew he couldn't just come in the front door and ask to see Alvin. Children were not allowed to visit other children, and, according to what Alicia had said, Alvin's own mother couldn't see him.

That made William more determined.

There was no moon that night, so William easily made his way through the darkness to the clinic with almost no fear of being seen.

He would enter as he had before—via the back en-

118

trance of the clinic by the loading docks. This time he would go up to the other floors in search of Alvin. He considered taking the elevator, but as before, he knew it was way too risky. He searched along the hall till he found the entrance to the stairwell.

He ascended the steps quickly to the second floor landing. He peered through the window in the door there, and, seeing no one, pulled it open and stepped in.

It was very quiet. He walked along the hall, ready to duck into a room if he saw a nurse approaching and noted most of the rooms were empty. He reached the nurse's station, but the nurse on duty was not there.

He glanced around and saw no one else, so he stepped into the station and found the list of patients. He scanned the short list and was perturbed by two things: one, the list recorded only the patients on the first, second, and third floors and Alvin's name was not among them; second, no one was listed for the fourth floor. So, of course, Alvin must be up there if he was anywhere. As his intuition had told him before, he felt Alvin was in serious condition—so serious he was being hidden by the doctor.

William returned to the stairwell and went up to the fourth floor. The door was locked.

Temporarily stymied, William considered giving up and returning home for the night, but he realized there was another flight of stairs. He went up and found a door that opened onto the roof.

The roof was flat and covered with tar and gravel. Several turbine ventilators dotted the roof, their fins spinning slowly in the wind. Smoke poured out of two chimneys from the furnaces. A third, taller chimney was not active. William approached it out of curiosity and stood on his toes to peer down inside. He sniffed an odor like burned meat and, almost retching, quickly jumped away.

As William turned from that chimney, he saw a rectangle of light near the south end of the building. He approached the rectangle and discovered it was a skylight over a lounge area on the fourth floor. Two of its windows had hinges and one of them had been left unlocked. William pried up the window very slowly, silently, and scanned the lounge. No one was present. He judged it to be a drop of at least eight feet to the floor below.

If he was careful, he could fall that far without breaking anything. He'd come this far, so he had nothing to lose by trying. He eased himself backwards down through the opening until he hung by his fingers from the metal edge. He took a deep breath and let go, rolling as he landed on the carpeted floor, just missing a table.

He sat up and listened. Apparently he had set off no alarms; he heard no one coming.

The lounge had two small couches, half a dozen chairs, and several small tables with lamps on them. A thick layer of dust covered everything. This area had not been used for some time—probably, William thought, because there were no visitors to this floor. The lounge area was open and flush with the outer hallway wall. William went to the edge and peered down the hall. He spied the nurse's station where a patrol man and the night nurse were talking quietly. They would certainly see him if he stepped out now.

William retreated and waited a few moments. He heard footsteps. He raced for one of the couches and hid behind it. He listened as someone passed by. He bent down and looked underneath the couch and could see the patrol man's feet as he walked back in the other direction.

He heard a door close.

William rose carefully, climbed over the couch and peeked into the hall again. The nurse was back in a corner, working at a CRT. The patrol man was nowhere visible.

William edged his way along the hall keeping himself flat against the wall. All the rooms were dark except for glowing night lights in consoles next to the beds, which did not provide enough illumination to see or identify the patients.

There were nameplates next to each door, however. Searching frantically, his whole body on readiness to run if the patrol man happened out in the hall, William eventually found a name plate that read, "Lawson, Alvin B."

He took a deep breath and stepped into the room, closing the door behind him, and made his way to the single bed where his friend Alvin lay.

He turned on the lamp next to the bed.

Alvin stirred, but he didn't awaken.

If that *was* Alvin.

The child William saw looked more like a shrivelled-up old man. He was completely bald. His eyes were sunk deep in their sockets; his skin was ashen and covered with deep brown spots.

Yet the eyes, the nose, the overall size and shape of the sleeping old-man/child was unmistakably Alvin.

William felt his heart pounding. He reached out to touch the boy and was shocked by the dry, thin texture of his flesh. A tear ran down his cheek.

He recoiled, and a sound of horror escaped involuntarily from his mouth. It seemed to echo in the room.

Maybe it echoed throughout the fourth floor.

He had to act fast.

He turned the lamp off and opened the door. He darted out into the hall and was frozen temporarily. He couldn't go back the way he'd come. There was no way he could jump up to the edge of that skylight.

He had to find the stairs. He inched his way towards the nurse's station. Apparently neither the nurse nor the patrol man had heard anything, or one of them would have come running. When he was almost opposite the nurse's station, he dropped to his knees and crawled by. Then he uprighted himself and walked quickly towards to the stairwell door. Fortunately, it opened from the hallway. He let himself out, then raced down the stairs to the first floor.

He stopped to catch his breath.

What had happened to Alvin? What had they done to him? How many other children were up there?

Were they all old people in children's bodies? Was that the awful secret that made the doctor keep them hidden? That had to be it, but it didn't explain much. What kind

121

of disease did the children have? Was it contagious? Why keep them hidden?

William needed some answers. He went through the first floor door and walked boldly towards the doctor's office. Its door, only a few feet from the main reception area, was unlocked, as if the doctor had nothing really to hide.

William knew better now.

He let himself into the office and turned on the lamp at the desk. He didn't know exactly what he was looking for.

The file cabinets were locked. So was the desk. William knew he couldn't break into either of them without it being obvious later.

Frustrated, he was about to leave, when he noticed the bookshelves. Maybe there was something there. He scanned the volumes of medical knowledge, still uncertain of what he was seeking. They seemed to be standard books on anatomy, disease, etiology, and many other "ologies" William had never heard of.

At last he came upon a very interesting book. Its title was *Children Who Grow Young*. Its author was Warren Barry, M.D. It was a small book and might not be missed. The dust on top of it indicated it was not consulted very often.

William tucked the book inside his jacket. He left the office, crept down the hall and exited by the rear doors.

As he walked along the dark streets, he trembled with fear and apprehension. The image of Alvin, deteriorating like an ancient man, haunted him.

It was not something he would ever forget.

William was a block from his house, walking with his head down, not paying much attention to his surroundings. He was so distracted he didn't notice someone approaching in the opposite direction. In fact, he ran into the person and almost knocked her down.

"Hey!" she protested.

Smelling feminine perfume, William thought the person might be one of the mothers, but the voice was too young. It was a girl close to his own age. He recognized her from school, but had never paid much attention to her before. That she was out at night, apparently prowling around as he was, intrigued him immensely, though.

"Sorry," he said, helping her up. "I didn't see you."

She squinted at him in the darkness. "You're William Wesley. Right?"

"Yeah."

"What you doing out here?"

"None of your business. You're not supposed to be out, either, girl."

"Don't call me 'girl,' You know my name is Mandy."

"All right, Mandy. What are you doing out here yourself?"

"Looking for my brother Danny. The little twerp ran outside the minute my mom went to sleep. I have to get him back, or I'll get into trouble. I'm responsible for him."

"I'll help you look for him," William offered.

"Did I ask for your help?"

"No, but why can't I help?"

Mandy was an attractive twelve-year-old, just heading into puberty. She wore a long coat, under which she had on jeans and a sweater. Her hair was reddish blonde and she had clear blue eyes. She thought about William's offer, then said, "I guess it's okay, if you really want to."

"I do."

They walked along a few feet, then William said abruptly, "You're not afraid of me, are you?"

Mandy almost laughed. "Should I be?"

"Sure. Everyone else is."

"Not everyone. Kevin Hamilton isn't."

"He's afraid; he just doesn't show it."

"Well, I'm not. I'm not afraid of anything or anybody."

William remembered Alvin. "Maybe you should be," he said.

"What does that mean?"

"Nothing."

"Come on, tell me."

"There's something going on at the clinic."

"Like what?"

"I don't know yet, but I'm going to find out."

She stopped briefly. "Are you trying to make me scared or something?"

William considered telling her some of the things he had seen, but he did not really know her. He had to be suspicious of everyone. "No," he said at last, "I'm just scared myself."

"You scared?"

"Everybody is scared of something."

"Maybe," Mandy said conditionally, apparently unaware she was contradicting herself, then she started walking again. "Right now, I'm scared I'll get my butt in trouble if I don't find my brother. Are you going to help me or not?"

"Sure," William said, catching up to her. He didn't want to go home and be alone just yet, so he was glad of the company she provided. He was still apprehensive, though, not about her so much as he was about everything else.

The book tucked inside his jacket seemed already to be having an ominous effect on him, its closeness to his body making him feel highly uncomfortable, as if its contents were leaching into his flesh somehow, poisoning him with whatever crazy ideas the doctor had when he wrote it. What secrets, he wondered, would the book reveal to him?

Would he be better off not knowing them?

Chapter Fourteen

William's Voice

It's like a nightmare—this thing with Alvin. I don't know how to handle it. It's not like something you would ever see in real life, but I'm sure I saw it, and seeing means it's real, unless a person is crazy, and I'm not.

I woke up this morning and still had bad feelings about Alvin. I wish I could get him out of that place, only I don't know what I could do for him. I'm not a doctor. Of course, I'm not sure Dr. Barry is a real doctor sometimes. He doesn't seem to cure people. He let Pete die and all Pete had was his toe cut off, and people don't die from things like that.

I feel sorry for Alvin. He's just a little kid. Okay, he's only a couple of years younger than I am, but that's a big difference at our age. Like I'm starting to get hair down "there," and looking at girls, and the only girls Alvin looks at are his sister and their next door neighbor Dawn.

What happened to Alvin really bothers me, because I think it's happened to some other kids. I wish I'd had the time to look in some of the other rooms when I was up there, but I couldn't take the chance.

I don't know for sure, but having the whole top floor of the clinic locked up makes me think the doctor is definitely trying to hide something. Otherwise, the patients for the fourth floor would be listed on the clipboard I saw on the other floor. So it's some kind of secret.

I wonder if the disease Alvin has is something I can get.

I'd hate to look like that.

This book I took from the doctor's office is really dense. The title makes it sound simple, but it's full of philosophical stuff, and makes my head hurt. I keep trying to make sense of it, but I got about thirty pages into it and it seemed to go around in circles, talking about "population control" and "exponential problem factors" and "societal pressures," and other things that sound like they might mean something important, except I don't know enough to understand it. One of the chapters is called, "The Problematical Concerns of Eugenics and the Realities of Social Management." I mean, how am I supposed to figure that out?

I tried to tell Mom about Alvin, but she wouldn't listen. Of course, I didn't tell her I broke into the clinic. I just said I heard Alvin was really bad off, and his mother ought to know about it, and Mom asked me how did I know what his own mother didn't know, and I couldn't think of a good answer.

You have to think ahead before you start in on a lie, especially when it gets complicated, because mothers—even when their minds are foggy from the happy candy—have this instinct about lying. Or maybe it's just that they mistrust their own children. (Sounds like a "societal pressure" to me.) Mothers never accept the things we children say without asking a lot of questions until you give up trying to explain at all.

I think I'd be better off talking to Alvin's kitten.

That kitten is strange too. Alvin's had it about six weeks and it hasn't gotten any bigger. From what I remember cats grow up pretty fast. But Alvin's isn't growing. Neither is Alicia's. In fact, I've never seen a grown cat or dog anyplace in Jamay. It makes me wonder if they're toys. Maybe the mothers secretly wind them up when we're not looking, or they put new batteries in them.

Maybe all of us are just toys. Maybe we're all like the dolls where my mother works. We're not just children but toy people. It's not the same as being small people. A

126

toy is something you can throw away, and I wonder sometimes if the mothers of some of us would like to throw us away like broken toys.

Everything seems like a toy in Jamay. We've got toy Bibles, and a toy library, and a toy school. Nothing is serious; everything is a plaything.

I guess I'm just a big toy. A toy boy. A toy boy with no joy.

I bet Kevin's mother feels that way about him—like he's a broken toy she'd like to throw away. He gets into so much trouble she's always having to apologize to somebody and try to make it up. Then she takes Kevin in the house and whips his ass good, which is supposed to be against the rules. I don't care, since Kevin deserves anything he gets, but if I was a rat, I'd tell the doctor about it. But I'm not a rat, and I'm not sure the doctor would do anything, because I don't trust him very much myself, especially after what I saw at the clinic. I bet if I went there *every* night, I'd see lots of weird stuff going on.

Of course, if I was really a rat, I could make life miserable for lots of people in this town. Dawn's mother, for example. I know she's been screwing with that patrol man at least two more times. The patrol men aren't supposed to mess with the women, and the women are supposed to know better. I bet Mrs. Henderson either isn't eating her happy candy or she's getting too much.

Last night was strange because I ran into Mandy Snyder walking around in the dark. I've seen her before—in school and sometimes in the library, and she's a lot smarter than she lets people know. Maybe that's the smartest thing about her. I go around showing off how smart I am, and it gets me into trouble. But I can't just act stupid because I'm not stupid. Maybe Mandy knows something I don't about being smart; maybe she's sly. Maybe the best way to use intelligence is not to let anyone know you're using it. I could see how that might work.

Anyhow, Mandy is the only kid I've met who doesn't look at me like I'm some kind of nut-case. She's not afraid

127

of me, and she isn't afraid of much else. So she says, anyhow.

I walked around with her for about an hour, and we finally found her brother, Danny, who's six or seven I think. He was hiding behind some trash cans in an alley. The way we spotted him was we saw these flashes of light down the alley, and when we went to investigate them, we saw Danny sitting there with a box of kitchen matches, lighting one, letting it burn almost down to his fingers, then lighting another one. He was having a lot of fun. It was almost a shame to take him home, but when Mandy spoke to him, he acted like she was his mother and looked like he was going to pee his pants. Mandy took the matches away from him and gave him a long talk about burning himself up.

That made me think about the fire at the church and my face felt hot, because I didn't want Mandy to think I set it. I didn't say anything about it, though. Of course, I guess I shouldn't care what Mandy thinks about me.

I walked home with Mandy and her little brother, and they live around the corner from my house. I never noticed that before. We went up on the porch and Mandy actually thanked me for walking her home. I said it was okay.

Mandy said she wasn't afraid of anything, but she wasn't as strong as a boy, and she heard that one of the patrol men was caught looking at little girl like she was a woman, and some people say he even tried to rape her, but Mandy couldn't find out for sure. She said she might be afraid of something like that, but she would fight if anyone tried to do something with her. Her Mom told her how to kick a man where it hurts. She said she would do it without thinking.

I didn't know about that stuff—about the patrol men maybe raping little girls. I wonder if the doctor knows about that. I wonder if the doctor knows what's going on behind his back. Or his front.

I said good-by to Mandy and her brother, and went out to the street to go back home. I saw Mandy's mother come to the door and get all excited about her kids being out after dark. Mandy said something that quieted her down real quick. Her mom has red hair just like Mandy—only Mandy's is lighter.

It was only a short walk home, but I kept thinking about things. I kept remembering how Mandy smelled like a woman in the dark, and how she was so brave about everything. I thought most girls were scaredy-cats. I guess I was wrong about that. Or maybe Mandy isn't like a regular girl.

The house was dark when I got inside, and for some reason that was scary to me, though I never was afraid of the dark before. Maybe it's because I was thinking of Alvin up there on the fourth floor of the clinic—maybe dying in the dark.

I got things figured out now, even if I can't figure out the doctor's book. Jamay Lake is a place for a bunch of nutso people, and the doctor is watching all of us, and some day he might just kill us all or something. That's my theory. That's why all these weird things happen. Something's really wrong with this place.

I got to get out of here. That's why I wrote this letter to my dad:

Dear Father,
This is your son, William. Maybe you forgot about me and mom. I don't know if you care about us, but I have to tell you we're in a very strange place. It's a city called Jamay Lake, up in Indiana somewhere, and that's about all I can tell you. It's out in the country, and when you come to the front, it won't say Jamay Lake, it will say Cummins Military Academy on an old sign. There's a gate there. But you can't get into it unless you have a gate pass. The man who watches the gate will shoot you if you don't have one. I will get you one somehow.

This place is really screwed-up. There's nothing but mothers and children here, and a few patrol

129

men who are like police. Some crazy things are happening. I don't want to grow up in this town, but I think mom will keep me here forever if you don't do something.

This place is so crazy that you will have to pretend you are a delivery man or something, even with the gate pass. You should have a van or a truck, so you'll look like one of the delivery guys. Maybe you ought to have something in your truck, like paint or something.

If you get inside, you'll have to be careful. People will watch you. If you can get away, you need to come to the house we're living in. I drew a map to go with this letter so you can see how to get here.

If you still love us, you'll come and rescue me. Maybe Mom will want to come too, but I can't say for sure, because she's taking drugs all the time—not serious stuff, but this tranquilizer they put in candy for all the mothers to eat.

I guess this sounds pretty weird to you. Well, I live here and it definitely is weird. I don't want to stay here any more. I'm afraid something bad is going to happen to all of us very soon. I've seen some things that are really scary that I can't even put in a letter, because I'm not supposed to know about them.

Love,

Your son, William

I don't know if Dad is alive or not, or if he cares or anything, but I'm going to find a way to get this letter to him. Alvin's mother works at the place where the mail goes out and comes in, but she probably won't help me. I'll have to be real sneaky.

The other thing is I've got to get a gate pass. Like I told Dad, nobody can get into this crazy town without one.

Kevin will have to help me with that. He's been going around bragging and showing kids things he has that you're not supposed to be able to get: like dirty pictures of women, and cigarettes. Kevin has got a source of some kind for getting that stuff.

I'll find out what it is if I have to beat his ass or kill him. It's about time I showed him who's in charge around here anyhow.

Chapter Fifteen

Brenda's New Baby

They came through the front door around noon. They didn't knock. They didn't call out first. They didn't ask permission to come in.

Two patrol men, Lester Stultz and Harold Thomas, just burst through the door.

They came up the stairs after Brenda Stowe, and found her in the nursery giving a bottle to a baby boy. One man grabbed the baby from her arms; the other started dragging her out into the hall. Her robe caught on the hinge of the door, and he ripped it loose.

The baby squealed.

"What are you doing?" Brenda demanded indignantly. "I've done nothing wrong." The men didn't reply; they merely grunted. They read her no rights. Nor did they say what she was charged with. They operated without any particular rules, except what they themselves judged to be right and proper.

"You can't take my baby!" she screamed at the younger man.

"Dr. Barry will decide that," he said. He held the baby close to him, carefully, making sure its blue blanket was tucked together properly. The baby continued to exercise its vocal chords.

"Leave me alone!" Brenda struggled in the grip of Lester, the older of the patrol men, who had rough features set in a porcine face. He backhanded her without hesitating.

"Shut up, bitch!"

Brenda held her face and whimpered. Lester twisted one of her arms behind her back and started pushing her down the stairs.

"There wasn't any need for that," Harold protested. "The doc said to take it easy on her."

"She's not making it easy. You just take care of the kid, and I'll take care of the woman."

"Just go easy, that's all." Harold glared at Lester, on his face a silent threat to inform on him.

Lester knew he'd do it too, to get him in trouble. Harold was young and inexperienced. He'd been a cop at one time, but not in a big rough city. He didn't know how people needed to be treated to get them to do what you wanted. He was too easy on everybody, including the kids. Some day, Lester thought, he'll turn his back at the wrong time. He'd wish then he hadn't been so trusting.

"All right, kid," Lester said, grunting with the effort of pulling Brenda out to the patrol car. "Just make sure you do your own job right."

Harold said nothing further. The baby suddenly became silent as the car pulled away.

Brenda was still hysterical by the time Warren came to see her in a room at the clinic on the second floor. She had been strapped to a bed and injected with a tranquilizer, but she was still wide-eyed and struggling.

"Miss Stowe," he said quietly, "there are things you have to understand."

"They took my baby and they tied me up. I understand that all right, and I don't like it. And they tied me up so I can't move!"

Warren stood by the side of the bed. "This probably wasn't necessary," he said, undoing the restraints from her left arm. "I'll take these off, if you promise not to try to run away, and let me talk to you about everything."

"I don't know about that. I want my baby."

"If you try to run from me, the patrol men will just catch you and bring you back, and we'll have to keep you

133

under restraint. You make the decision."

Her face relaxed a little. "All right. I won't run away."

He unfastened the remaining straps. "Now, is that better?"

She nodded.

"You know, of course, that baby wasn't yours."

Her face registered total disbelief and outrage. "Yes, it is. It's my baby, or I wouldn't have it. Now would I?"

"Think, Miss Stowe. Try to remember. You took that baby away from one of my nurses. Did you believe it would be so difficult for us to figure out who would have taken it?"

"I had that baby myself," she said defiantly.

"You never had a baby." Warren patted her arm, trying to calm or comfort her, but she jerked away.

"Yes, I did. I can prove it too." She pulled down the front of her gown and squeezed her left breast. Milk dribbled out of the nipple. "See? I'm starting to get my milk back . . ."

Warren was startled in spite of himself. He touched the tip of his finger to her nipple and held it up to his eyes and nose. The milk was real.

He thought about it and realized he shouldn't be all that surprised. If she could convince herself in her state of mind that the baby she had taken was hers, it might not be that great a step to convince her body it had given birth and that she should be lactating. He recalled cases he had read about in the medical journals about spontaneous lactation; in folklore it was called "witch's milk." It was possible for a child, or even a male to produce milk, if certain hormones became unbalanced in the body.

Warren reached over and covered her breast, tenderly pushing the gown back in place.

"That's strong evidence, Miss Stowe, but it's not proof. Milk production is possible without pregnancy. Besides, you and I both *know* you have not been pregnant in the last year. You also know that you can*not* get pregnant. Don't you?"

She seemed genuinely confused. "But where did I get a

134

baby before? I had Donna Marie. I took her to the picnic and showed her to the other mothers. It was because Pete died. I needed to have a baby, so I did."

"Think," Warren gently coaxed her. "Remember."

"I was pregnant . . ." Her blue eyes watered. "No, I wasn't even with a man. I—but I had Donna Marie, and somebody stole her and left a *doll* in her place! That's what happened. I had to go find her. I had just bought formula for her, because my milk was drying up, but now it's coming back, and I can nurse her again. Donna Marie is my baby. I love her." She stared down at her own hands. "I don't understand."

"The baby you had with you this morning—it was a boy."

"No, that's not right. My baby is a girl."

"You never had a real baby." He realized how foolish it had been to give her the doll, but at the time it seemed a kinder way of dealing with her son's death than just making her live with the misery. "I gave you the doll, and because of the heavy doses of tranquilizers you were taking, you convinced yourself it was real. Or perhaps it was because you wanted to believe it. Either way, I was wrong to have done that."

Brenda hunched forward. She flexed her hands and studied the way they moved, as if she had never realized they did that before. Then she fixed her gaze on the end of the bed. "You gave me Donna Marie?"

"Yes."

"You're her father?"

"Miss Stowe, I just told you she was a doll. She had no father. She was not a real child."

"My milk was real."

"Yes. Your mind convinced your body of that. The mind is capable of causing all kinds of things to manifest—such as stigmata, odd-shaped scars—and mother's milk."

"But I *am* a mother."

"You were, yes. But your son fell ill."

"So I'm not a real mother anymore."

"I'm afraid not."

"Nothing is real," she said flatly. "Nothing."

"Now, Miss Stowe, you have to get over this. You know Pete is dead. You never had a baby. You'll have to learn to cope with that, and then, maybe, we can put you somewhere so you'll be with children again. But you've got to. . . ."

"That bastard hit me," she said quietly, almost in a childlike manner.

"Who?"

"The patrol man."

"Which one?"

"The ugly old one. He hit me and the other man took my baby right from my arms."

"I'll see that he's disciplined."

"It doesn't matter. Because nothing is real. Nothing at all. This is a place of dreams that don't work out. We are not real people anymore. We don't have . . ."

"Miss Stowe?"

Her eyes rolled back, and she slumped against the back of the bed. A short gasp escaped from her lips.

Warren felt for her pulse. He put his stethoscope to her chest. He shook her.

She was dead.

Warren stepped away from the bed, suddenly feeling a great depression. Brenda was like the woman from the fire; she had just simply given up and died.

For no physical reason. She died because she wanted to.

Later that evening Warren sat in his office. Only his desk lamp was on. He was bent over a sheet of statistics which he had scribbled in cursive on a sheet of notebook paper:

Two women dead.

One baby dead.

A state trooper murdered.

Eight children on the fourth floor of the clinic. Probably terminal.

Signs of neurosis among general population.

136

Rumors of troubled children.

Unsubstantiated rumors of sexual activity between staff men and mothers.

The Cherished Ideal.

He scanned his list, then underlined the last item. "The Cherished Ideal" was not doing so well.

Brenda's death was even more disquieting than the other woman's. Because now he realized what their deaths represented: the gradual death of "The Cherished Ideal."

They had both died of shock—shock induced by an abrupt choice to no longer live. They were like people found dead at disaster sites who had no injuries; they had died simply because they had seen enough of life. Such cases usually occurred around earthquakes, volcano eruptions, or other catastrophes. The human mechanism, when faced with the overwhelming, sometimes just refused to continue.

But the catastrophes here were not overwhelming. Maybe, in Brenda's case, if he had made her face the truth sooner, she would not have given up. But the other woman had been exposed only to a fire in which neither she nor her children had been injured.

How these two women died was also troubling because it was a symptom of how they perceived the world they lived in, the world he and Sondra had put together.

He chuckled. Now he was counting his wife among the blameworthy. Typical of the mind to try to find either a scapegoat or someone to share the blame.

He knew, of course, it was all his own doing.

If these women gave up life so easily, he wondered exactly what was missing from their lives? People faced tragedies every day and survived. Why were these two women so vulnerable?

He took a pencil and crossed out everything on his list in anger. Then he wadded up the paper and threw it across the room.

He had to change things somehow, take charge of the situation. But he knew there was no quick and easy fix. He needed time to consider ways of bringing his society

137

back into balance. He took a new sheet of paper and wrote down three things to do immediately:

Increase dosage in pharmaceutical sweets.

Have patrol men monitor women/children more closely.

Consider closing the church temporarily.

He didn't really want to close the church, but he had a number of good reasons for doing so—not the least of which was how obvious it was when the congregation was gathered together that some of them were missing—which would generate more and more questions that he wanted to put off answering as long as he possibly could.

Besides, he could no longer readily think of uplifting subjects on which to preach. Anything he might say to them would be a lie at this moment.

His resolutions made, Warren turned off the lamp and left his office.

He had another body to commit to the flames of the crematorium.

Chapter Sixteen

William's Covert Activities

It was a Tuesday afternoon, and starting to turn chilly as November approached. Still, the sun was shining and there was little wind. It was not unpleasant to be outside.

Except for Kevin Hamilton.

William had trapped him behind the library where a fence prevented his escaping. He was threatening him with his presence only at the moment, but he was willing to do more if necessary. In fact, he hoped to do more.

"Where'd you get that stuff?" he demanded harshly.

"Twat did you say? I cunt hear you." Kevin had a strange smirk on his face, as if he couldn't decide whether to fight or not, but he wasn't as cocky as William expected him to be.

"Quit that crap. Where'd you get the stuff?" William took a step closer. He was almost nose-to-nose with Kevin.

"What stuff?" Kevin said innocently.

"The pictures of naked women, the cigarettes. And whatever else you've got."

"None of your business, dumbass."

"I'm not a dumbass and you know it."

"I don't have to tell you nothing, and if you don't be careful, I'll kick your ass."

"As if you could do it."

"I could, and I will. I've had enough of you. Everybody has. Everybody hates your guts."

"I don't care who hates me. I just want you to tell me

where kids get stuff like that."

"Maybe you can get anything, if you got the smarts. I guess you're too dumb, or you'd know."

"Tell me."

"I'll tell you something—I saw you set that fire by the church. If you want some real trouble, I'll get it for you. What do you think the old doctor would do to you, then? He'd give you a shot that'd kill you, that's what."

William laughed. Kevin seemed dumbfounded. "What's so funny, creep face?"

"I've been making people think *you* did it."

Kevin's face whitened, then turned red with anger. "You goddamned liar." He drew his fist back to hit William, but before his arm was halfway up, William had punched him hard in the stomach, slamming him against the library wall.

Kevin doubled over. "You . . ."

William hit him again. In the jaw. Kevin slid down to the ground. Kevin kicked him in the side.

"Wait till I get up! I'll break your head."

"You're not getting up." William stomped on Kevin's right kneecap—just enough to sting, not enough to break it. Kevin howled like a dog.

"Had enough?"

"Drop dead," Kevin spat between bloody teeth.

"I'll half-kill you if I have to. I don't care what happens. You understand? I don't care. You can go cry to your mama, or tell on me to anyone you like, and it won't make any difference to me, because I don't care."

Kevin looked up at him warily. "Asshole."

William squatted, shoved Kevin forward, and twisted his left arm until Kevin's fist almost reached the back of his neck. Kevin grunted, trying to endure the pain silently, but it was too much for him.

"All right, sumbitch! All right! I'll tell. . . ."

William let go immediately, stood, then helped Kevin up. Kevin's defiance was somewhat abated as he rubbed his aching shoulder.

"Okay, where do you get the stuff?"

"You won't like it."

140

"Are you trying to fink out on me? You want that arm jerked out of your shoulder?"

Kevin's right hand darted into his pocket and brought forth a switchblade.

Click!

William grabbed Kevin's wrist, twisted it with all his strength, and the knife fell out of the other boy's hand. William bent down and picked the weapon up, folded it shut and dropped it in his jacket pocket. "Thanks for the neat knife. I might need it if I have to cut your nuts off."

Kevin apparently knew he was defeated.

"One of the patrol men . . ."

"Which one?"

"Stultz, the ugly guy. You know, the one who looks like a pig. He'll get you just about anything you want."

"What's he want in return?"

"Nothing much," Kevin said, smiling nastily.

William didn't like the way Kevin smiled. "Like what?"

"You just gotta bribe him, that's all."

"With what?"

Kevin wiped his mouth on his sleeve. "Depends."

"Depends on what, damn it?"

"What *he* needs. You need something. He needs something. You just trade."

"What would I have he'd want?"

"Maybe a pair of your mom's panties. Dirty ones. I got a pack of smokes off him with a pair of *my* mom's panties."

"What the hell would he do with panties?" William asked suspiciously.

"Maybe he sucks the juice out of them."

"Baloney."

"I don't know. He's a queer or something, I guess."

William sensed Kevin was either lying or still being a smart alec, but he didn't feel like beating him any more. There were limits to what he himself would do, and he suspected Kevin was just cunning enough to avoid the whole truth, no matter what he did. He had the name. That's all he needed.

141

But just to be sure, he said, "If you're lying to me about Stultz, and it's somebody else, I'll come back and finish what I started—with your own knife, asswipe."

Kevin's face showed no concern. "It's Stultz all right. Go find him. Tell him what you need. Tell him I sent you. He'll fix you up. He can get anything. Take a list with you. Maybe you oughta get some of your mom's pants before you go."

"Leave my mom out of it," William said.

"Piss on your mom."

William drew his arm back, then let it drop to his side. Kevin was just trying to get in the last word. What difference did it make what he said about his mother? There was no one else around to hear it, so there was no honor or duty involved.

"Aw, go to hell." William turned and walked away, massaging his knuckles. They were badly bruised from the fight. He was worried too. Kevin was holding something back. It wouldn't be like him not to.

But maybe Stultz liked to wear women's panties, for all he knew. There were probably people who did weird stuff like that.

Stultz looked like he could be one of them.

The patrol men were usually easy to locate. Since there were only a few of them and Jamay Lake was so small, tracking them down was a matter of patience.

William knew better than to ask anyone, though. He'd have to find out on his own where Stultz was.

He went first to the patrol men's main quarters and discovered Stultz was not there, which meant he was on patrol, probably walking around somewhere killing time, or in the pharmacy, the clinic, or a number of other places.

After wandering around an hour or so, William spotted his man out in front of the school. He was just coming down the steps. As Stultz started to get in his car, William ran up to him.

"Officer Stultz?"

Stultz' expression was one of disdain. He wasn't a particularly friendly person and had no love for children; he had been hired to do a job as far as he was concerned. It didn't have to go any further than that.

William was startled by how clear Stultz' eyes were. He was obviously very alert—very attuned to his surroundings at all times, like an animal of prey.

"What you want, kid?"

"A friend of mine . . ." He tried to read what was in the man's eyes. Kevin may have lied, may have set him up, despite his threats. Stultz didn't look like he would help anyone.

"Yeah?"

"Kevin Hamilton. He said—he said you can get things."

"Kevin said that?"

"Yeah."

"I wonder why he said that?"

William's resolve started to crumble; Stultz was a big man, a dangerous man too, no doubt. He might rat on William for even asking. There might be hell as a result; maybe the doctor did have a death shot for kids who got out of line.

But he'd already started his query, and he had no choice but to continue. "Because I asked him where he got the stuff he had."

"Oh, and he told you?"

"He said to tell you it was okay."

Stultz stared at him a moment, then entered the car. "Get in, kid. We can't talk out in the open."

Stultz leaned across the front seat and unlatched the passenger side door. "Come on."

William slid in reluctantly and closed the door. Stultz started the engine and cruised down the street slowly.

"Okay," he began, "let's say, for the sake of argument, that I got some stuff for Kevin, though I ain't saying that's true for sure. But let's say I did. You didn't think I'd do that for nothing, did you?"

"No, of course not. He said you'd want a—a trade."

"That's a nice way of putting it." Stultz turned a corner and headed back towards the church. "Of course,

143

it all depends on what it is you want. You see, everything has its price according to what it is. Cigarettes ain't too bad. Pictures of tits and ass cost a little more. A video, say, of something you don't see around here—a video of people screwing—that costs quite a bit."

William blushed at the man's coarse language, not because of its content so much as by the blunt, casual nature with which he used it in front of a child. He also found himself intrigued by the idea of getting a sex video, but quickly banished that notion from his mind. His particular need was more important than any voyeuristic impulse.

Stultz pulled the car up in front of the church garage. He reached over the sun visor and brought out a remote control on which he pressed a button that caused one of the garage doors to rise. He drove in, worked the remote again, and they were alone in the garage with the door shut.

"This here's my hideaway. Nobody uses this old garage, so I got a good stash here. Just about anything a kid might want that he can't get otherwise. Like the stuff I mentioned before, and other things. Girlie magazines. *New* comic books. Cookies without the hit in them . . ."

"What do you mean?"

"God, you're a dumb one, ain't you? You don't know the cookies got dope in them? Well, I guess, maybe you're too big and don't eat those cookies. You have to get shots, don't you?"

William nodded numbly. "What's in the shots?"

"Never mind."

"What's the doctor doing to us?"

"Say, I ain't here to sell secrets. If you want secrets, you got to find them by yourself, kid. I got merchandise—contraband is what it should be called—and I got lots of customers. I don't have to take squat from you, or tell you anything I don't want to. Now you tell me what you want, and I'll give you the price, and then we'll settle. A simple little business transaction."

William realized he was sweating. Being alone with this ugly man in the garage was a threatening situation, and he was beginning to lose his courage. Maybe he should forget about his plan, form an alternate one—anything to get out of here.

"Maybe," he said carefully, "you don't have what I want."

"Look, kid. You're wasting my time. Tell me what you want and get it over with. I ain't got all day to mess around."

"All right. I want a gate pass."

Stultz' brow wrinkled. It was difficult to tell whether he was frowning or just thinking. "A gate pass? What the hell would you do with that?"

"I just want one. Do you have to know what I need it for?"

Stultz rubbed his chin. "That's a tall order. Not that I can't get it, of course, but I have to figure out what it's worth."

"That's all I want," William said. "I wouldn't bother you for anything else. Ever."

"You wouldn't, eh? A gate pass." He swiveled around in the seat and appraised William in a way that made the boy feel very uncomfortable. "You're not a bad-looking kid. I might make you a pretty good deal. Kevin, I charge him a lot, because he's a little creep, and I just don't like him that much. A kid like you—man, what you could do on the streets of L.A."

"What?"

"Los Angeles. I used to work the Strip. I saw every kind of human scumbag there was. Mostly whores, but also a lot of kids like you, hanging out on the corners, turning tricks with rich old farts."

"Tricks?"

"You know—queering them. Letting the old guys suck them off or screw them in the butt. Ain't you ever heard of that?"

The skin on William's neck felt like it was creeping up. "No," he said hoarsely.

"You're a little virgin, then. Ain't you? A cherry."

William remained mute. It was beginning to sink in on him. Stultz *was* queer.

145

"Look, I know what you're thinking. You're thinking this stuff is nasty. Like, you wouldn't ever let somebody touch you or play with you. Sure, it's nasty. That's why people pay for it, because ain't too many kids willing to do it. The kids out in L.A., they're runaways. They got drug habits. They'll do anything for money. Anything at all. Girls fourteen years old are turning tricks out there. And boys. The world's a screwed-up place, kid, and you just don't know it. You don't know what life is all about."

"I don't want to know. I just want a gate pass."

"Then you're going to have to put out."

"What's that mean?"

"Put out, damn it. Do what I say. Bend over. Let me do what I want. Hell, kid I won't *hurt* you. It all comes out in the wash."

William's eyes were wide with unsought truths. Now he knew what Kevin had meant about not liking what Stultz would want. He felt like kicking Kevin's ass for not telling him exactly what the price would be.

"Kevin said you were a queer."

Stultz' face reddened. "I ain't no queer. I like snatch as well as the next man, but you can't get it around here without raping someone, and the doctor ain't too kind on that sort of activity."

William remembered Mandy telling him about how one of the patrol men attempted to rape a girl. Could that have been Stultz? He glanced at the man's unprepossessing face. Stultz looked like he was capable of any act.

"It's like in prison," Stultz explained. "You take what you can get. Men do each other all the time in the joint, but it don't mean they're queer. It's just the way they get by without any women around. Now, since I don't have anything against you, I won't 'charge' you like I would Kevin. You just put out—oh, I don't know—four or five times, and I'll get you a gate pass."

William edged towards the door. "No!"

Stultz touched William's left hand. "Come on, kid. It ain't that big a deal."

William yanked the door handle and almost fell out of

the car. He was on his feet quickly, though.

"I'll tell!" he yelled. "I'll tell everyone you're queer." He searched around frantically for a way out. All he saw was the door to the church.

Stultz got out on the other side of the car. He made an obscene kissing noise. "Hey, boy, how about a kiss? You cherry!"

"I'll tell the doctor."

"He won't believe a troublemaker like you."

"I'll tell him about the stuff you got here."

"I don't see any stuff."

William's eyes darted around the garage; it did seem empty. Stultz had lied. It was all a setup to get him into the garage.

"Come here, cherry boy."

William pulled out the switchblade he had taken from Kevin, brandishing it at Stultz.

"Oh, a knife fighter, eh? I'm really scared." Stultz jumped forward and deftly kicked the knife from William's hand. He picked it up and put it in his shirt pocket. "I hate to tell you what Kevin had to do to get this. Too bad he lost it."

William backed away, leaned against the door to the church, and it fell open behind him. He dropped to the floor.

Stultz' laughter sounded like a bullfrog croaking. William got to his feet and ran through the church towards the front entrance. He pushed his way outside just in time to see Stultz' car driving away.

William ran down the front steps and headed for home.

Later, William realized he could not rat on Stultz. He would deny everything. So would Kevin. So would any other children who had to "pay" for things they wanted. And William's own credibility was suspect—as Stultz had rightly pointed out.

Despite William's intelligence, despite his smug feeling that he knew it all, he had never even considered a patrol man would want sex from him.

Such a concept was unknown in the world of Jamay Lake—at least to William, and he had thought he had more intelligence than any other child. Maybe he had brains, but when it came to the seamy side of things he was, as Stultz had called him, a "cherry boy."

The doctor had done a good job of sheltering the children from certain ideas. William felt painfully naive.

And he still didn't have a gate pass.

His mother was at the doll shop. He was alone in the house. Too alone. He felt betrayed, vulnerable and desperate. He needed company.

He decided to see if Mandy was home.

William sat with Mandy on a bench in the back yard. She had put on a light blue jacket that contrasted nicely with her colorful hair and matched her eyes. Just looking at her made William feel a little more hopeful.

Mandy remained silent. She could see William was upset, but she had the sensibility not to press him into revealing what was wrong until he was ready to. She had learned how to handle moody people by dealing with her mother.

After a prolonged period of staring off into space, William said, "You have to take shots?"

Mandy was surprised. This surely wasn't the reason for his being upset. But she answered anyhow. "Yes. Once a month, like all the bigger kids. Why?"

"Ever wonder what's in them?"

"Doctor Barry says they're special vitamins."

"Why do we need them—and so often?"

"I don't know. Because they're good for us? Why are you talking about shots? It's bad enough we have to take them, without reminding me of it."

"Because of something somebody said to me." William looked mysterious. "The shots aren't what we think."

"What?"

"It doesn't make any sense yet. It's another secret."

"Another one?"

148

"There are a lot of secrets here. Like in the clinic. There are sick kids up there. Really sick kids. And the patrol men aren't here just to protect us, either."

"What do you mean?"

"They're here to make sure we don't get away."

"Who ever tries?"

"I know no one tries, but if they did, one of the patrol men might just shoot . . ."

"William, you worry too much, especially about things that aren't even happening. Your imagination goes wild."

"It's not imagination. I've seen things myself. We got to get out. We got to do something."

"Why? We have everything we need here. My mother says . . ."

"The mothers are in on it. Everybody knows the secret except the kids."

"William, you're scaring me."

"Look, you should be scared," he said earnestly. "Something big is happening here. Big and bad. We need help from the outside, and I think I know how to get it."

"How?"

William told her about finding the letter with his father's return address and how he had written him. "So, all I need is a gate pass, so he can get in and take me—us—out."

"All of us?"

"You can come, if you want."

"I don't know if . . ."

"You don't have to decide now. I don't even know if the letter will get to my dad. I'm not sure he's really alive."

"How do you know he'll help you?"

"I don't. I don't know anything, and I know too much. See? That's how screwed up it all is."

"You don't make much sense sometimes."

"I need your help, Mandy. I can't do it all by myself. I tried, and I almost got . . ." He paused. He didn't think he could tell her about being threatened sexually by Stultz; it was too bizarre. It also made him sick even to think about it. "I tried," he repeated, "and failed."

"Okay, I'll help you."

"You don't know what I want you to do."

"That's all right. Just tell me how I can help."

Her face was completely bereft of suspicion. She actually trusted him, and William had never seen that from another human being, except from Dawn, who didn't know any better. He wished he could just sit there and be with her, without having to do anything else. He was beginning to like her very much.

Strange—William Wesley liking a girl. It didn't sound possible. But it was happening. She wanted to help him; all she asked was how.

"It'll be easy," he said finally. "I think."

Just before dark, Mandy ran up to the sentry station by the gate and knocked on the window, rousing the troll.

"What is it?" Max asked gruffly, barely poking his misshapen head into view.

"You have to come right now," Mandy said excitedly. "I don't have time to explain. It's my little brother."

Max muttered but the call to duty was too strong to resist. He was, after all, responsible for the well-being of everyone in the community.

"Hurry!" Mandy pleaded.

Max opened the door and stepped out. He started to lock up, but Mandy pulled on his arm. "We have to get to him right away."

Max left the door slightly ajar, then walked/limped as fast as his built-up shoe would let him while he tried to keep up with the young girl.

A minute later, William ducked into the station, after having first made sure no one was watching. He found the pad of gate passes, took one from the middle, and tucked it inside his jacket. He was out in another minute and running back down the street.

Max returned shortly, cursing under his breath.

"I really thought he was hurt badly," Mandy said. "I'm sorry. I didn't mean to waste your time."

"Okay, already," the troll spoke. "You just be careful in the future. I'm a soldier and I'm not to leave my post. What if the enemy came up on us? Why, they'd be in here murdering and pillaging and everything. Like in 'Nam."

"I'll be sure before I bother you again. I promise."

Mandy led her little brother home, giving him a big kiss first for being such a good actor. He had lain very still, pretending to be unconscious while Mandy and the troll fussed over him. He deserved to be rewarded, so Mandy promised him an extra cookie when they got home.

The next morning, William had one more bit of subterfuge to pull off. He had to get the letter with the gate pass in it into the outgoing mail.

Myrna Lawson was in charge of the mail, which was part of her duties at the free pharmacy on the days she worked there.

William came into the free pharmacy, acting non-chalant, though he was afraid the letter inside his jacket might fall out at any minute and betray him.

"What do you need, William?" Myrna asked. She was putting the mail in bundles. Most of it was business correspondence. Very little personal mail was allowed out, unless it was approved by the doctor.

"Maybe a candy bar. I don't know what I want for sure."

"Well, don't break anything while you're looking around."

"I won't."

William went up and down the aisles a couple of times, making a good show of looking over the merchandise, but he was really waiting.

Finally, the phone rang. Myrna had to get up to answer it in the back room.

Mandy was calling and would engage her for at least five minutes as they had planned.

William rushed over to the counter, looked down into the mail and started to slide his letter into one of the bundles already made-up.

Then he realized he needed a stamp.

He looked around frantically but saw no stamps. Mandy would hang up in seconds, and Myrna would come out before he accomplished his mission. Thinking quickly, he jerked a letter out of the pile that was already stamped, pried the stamp off carefully, then attached it to his letter with cellophane tape from a dispenser on top of the counter.

He slipped his letter into one of the bundles, tucked the other letter in his jacket and grabbed a candy bar—mere seconds before Myrna returned.

"Silly girl," she mumbled. "Just wasting my time with a lot of . . . what are you doing by the mail?"

"Nothing. I was waiting for you." He held up a Hershey Bar. "Just wanted to show you what I'm getting."

She eyed him suspiciously as she entered the candy bar on the register.

William's heart was racing. If she decided to check over the mail—all his hard work and planning would be for nought.

"How's Alvin?" he asked.

Myrna's face betrayed great concern, distracting her from her present purpose temporarily, just as William had hoped.

"He's—well, he's just fine, I'm sure," she answered irritably, "as if it is any of your business." She grabbed several bundles of mail and dumped them in a battered canvas bag, then set the bag on the counter. William was certain the bundle he had put his letter in was in the bag.

As he walked out of the store, he turned the corner and took out the letter he'd stolen the stamp from. It was to an address in Kentucky, a store of some kind. He opened the letter and found a statement for a delivery of dolls. He tore the letter and envelope into tiny pieces and deposited them in the nearest wastebasket, many of which lined the streets of Jamay Lake.

He continued down the street, trying to visualize his letter getting to his father and his father opening it. He

152

realized he could form no clear mental picture of the man. He wasn't certain he would even recognize him, but writing the letter was his only real hope of getting out of Jamay Lake. He prayed it would reach its destination with the taped stamp on it.

And he hoped someone would really be there to receive it.

PART TWO

THE MICROCOSM

" . . . some species remain half-developed; a Peter Pan species. Imagine what would happen if some strange genetic mutation caused human beings to achieve sexual maturity at the age of two. They would begin to have babies at the age of two and might well die at the age of ten, worn-out by child rearing. In a few generations, older people might disappear, never to be replaced, and we would become a race of children."

—Colin Wilson, *Mysteries*

Chapter Seventeen

Prehistory

"You understand your decision will be permanent. At this time, I have no counteragent, though I expect to in the future."

"I understand," Brenda Stowe replied uneasily.

"You have no reservations?" Warren continued.

"No, I don't think so."

The two of them sat in a small rented office in Fort Wayne, Indiana, where Warren had conducted most such interviews. The office also served as a mailing address for Warren's various enterprises. Sitting nearby was Sondra, his wife, there to act as witness to the agreement and remind Warren if he forgot any details. She had also helped to recruit Brenda, though she had a few misgivings about the woman's age. She was younger than the others and maybe not so sure of herself or her desires.

"You have to be sure," Warren continued.

Brenda nodded her honey-blonde head.

"You also agree to the second condition of the contract?"

"Yes."

"You thoroughly understand you will be surgically sterilized by means of a tubal ligation, and that it is, for all practical purposes, an irreversible operation in women?"

"Yes, I do."

"Finally, you will live in the confines of Jamay Lake, Indiana for a period of not less than three years. You will further sign a non-disclosure commitment, stipulating that if you choose to leave the community, you will not disclose its whereabouts to anyone. Nor will you ever inform anyone you have been there or tell anyone the nature of the experiment in which you will be involved. Nor will you contact anyone in the outside world without prior permission while in the community."

Brenda's eyes showed she was not totally decided. "Does it have to be so final?"

"These stipulations are necessary to the successful completion of the experiment. Any experiment, especially one of this magnitude, must have certain controls. Remember, all your needs will be taken care of: food, lodging, clothing. You will be given work. Your work time will accrue against an account set up in your name, the whereabouts of which will be revealed to you upon the conclusion of the experiment or the end of your period of commitment, should you decide to leave.

"Your child, Peter, will receive excellent medical care throughout the experiment. The drug he will be given will not harm him or affect him in any way except as specified. You will be required to maintain a drug program designed to make your stay in the community more pleasant; no ill effects have ever been observed with this drug. If any side effects occur, your medication will be changed."

"This sounds like a speech, or something." The implicit criticism was a form of defense; Warren had observed it in others he had recruited. It was the natural human tendency to refuse to commit, to make a choice—especially if it would change the course of a person's life—whether for worse or the better.

Warren allowed himself a small smile. "I've repeated it so many times, I suppose it sounds cold by now. I apologize for that. Legal ramifications, you know. If there's anything you don't understand, feel free to ask."

"I understand it. I just don't know if it's the right thing to do."

"The rightness of anything is difficult to determine, Miss Stowe. We all have to do what we feel is right for

158

ourselves, in our own hearts. Like it or not, that's all we have; that's all the rightness there is to anything. What I am asking of you is not a simple matter. I'm well aware of that. It's a very big step. Only a few women have been brave enough to take this step so far. But ours is a thriving community now. We have a degree of peace and solitude I would venture to say no other community in the nation enjoys. We have no crime. We have none of society's greater ills. Ours is an ideal society."

The doctor slid the forms across to Brenda. "Don't sign, unless you're truly certain, Miss Stowe."

She flipped through the forms, barely glancing at them. Warren could tell she knew exactly what everything he had explained meant; she was not ignorant or stupid. She was only hesitating. She had doubtless been taught not to sign anything without making it an involved, questioning process.

She took the pen Warren offered, and bit her lip. Something was troubling her, something not connected to this commitment at all, but she had been holding it back, perhaps from embarrassment, perhaps because of uncertainty, maybe even an unspoken fear that there was a catch she would find out about later that would make her regret her decision.

"There's only one thing I have to know," she said after a moment of intense silence.

"Yes?"

"Will Everett be able to find me?"

"Everett?"

"Pete's father. The guy who . . ."

Warren knew how to finish the sentence. She meant the man who had beaten her constantly, the brute who had terrorized the mother of his child, and the child also.

"No. He cannot find you. I've gone to great pains to make our little society virtually invisible to the outside world. We have layers within layers of security. I doubt the F.B.I., C.I.A., or any agency could get through them. By the time they did, we would have moved elsewhere. We have many contingency plans."

"You don't know Everett. He's mean, but he's also

159

smart. He's tracked us down before, just so he could abuse us—he thinks he *owns* us."

"I'm well aware of his type of man, and the character of such men. Most women in our community have a similar problem. Once you move in, though, you will become, for the record, a person who works for one of the various enterprises in a town that theoretically does not exist. We will have power of attorney on all business matters. Tax forms will be filed for you; all outstanding debts you have will be taken care of. There will be no reason for anyone to come looking for you, so there will be no trail for anyone else, such as your Everett, to follow. We have had no trouble with insensitive husbands or mates since we founded our community. None. They cannot find us. If they even got close, we would steer them in another direction altogether." Warren appeared pleased and proud. He enjoyed having been so successful in his experiment.

"But, what if he did find—somehow found the town."

"That's, as I said, just about impossible. But, unless he's Superman, or had means unknown to me by which to penetrate our security levels, and he showed up at our town one day, he could not get in. We have only one entrance, which is guarded by a man with a surly disposition who is likely to shoot this Everett and ask questions later."

"He'd *shoot* him?" The concern in her face irritated Warren. These women hated their men, yet they had strange affection for them, some variety of unreasonable "love," despite how much they had suffered at their hands.

"I was exaggerating. Rest assured, Everett could not get in. He couldn't climb the walls, and if he could, he'd find himself entangled in electrified barbed wire. He would also set off a number of alarms that would bring our security force running before his feet hit the ground."

"I guess you've got it all figured out," she said.

"I like to think so."

Brenda took a deep breath; her face showed renewed

determination. She signed all the forms hurriedly, with a flourish of decisiveness.

"A place with no Everett sounds like heaven to me," she said, shifting the forms back to Warren who signed them also and handed them to Sondra for her signature as witness.

"It's not quite heaven," Warren said, smiling broadly now, "but very close indeed. We welcome you."

That had been a little over a year ago. Brenda was the last woman to be admitted to Jamay Lake. With her in the population, Warren felt he had a good balance of mothers and children of various ages. The colony had been in existence close to three years, when Brenda was recruited through a contact Sondra had in a center for battered wives and abused children in Indianapolis. The center itself was difficult to locate. Warren could not even go there, because he was a man. More and more facilities were being opened across the country, as the problem of wife battering and child abuse grew.

As the family unit broke down, the traditional values eroded as well. Wives (legal or common law) became less than human to often brutish males who beat them anytime they wished; children were reduced to objects, human punching bags. Divorced women, driven to work two jobs to make a living, had to leave their children at home alone. They themselves often became child abusers—out of frustration with their situations.

That this intolerable situation could exist in a modern society, in one of the richest nations in the world, had tormented Warren for years. It was an abomination, and there were not as many people who cared about correcting it as Warren thought there should be. Indeed, people shrugged the problem off if it didn't directly affect them.

Warren's concern had started when he was an intern and worked the third shift in a hospital near the worst section of town, where he almost nightly saw the hell many women and children had to bear. And he himself so loved children he could barely tolerate his job, seeing how they were beaten with sticks, or belts, or whatever was handy, while their mothers, themselves often bruised and battered, made lame excuses such as their child had merely fallen or had run into a door.

Then, when he became an M.D. and left that hospital and its environment, he moved up to a facility in the suburbs, where he did not often witness such things. So he forgot for a while how it was for many women; like most of society he suppressed his awareness of the problem and went about enjoying his own life.

Yet it was still there, in the back of his mind, festering; it could not be absolutely ignored—unless one didn't read newspapers or watch television.

Warren decided to bury his head in the sand, to go underground, as it were, by hiding out in his own little world. He went into research after he worked at the hospital for two years, deliberately putting a distance between himself and the problems of human beings, while he played with Petri dishes and chemicals.

But still the problem—and his concern about it—surfaced occasionally, often at odd moments when he was deep in concentration, his eyes focused on a slide under a microscope, where he observed microbes and diseased cells and liked to pretend he was as isolated from the world as the organisms on the slides were. Yet, he mused, if he were to turn a microscope on the slide where he fancifully hid away, what kind of germ would he consider himself? What part of the disease was he? How did he fit into the etiology of the problem?

Why did he feel so responsible?

His own childhood had been pleasant and normal. His parents had never abused him. He had grown up in the reasonably comfortable surroundings an upper middle-class family enjoyed. He was always insulated from the seamier side of life, even in high school, though he knew there must have been children with problems around him all through his own childhood years; he just didn't see them. Why should he? He was not compelled to interact with anyone below his social caste. He was college-bound—a serious student with preset goals. He had known almost before he could pronounce the word that he would be a physician.

In college he was also insulated. He had to earn money for the extras, but most of his expenses were paid by his parents, supplemented by scholarship and government loan funds for which he readily qualified.

It was not until he left the confines of the university campus that he was exposed to the truisms of human suffering—not the physical suffering described as "trauma" in a medical textbook—but the emotional and psychological suffering from which there was little respite and for which there were no easy cures or solutions.

When he was not totally involved in research, he would try to analyze the problem as he saw it, attempting to fix it within the context of a world-view that made some sense. But the problem resisted sensibility. It was senseless. It need not be. It was an enigma—yet there were aspects to it that pointed to its origins.

For one thing, Warren had observed there was a particularly vicious cycle involved: women got pregnant, their husbands or mates were uncaring; the women were abandoned; they had more children, often by any male who was convenient, sometimes in order to receive more federal aid. With more children came more pressure, more possibilities for abuse. The women became pregnant again. They added to the surplus population— but their addition was in the form of ciphers—zeros that contributed nothing to the mass of people other than more people with even more problems—such as more and more unwanted children, street gangs, drug use among children, child prostitution and pornography—all the ills the population experts had predicted when there were too many people—especially in a society that could not apparently guarantee a reasonable standard of living for all of them.

How to break the cycle? It would seem that if the origins and causes of any particular problem were known, then it should be a simple matter to solve the problem. Of course, problems having to do with people were complicated by the totally unpredictable human factor—which could obscure the potential solutions.

There was an element within the cycle of events which Warren could not identify. In his off times, he read widely in sociological texts. He gathered statistics. He studied population control methods. But he couldn't seem to get at the core of the problem. What kept women going on this way? Where were the answers he desperately sought?

What was he overlooking?

Then, he made a breakthrough in his own research, creating a new breed of tranquilizer that had few of the side effects that made doctors reluctant to prescribe drugs presently in use. It was at this point that Warren realized he had to compromise some of his principles for a greater good, especially those involving his fealty to the company for which he worked. He knew that most researchers made only one such discovery in their lives, and that he had to make the most of it.

He had to use this discovery to achieve independence, so that he might bring about changes in society that he really cared about.

He resigned his position, having first taken great pains to hide all the results of his research, taking files with him, erasing files from computer banks, absconding with his notebooks, slides, and chemical formulae in the middle of the night, like a common thief.

He filed his own patent on the drug, hired a very smart attorney, then put the formula up for auction. He ultimately re-sold the patent to the pharmaceutical company that had given him his research grant, with a proviso for royalties on every sale made as long as the drug remained proprietary to the company—that is, it was not available in generic form. After FDA approval—which was not as involved as usual due to the new drug being chemically similar to other previously-approved medications—Warren's discovery was put on the market.

Suddenly, Warren awoke one morning and realized he was rich. He could do anything he pleased. He had the independence he needed, and he knew how to protect it. Being a prudent man, he hired an investment counselor who kept his money from being gobbled up by taxes while providing him with a steadily-increasing fortune. Six-figure checks became commonplace in his life.

The doctor spent some time just traveling, wandering the world, going to the places he'd always wanted to see. He was indulging himself only temporarily. After this tour, he planned to do some hard thinking and planning. He needed some space, however, to recharge his mental facilities. He had been locked up in the confined world of research too long.

After two years of extensive travel, he returned to Indiana. He volunteered to work at a hospital, so he could again observe what now was "The Problem" in his mind close-hand.

Things had gotten worse: more teenage pregnancies, more abused children, so many wives beaten that special, almost underground, homes were set up for them to hide them from their husbands or live-ins.

Yet these women continued to have children.

The cycle had become even more pernicious as society basically refused to acknowledge the problems involves. Child abuse, wife battering, abortion—they made good subjects for television movies, but few people were really caring enough to help directly.

They fooled themselves that their contributions to the United Way were sufficient; their consciences were wonderfully bereft of guilt.

Warren left the hospital after less than a year, and he founded his own facility for child abuse and battered wives. He was the only man on the staff. He hired two women doctors, and a handful of caring nurses and counselors. One of the doctors was Sondra Scott, whom he would later marry.

There were problems in starting up. He had to move three times to avoid detection by vengeful husbands. The third move was precipitated by him having his own nose broken by a berserk father who had come, he said, "to collect my old lady and my kid."

He operated the facility for almost three years. All the while, he collected data from the women who came there. He talked to them at length, and developed psychological profiles. He felt the key to understanding the perpetuality of the cycle was among the people it affected most.

As it turned out, the missing factor was basic:

Mothers liked to have babies.

That was fine. That was nature. That was the supposed purpose for living—to procreate, to be fruitful and multiply, to maintain the survival of the human species. But this natural drive was an anachronism in a world that was becoming overcrowded and inclined to violence.

Population control was a controversial subject. People should be allowed to choose to have as many children as they wanted—which was the philosophy of the United States, at least. But population control was essential if there was ever to be a better world. The people who really believed in it practiced it well enough, with the result that most educated women had only so many children as they sincerely wanted, while undereducated or ignorant women seemed to have an excess of children—more than they could possibly want.

Intellectuals would debate endlessly the proper means of birth control: pills, condoms, sponges, implants—or, if absolutely necessary, abortion.

But women still wanted children. They could have six kids and be barely capable of sustaining any kind of decent lifestyle, yet show up pregnant at their next examination.

Why?

Warren used to pose the question to Sondra over and over. She thought it was "maternal instinct." It was a difficult imperative to ignore, even among educated women.

Why? Warren kept agonizing over that single *why*.

Then one day, one of the women he cared for at his facility provided the answer. He probably had heard it a thousand times before, but it hadn't sunk in, it hadn't seem to fit into the puzzle The Problem had become.

166

Her name (he would never forget it) was Ruth Ann Walker. She had never married, though she had four children. She had dropped out of high school at age fifteen to bear her first child. At twenty-two, she now lay on the examining table in his office, pregnant once more. She had been away from the center about ten weeks, set up with a decent job, safely hidden from her old boyfriends—and duly instructed in all methods of birth control. She had to have gone out of her way to get herself in her present condition.

"Your suspicions were correct, Miss Walker," Warren told her with some sadness. "You are pregnant. Four to five weeks."

"I knew it," she said.

Warren usually just sighed and gave the woman a diet to follow and a list of things to avoid. But this time he was overwhelmed. After all the years of thinking about the cycle and how it refused to be broken, he could no longer play the polite doctor who accepted anything his patient presented him.

"Why, Miss Walker?" he asked, his voice trembling, almost on the point of rage. "Why do you keep getting pregnant?"

Ruth seemed unaware of his emotions. She sat up, swinging her legs over the edge of the table. "I like kids," she said, as if that were all the explanation necessary.

"But doesn't the quality of life mean anything to you?"

"I don't understand that."

"The more children you have, the more difficult it is for you to take care of them. We went to great pains to find you a respectable job and get you started on a new way of life. We showed you every method of avoiding pregnancy. And you show up here pregnant again. It makes no sense to me. If you really like kids, you should stop having them, so you can properly care for the ones you have."

Ruth's eyes were glassy with profound ignorance, almost as if she wasn't absolutely sure where children came from.

167

"But I like kids."

"You said that. Get a job in a nursery or a day-care center. Become a teacher's aid. There are many ways to be around children without having them."

"It's not just kids," she said, finally yielding the precious information the doctor sought. "I like *babies.*"

"What?"

"Little ones. Once they start getting big on you, you can't love them no more. You can't hold them no more, and you can't kiss them, and when they get bigger and bigger, they get sassy. They're the most fun when they're babies."

Warren's mind processed this notion in a variety of ways, one of which led to a strange conclusion: if women had babies only, they would have *fewer* babies.

At first, it made little sense, even to Warren. But it was the clue to halting the cycle. He felt that instinctively.

"Thank you, Miss Walker," he said, his manner becoming more affable.

"For what? I didn't do nothin' except get knocked up again, and I can tell you're mad about it."

"Not any more. I'm happy for you. If having a baby in your arm makes you happy, who am I to spoil that?"

Ruth was totally bewildered.

"You may get dressed now. See the nurse out front. She'll give you the necessary paperwork."

Ruth shook her head in wonder, knowing she would never understand doctors—or anyone else with more than a high school education. She dressed hurriedly as if she couldn't wait to get out of this madman's presence.

After she left, Warren went into Sondra's office.

"I've got the answer," he said.

"What's the question?"

"Never mind. I have the answer; now all I need is the solution."

Warren set up a small research facility, leaving the primary duties of the center to Sondra, who was more than capable of assuming his responsibilities.

168

He knew enough about genetics to get started. But he had to learn more about growth abnormalities: he studied obscure texts and monographs at university libraries. He traveled to hospitals and clinics dealing with human growth problems. Then he had to take everything he learned and turn it inside-out; what he had learned was for treatment of people who wanted to grow, people who might otherwise be dwarfs, or whose metabolisms and natural growth rates were affected by drugs—such as those given to kidney-transplant patients.

Warren wanted exactly the opposite effect. He wanted to stop growth altogether. There were drugs that were meant to regulate growth, to help prevent giantism, for example, but nothing that would halt *natural* growth as Warren intended.

He had formulated a theory, which he postulated in his book, *Children Who Grow Young*, about how halting the growth of children could theoretically benefit the population as a whole. The book, which he had to publish on his own, was met with derision and scorn by those in the medical and scientific communities. Socialists denounced it as "tantamount to a neo-Naxism;" ministers called it "tampering with God's plan." Finding no support among his peers—or anyone else for that matter—Warren withdrew the book from circulation.

Its disappearance was barely noticed, and Warren faded into the obscurity reserved for all of those who dared to present outrageous new theories to the world. Warren decided he didn't need anyone else's acceptance of his ideas and continued his research.

Even before he wrote the book, however, he had begun to experiment with means of achieving the plans outlined in his writings, first with animals. He worked with complex organic compounds derived from pituitary glands and other glands in the endrocrine system related to growth regulation. He had many early failures with monkeys; growth was stopped, but with disastrous side effects, such as deformities similar to those caused by the disease acromegalia, an affliction that occurred in humans when growth hormone was secreted in adults.

But even the failures taught him something positive—that he could manipulate growth. He felt he needed only to refine the compounds he had synthesized. He resumed his experiments with lower animals, whose maturity was achieved over a shorter period of time.

Eventually, he succeeded in arresting the growth of rats. With a simple injection, he could stop growth at any predetermined stage. One week, two weeks, and so on. He refined his formula again and started experimenting with dogs and cats. Cats were especially good subjects. He could stop a cat's growth easily at two months, and maintain it *indefinitely*.

That was the desired effect, the solution he was seeking.

He tried again with monkeys—success. Then with lower primates—success. Not just success, but success without undue side effects. The animals whose growth was halted remained physiologically and metabolically immature with no observable ill effects whatsoever.

In theory, then, the formula, refined one more stage to interact with human metabolism, would work on children. That, of course, was not something he could test so easily.

Before he could even begin experiments with humans, he would have to get FDA approval. With such a new drug—which was formulated to make possible a society the premise of which had been severely judged and denounced—fostered by Warren's own foolish publication of the book—it could take years to get permission merely to test it on human subjects. He might, in fact, never get approval. The FDA was notorious for its reactionary stance regarding new drugs and cures, especially those which had controversy behind them, such as the so-called "abortion pill" that had been approved in France for years. Most other countries had access to drugs the FDA was still withholding from the American public.

Warren could not abide the idea of his drug being tied up in the great American bureaucracy. He wanted to put it to use immediately, to start helping people now, this century—within his own lifetime.

He devised a plan.

Several years had passed. But Warren had the solution. He brought Sondra, whom he had found time to marry at some point during those years, into his lab and showed her the results of his years of toil.

It was a warm night in September. An ordinary night with nothing to distinguish it from any other except that Warren was about to embark on a scheme that few men would have the courage even to contemplate.

Sondra had only rarely been invited to his lab, and on those rare occasions she had restrained herself from asking her husband exactly what he was doing. Tonight, he promised, he had something to show her that would at the very least astound her.

"I hope you haven't been doing Frankenstein stuff in here," Sondra said teasingly. "Or gene-splicing. Or playing around with DNA . . ."

"I assure you it's nothing as ordinary as any of that."

Sondra smiled. She wasn't joking now. "Oh, I'd never expect anything ordinary from you, Warren." She had read his book, advised him not to publish it, but demurred when he insisted, and stood by him through the controversy.

"Thank you, dear."

"Well, what is it you want to show me?"

"Wait here." He went to the rear of his small lab. Sondra could hear the creaking sound of a cage door opening. Warren came forward, holding a small furry bundle in his arms. She displayed mild surprise when Warren placed a gray kitten in her arms.

"Eureka!" he said.

"Hi, kitty."

"You approve?" Warren was delighting in his discovery, yet he didn't want to reveal it all at once. He wanted to savor it, let it out little by little, so it would have maximum impact on Sondra.

"It's a nice kitty, Warren. Did you make it yourself? Or does it talk or do calculus?"

"This 'kitten' is a over a year old."

Sondra's expression changed from surprise to dismay. "A midget cat?"

"It's not a midget, or a dwarf. It is, physiologically, physically, and any other way you want to consider it, a *kitten*. I stopped its growth. It will remain a kitten as long as I want it to. All I have to do is to give it an occasional booster shot."

Sondra didn't know exactly how to react now. "But what's the use of it?"

"Well, if you liked kittens, but you loathed cats, you could always have a kitten—without the necessity of replacing your cat once it grew up."

"Yes, but . . ."

"Therefore you need not let so many cats get pregnant."

"I guess I follow you, but is it humane?"

"This cat 'thinks' it's a kitten. It acts like a kitten and nothing more. It doesn't know what it's like not to be a kitten, so what harm have I done it?"

"Well, you've upset the balance of nature or something akin to that, I suppose," Sondra replied reasonably.

"We put millions of unwanted animals to death every year."

Sondra's expression changed to one of reserved acceptance; she had yet to achieve the excitement Warren hoped for, however. But she seemed to see some of the possibilities. "I see. That's great, Warren," she continued on a somewhat more somber note, "but is this the solution to society's problems?"

"Yes, it is."

"Kittens for everybody?"

"No." He placed his hands on her shoulders and gazed into her eyes steadily, trying to convey some of his sense of accomplishment to her. "You see, dear, this will work for human beings as well. Think of all the unwanted children."

At first, Sondra was against the whole idea. She had

read his book and knew he believed in a rather radical method of birth control, but it never occurred to her he was seriously considering a way to put such a method into action.

Stopping the growth of human beings—of children—seemed to go against nature, much more so than with animals. It simply wasn't the same as it was with a kitten or a puppy. Cats and dogs were already altered to suit society's needs. They ate manufactured foods; they were spayed and neutered; they were bred for man's own purposes. "Adjusting" their growth would be for man's convenience; it would be a matter of choice too. No one would *have* to keep such a pet.

It was an altogether different scenario with human beings. For one thing, Sondra pointed out, the very concept was too close to eugenics—to the idea of race purification practiced by the Nazis, as critics of Warren's book had harped on. Who would choose who was allowed to grow up? What would be the consequences of having "perpetual" children?

Warren's theory could be put into practice by a mother like Ruth Ann Walker. She liked babies, but not children. If she wanted a baby all the time, then give her a baby that was always a baby, so she wouldn't need to get pregnant over and over. It was such women, usually uneducated, who continued to have children so they could have babies—infants—offspring they could control. With Warren's drug, such a woman could have her child's growth arrested at any age she preferred. No children would be allowed to grow past twelve and become teenagers, "when they are a most troublesome age," Warren proclaimed, "and they become unruly and difficult and turn on their parents."

Use of his drug would wipe out the The Problem within a generation.

"Not all women would choose to use it," Warren continued. "Only those who pose problems. Educated women, middle-class women, would continue to have their children and allow them to grow up. A true zero population growth would be achieved."

173

Sondra pointed out that the child's free will was not considered.

But, Warren countered, the child would not be hurt. It simply would not grow up.

"Like Peter Pan," he said.

Sondra argued with her husband for days over the matter. "But society will still have its say in the matter. Look at the abortion issue, and sex education, and the pill—let's say your solution were viable, would our society tolerate it? After all, you only hinted at such a thing in your book and people were ready to crucify you."

"Probably not," Warren admitted. "But we must try."

"Warren, you're forgetting something here. How long would the child remain a child? Wouldn't that be a problem? Wouldn't there come a point when the child was owed a normal life?"

"You have a valid point," Warren agreed. "That's why there has to be a controlled experiment first."

"What do you mean?"

"I propose building our own society in which to experiment—by creating the microcosm—the Petri dish—whatever you want to call it, in which the experiment can unfold. I have the money to get it going. We will have no trouble finding subjects."

"Where?"

"You encounter them every day in the center. Women who want babies, but not children. Women who want kittens but not cats. Women who suffer as a result. Women who are a drain on society without really meaning to be. You and I, and whatever people we can trust—will build this mini-society. We'll make it ideal."

Sondra still had many reservations. "You don't intend to go through the FDA approval process first?"

"No."

Sondra started to warn him, but she knew her husband was well-aware of the chances he was taking by bypassing the system.

"You want to do it all on your own, in your own giant Petri dish. But, Warren, think of the difficulties of setting up a society . . ."

"A secret society."

"All right. There are so many complex matters involved. Schools, medical care, religion, sufficient income . . ."

"I've created a master plan that takes all that into consideration."

"Warren Barry's own Utopia, is that what it would be?"

"I've studied utopian societies. Most have failed. Mine will not."

"How can you *know?*"

"I can't. But since it will be an experiment and not a permanent society, its chances of failure will be limited, if only by the constraints of time."

Sondra was still dubious, but she loved Warren and she believed he was a man who truly desired to help mankind.

"All right, Warren. I'll go along with you, though this is dangerous and foolish, and perhaps even slightly insane, but only on the condition that you will set a time limit. If the experiment fails, if having 'permanent' babies does not make women content, then you will close the society and allow the children to grow up as nature intended."

"A reasonable condition," he replied. "I had already formulated a five-year plan, which should be long enough to judge the results."

Sondra should have known he would have everything all planned out. He was such a meticulous man, possessing an intellect that was capable of grasping complex concepts—and creating them.

"So what's the first move in your grand scheme, Sir Thomas?"

"First, I am going to write a very big check. I'm going to buy a town."

Chapter Eighteen

The Birthday Party

Warren had overseen every detail of his ideal community. He chose nurses and a pharmacist who were like-minded and willing to participate in the experiment. The doctor wsa also very careful in recruiting the proper type of women to populate his utopia. When he selected the mothers, he tried to find women who would have useful skills, plus fit his other criteria: they must have only one or two children; they should be willing to leave behind all of the outside world, including any mates or any relatives, since he believed their presence would interfere with the experiment; and they had to be willing to be sterilized.

While many of the women lacked higher education, there were among them educated women as well— women who simply had trouble with men, and who had needed men in their lives primarily only to provide them with children. Just about all the women didn't like men that much, due to having had so many bad experiences with abusive fathers or mates.

He subjected each woman to extensive psychological testing as well, to make sure she would be able to cope in the microcosm of Jamay Lake. They had to be happy with the idea of the fact that no child would grow older than twelve during the course of the experiment.

Finally, they had to be willing to make the decision at what age their children's growth would be arrested: infant, toddler, any age up to twelve. There would be no unruly teenagers. And they had to realize the necessity of themselves taking tranquilizers; most of them were high-stress individuals who needed such therapy anyhow. If the experiment proved successful, Warren had planned to gradually wean the women from use of such mind-calming drugs, believing he was removing the source of much of their stress by encamping them in his town.

He never seemed to get around to telling them that despite all his continuing research, he had yet to come up with a drug that would reverse the effects of the anti-growth drug.

That was another compromise of his principles. He had kept that knowledge from Sondra for a long time—actually, until she had given the drug to herself.

She had thought his warnings to the mothers about possibly not being able to reverse the drug was only a matter of legal jargon.

Warren hoped she did not hate him too much for this sin of omission.

While he earnestly worked to find the counteragent, Warren didn't want the lack of it to prevent the experiment from beginning.

So he had gone ahead, as if everything would somehow take care of itself, perhaps by divine intervention.

He established Jamay Lake. He believed he had taken all aspects of maintaining such an experimental community into account. He had ways of making income; he had ways of keeping the women occupied; he had ways of protecting them. He even thought of closed-circuit television that showed only programs and movies that emphasized the happiness of being a child; he stocked the library with books that would reinforce that idea.

He bought the old Cummins Military Academy in northeastern Indiana for almost nothing. It was owned by a bank that had foreclosed on many notes to acquire it, and the bank was happy to be rid of it.

Indiana, he thought, was an ideal place to try his society. Indiana had always been a state where many disparate groups, often proposing truly outlandish philosophies, found homes. There was something in the

177

character of the state that allowed this, perhaps because of its central location in the Midwest and the stolid personality the location seemed to nurture.

After he bought the academy, Warren had it refurbished, spending great sums of his own money on fixing up the old faculty homes, and turning the various outbuildings into useful structrues.

Finally, he created the official "religion" of the community, of which he was the only minister. Its avowed purpose was to propagandize the ideal, but it was also designed to maintain peace and order. Besides, most of the women had strong religious convictions and would have insisted on a church of some kind. Rather than establish separate denominational facilities, Warren took the expedient step of declaring only one true religion, which, he believed, satisfied most of the needs of the congregation that would participate in the Nameless Church.

He had not recruited any fundamentalists, Catholics, or other strong-minded religious women who would demand more than a mere storybook church with a pretend minister.

He had thought of everything.

Now, five years after he had begun, he had to contemplate tearing it all down, because he had not thought of all the inevitabilities.

Among them, death.

Two weeks had passed since Brenda Stowe's death. During that time there was a fatality in the children's ward on the fourth floor too, and two more children had been brought to the ward.

Warren felt helpless where the children were concerned. There was no known cure for the disease they had. His only hope was the development of a drug to counteract his own drug, but his time for research was limited, and he knew many more would die before he could—if ever—discover such a drug.

Perhaps he was tampering with Nature, after all.

178

Perhaps this was the payback.

But why did innocent children have to be sacrificed—some of them only two- or three-years-old?

With a heavy cloud of depression hanging over him, Warren hesitated to hold the annual Founder's Day celebration—which was also the group birthday party for all the children in Jamay Lake. He had decided that if the children celebrated their birthdays all on the same day, it would help to distract their awareness from the fact that they were not really getting any older. No age was specified for anyone at the party. Each child had his own cake—usually baked by his mother if she were capable—with a single candle on it.

Warren usually looked forward to Founder's Day, because it had been always a happy occasion the first four years it was celebrated. But now it would be painfully obvious that people were missing. There might be potentially difficult questions put to him for which he had no ready answers. He even considered cancelling the celebration altogether.

On the other hand, a party might dispel some of the gloom that permeated the community. The picnic was supposed to have done that, but the unanticipated fire had ruined that plan.

After much soul-searching, he decided to go ahead and have the celebration. It could serve to renew the spirit of the residents of Jamay Lake.

It was usually held in the churchyard, but since that had yet to be fully restored, Warren decided to take the celebration outside the wall, in the open, where people could feel free and commune with nature.

He had a large tent brought in and set up in front of the wall just south of the gate. He had banners and colorful pennants put up. He bought a new P.A. system through which to pipe joyful music.

He vowed his people would be happy—one way or another.

"How old will I be today?" Alicia asked her mother,

179

Myrna, as they dressed for the celebration. "It's my birthday, isn't it?"

"Yes, it's everyone's birthday."

"We were all born on the same day?" Alicia thought her birthday was in July.

"Not really," Myrna said reluctantly. "But we live in a special place, and so we celebrate birthdays in our own special way. That way, all you children get a really big party, instead of a little one."

"Is it your birthday too?"

"No. It's only the children's birthday."

"Is Alvin coming?"

Myrna stopped buttoning her blue dress and sighed. "He's still ill. You know that."

"I thought maybe they'd let him out because it's a special day."

"You ask too many questions. Now put on your good shoes, and let's go. We don't want to miss anything."

The festivities began at twelve o'clock. Everyone was impressed with the tent and the decorations. There was a bountiful buffet with salads, cold cuts, and many hot dishes as well, four different flavors of ice cream, cake for everyone and plenty of cookies for the younger children. The sun was out, though it was early November, and there was need only for lightweight sweaters or jackets. This time of year Indiana weather was particularly shifty; offering hot weather one day, cold the next, rain, snow—the possibility of hail. The only weather types not anticipated were tornados and thunderstorms; those spectacles were reserved for the spring and early summer.

The single oppressive aspect of the celebration was the presence of all the patrol men, stationed on various sides of the tent, keeping watchful eyes on the celebrants. Warren disliked having them standing watch like storm troopers, but he felt they were necessary. He didn't want another disaster such as the fire at the picnic.

Some of the mothers, Warren observed, seemed a bit

apprehensive, but he felt that would pass, especially since most of the children seemed to be happy and enjoying themselves.

Unlike previous years, Warren did not give a speech about the importance of Founder's Day and the Big Birthday Party. He decided anything he said would be redundant and ponderous, and he wanted the affair to take its own direction.

So Warren wandered among his people, smiling like a city official running for re-election, while he secretly eyed children and adults alike for signs of disease or discontent.

Occasionally, after making a circuit through the party, he would wander over to one of the open sides of the tent and just stare into the Indiana countryside.

He suddenly felt like a prisoner gazing at freedom; it was just yards away—the outside world, the unconfined world—the world where normal things happened—where children grew up and did not have to be fed drugs or injected with them—and women didn't die without reason.

The world he had *not* made—the world God had made.

He wondered how many of the women felt the same way. Did they consider themselves prisoners?

Was his Utopia any more nearly perfect than any other? Was there a difference between Utopia and prison, after all?

Was he playacting at being God?

Sally Henderson arrived half an hour late with Dawn. She had been upset all that morning, when the period she expected still hadn't come. She was usually so regular, her menstruation cycle as predictable as the phases of the moon.

But something had happened to disrupt it, making Sally distraught and on the point of hysteria.

She had been with Paul, the patrol man, at least half a dozen times. Neither of them had taken any precautions; there seemed to be no need since she believed he wasn't

181

diseased, and he believed she had been sterilized.

Which was true, of course.

Yet she felt like she was pregnant. She could feel the morning sickness even now beginning to make her queasy. Was it possible the doctor had botched the operation in her case?

She had ambivalent feelings regarding the prospect of pregnancy. A baby might be nice. But having one would violate the "rules," and undermine the trust the doctor had in her. If she even *thought* she was pregnant, the doctor would know what she had been doing.

Could she keep her relationship with Paul secret? He would certainly be dismissed for having sex with her. She would be an outcast in the community, the object of everyone's scorn. That would be difficult to endure.

She sat at the end of a table, away from the clique she normally associated with, and agonized over what she had allowed herself to do.

This was not supposed to happen!

Helen Snyder, Mandy's mother, had left her children alone at the table and was mixing with the others. She had red hair, a richer, darker shade than her daughter's honey blonde, and a full figure. She was feeling very odd today. Something was stirring within her, driving her towards a goal she could not put into words.

She approached Wanda McCoy, a woman ten years younger, who sat at a table with other mothers in the clique that had infants to care for.

Wanda was not very attractive. She had light brown hair, thick thighs, and an ordinary face. She was also slightly stupid. She was cooing and talking baby talk to her infant when Helen tapped her on the shoulder.

"Baby's real good, ain't he?" Wanda was saying. "Baby's . . . what? Oh, it's you . . ."

"Helen."

"Helen. What you doing over here?"

"I just wanted to be sociable. I never talked to you very much."

"That's because you're one of the snooty bitches who don't like us with babies."

"That's not true."

"'Tis so. Well, we ain't missing your company."

Helen leaned down and whispered something in Wanda's ear.

Wanda turned and glared at Helen. "Go to hell, you nasty old bitch."

Helen gasped and backed away, her face flushing. She stumbled through the crowd, trying to hide within herself.

William wasn't quite bored yet. He had taken his share of the goodies—avoiding the cookies, of course—and was finishing his second dish of chocolate ice cream. This gathering, he had decided, was better than the picnic, but it would get old quick, especially with that num-num music blaring out of the speakers.

He left his empty dish on the table, nodded at his mother, and started walking around, as many others were now doing. He passed Lester Stultz from a distance of about ten feet. Lester gave him a nasty wink, accompanied by an obscene gesture.

William flipped the finger at Lester and walked away. Lester merely leered.

Then William found Mandy, sitting at a table with only her little brother for company. He sat down next to her and took a sip from her cup of punch. She didn't object.

"Happy birthday," he said.

"Happy birthday," Mandy replied. Then she whispered, "When's your real birthday?"

"In March—the 28th."

"Mine's in April—the 14th."

"That's interesting."

"What? Are you being sarcastic?"

"No. Your birthday is half mine, and we're both Aries."

Mandy thought about what he was saying a second. "So?"

183

"We have a lot in common. It's in the stars."

"Do you know about that stuff—astrology and things like that?"

"Not really. My mom used to read my horoscope to me every day from the paper when I was a little kid. Of course, she doesn't do that any more."

"Aries is the Ram, right?"

"Yep. You and me are goats."

Mandy smiled. "A ram is a male goat."

"Okay. What difference does it make?" he said without humor.

"Don't you ever have fun, William?"

William sipped more punch. He wondered if it had anything extra in it, but realized it was too late to worry about that now. "How?"

"I don't know. You could make your own fun if you wanted to bad enough."

"Do you have fun?"

"Not very much," she admitted. "Except when I write one of my little stories."

"You write stories? What about?"

"About things around here—about how the women are spaced out—like they're robots. Writing it down makes me feel a little better. You ought to try it."

"That doesn't sound like fun to me. I'd write weird stuff probably." He looked sideways at her brother. "Hey, kid, ever have fun?"

"Ice cream," Danny replied.

"Sharp kid." He drew himself closer to Mandy. "Look over there."

"At what?"

"Outside the tent. See those woods? We could just run like hell and get there before anyone noticed we were missing."

"Then what?"

"We'd keep running until we found a better place."

Mandy's face assumed a solemn expression. "And we'd have to keep on running and running. You know it wouldn't be that easy."

"You're right," he said.

"Why don't you have patience, William? There hasn't been enough time for your father to get the letter and *do* something about it."

"I know."

Mandy took the cup from his hand and finished the punch. "I'm getting bored just sitting here. Why don't you come with me and see if we can find my mother?"

"All right. I don't have anything better to do anyhow."

Helen had recovered from Wanda's vicious attack. She was now sharing the story of it with Georgia Burrfield, mother of Eddie, a nine-year old who she allowed to run wild, who had become another nuisance in the community.

Georgia didn't pay much attention to Eddie's misdeeds. She ate more than her share of the drugged candy and ingested many yellow and orange pills—the excess of which she had obtained by using her only reliable commodity—her body. A roll with one of the patrol men every now and then assured her a steady supply of anything she needed.

She was a slender woman with flat breasts and wide hips. She bleached her hair and wore more makeup than usual. She was the whore that Sally played at being, and she didn't much care who knew it or who talked about her behind her back.

Warren was aware she was a problem. But he needed a few women of her character to see how they reacted to the experiment. If it were ever to be put into action on a wide basis, her type would be the most likely candidates to embrace the concept behind the community. Or so Warren theorized. He was not aware, however, of her overindulgence in drugs or how she obtained them.

Georgia listened to Helen's bitching for several minutes, before she squinted and asked, "Just exactly what did you say to that bitch that made her talk that way to you?"

Helen cast her gaze down to the ground. "I don't think it's something you need to know."

"I ain't going to tell anybody." Her eyes were glazed. "Hell, people talk about me all the time, and I don't care. But I can keep a secret, if that's what you want."

"I'm lonely," Helen said meekly.

"Is that what you said?"

"No." She swallowed hard, then looked up into Georgia's eyes. She hadn't noticed how obviously high the woman was—stoned out of her mind as Helen's generation would have termed her condition. It dawned on her this might be an opportunity. "What I said is 'I'm very lonely and would like to touch you.'"

Georgia shook with laughter. "Hell, you ain't lonely, honey. You're horny."

"I wouldn't use that word exactly."

"A lot of us is horny around here. All them months without a man—it ain't natural. Maybe this place is good for the young'uns. I don't know. But it ain't good for a woman who wants to *be* a woman. Hell, why don't you grab one of them patrol men, hon? They don't none of them take the saltpeter or whatever it is the doctor gives them to make their peckers limp. All of them are available."

Helen trembled. Coarse language always upset her to a degree. But she was even more upset by the underlying message Georgia was conveying. Everyone seemed to be getting what they wanted—except her. It was all a big secret.

"You don't understand, Georgia," Helen said with a sigh. "I don't like men that much."

Georgia's dark brown eyes rolled in mock surprise. "Well, I do declare! So that's what you want." She pressed herself against Helen briefly with significant results. "I ain't that particular. I'll take care of you, hon."

Several minutes later, Georgia slipped out of the tent, in full view of a patrol man, leading Helen into the woods.

Kevin Hamilton sat in a corner of the tent alone, next to the dessert table. He was contemplating doing

186

something daring, as William had at the picnic, maybe setting a fire to the tent, or dumping one of the little kids in the punch bowl—anything to break up the monotony and prove he was as good at troublemaking as William.

But Kevin wasn't up to any mischief. Kevin's skin was tingling, and his stomach was doing flip-flops.

Maybe he'd eaten too much. Four dishes of ice cream and half a cake on top of all the other food he had consumed was quite a bit, although such gluttony had never affected him adversely before.

He fought the churning forces within his body a long time before he surrendered.

He threw up mightily on the ground, spewing forth, so it seemed, everything inside his stomach and half his intestines. At the same time, he fouled his shorts.

Indiana's weather had held back long enough. The temperature dropped ten degrees in as many minutes. Dollops of rain pelted the roof of the tent.

A patrol man rushed to unplug the P.A. system which was playing an instrumental version of "Bridge Over Troubled Waters" for the fifth time.

The mothers sought out their children and trotted towards the gate, covering their heads with placemats or napkins, or just pulling their jackets up over their hair, so that from behind they looked headless. They headed home, not one of them even thinking to take advantage of the rain to run away.

As the rain pounded more relentlessly on the tent, some people decided to wait it out for a while, knowing they would get soaked if they ventured forth now.

William and Mandy couldn't find her mother. William saw his own mother giving him that "get-your-butt-over-here" look, and reluctantly joined her. When there was a brief let-up in the rain, they sprinted towards the gate.

Mandy and her brother stood in the middle of the tent, searching the few people left behind over and over for signs of their mother. After nearly half an hour, during which the rain slowly became a mild drizzle, Mandy took her brother by the arm and dragged him home.

It would be just like their mother to go on without them.

Harriet found Kevin sitting in a puddle of his own vomit. He smelled of urine and excrement.

"What are you?" she reproached him, "a goddamn baby?"

"I'm awful sick, Mom."

"What a mess. Get up out of that." She smacked him lightly on the cheek. Then she felt guilty. His face was broken out, covered with small brown dots. "I'm sorry," she said, helping him up. "You really *are* sick."

Despite the rain, Warren thought the party had gone well. He had observed no undue behavior, no problematical situations, no grumbling or griping. It was a great big fun birthday celebration.

As the rain let up finally, Warren himself went home, leaving the patrol men to help the few remaining mothers and children reach their houses safely.

He could hardly wait to tell Sondra how successful the whole affair had been.

As it grew dark, the tent was empty. The rain was a mere annoyance now, barely noticeable, only a few molecules more than a mist.

Georgia Burrfield emerged from the woods, her clothing soaked and clinging to her, revealing everything beneath it, including her lack of underwear.

She seemed unusually happy. She presented herself at the gate and was allowed in without question, since the troll had gone off his shift, and the man now in the booth knew her.

A few minutes later, Helen Snyder came forth from the same woods, clutching a coat around her shivering body. Her face seemed frozen in awe. She had committed acts she had only fantasized about the last few years, with a woman who was nasty and disgusting.

She was not very happy.

She felt deeply ashamed—not because of her desires, but because of her having given in to them with a person who in the outside world she would not even talk to. She considered herself the worst of all whores.

She kept rubbing the back of her hand across her mouth, trying to erase the taste and smell of Georgia's lipstick. As she approached the gate, she pulled her collar up around her face to hide what she thought must be a hideously smeared face—one on which her recent activities must be clearly etched.

The man at the gate said nothing. He barely glanced at her as he let her enter.

She took half a dozen steps forward.

She fell on the rain-glistening pavement, watching her own reflection in a puddle as she plummeted face down.

Her heart stopped.

A few miles away, Indiana State Troopers were having a party of their own, although it was marred by a particularly morose atmosphere.

Early the day before, a man and his son, fishing in the Salamonie River, had found the contents of a state trooper's car glove compartment washed ashore on the southern bank not far from Salamonie Lake. They found a ticket pad, a vehicle registration form, and a small box of tissues.

They decided these things might provide clues to the whereabouts of the missing state trooper whose face had been in every Indiana newspaper and on every Indiana TV station news report several times in the last month or so.

They took their find to the nearest state police post.

The Salamonie was dragged in both directions for hours, crews working all through the night. Late the next morning they found the patrol car. A wench was used to pull the weighted vehicle up from the shallow river bed.

Whoever had deposited it here certainly didn't know how low the river got when the summer rains were over.

The troopers were disappointed that their fellow officer was not in the car—though that provided a very slim hope he might be alive somewhere.

None of them actually believed that, however.

But they celebrated just the same. The car was covered with fingerprints, most of them smudges, of course, but several were quickly identified as those of a former Joliet Prison inmate—a notorious child molester and rapist—who had eluded the law for nearly a decade.

Those prints belonged to Lester Stultz.

Chapter Nineteen

Chorus

Dawn:

Happy Birthday to me. Happy Birthday to everyone. It's kind of a great big party, and it's *everyone's* birthday. I used to have my own special day for my birthday, but Mom say's this way is better, so we don't have to be jealous of each other. I don't understand all of that. Why would somebody be jealous about a birthday?

I guess it's Shirley's birthday too. I should've asked Mom about that. I don't know if dolls have birthdays. Shirley's a pirate too, and I *know* they have birthdays. So I can pretend Shirley's birthday is today too. I think she is twenty-seven, because you have to be old to be a pirate.

I sat down with Alicia. It was okay with Mom, because she's not feeling very good. She acts like she's going to throw up. I hope she isn't getting what Alvin has.

Alvin has been gone a long time, maybe two or three weeks. I get to stay with Alicia a lot, because she's alone except for her kitties, but I wish Alvin would come back too. He's a boy, but he doesn't mind playing with girls, I guess because he has a sister.

This party is also "Founder's Day." That means Jamay was started on this day. Usually, the doctor makes a speech, but this year he didn't, and I was kind of glad about that, because speeches are boring.

There was lots of ice cream and cake, and we got to have our party in a big tent outside—really outside! I don't remember being outside the wall in a long time. It's pretty out there with lots of trees and stuff, and you can hear birds and animals running around in the woods. I saw a raccoon out there. I don't remember seeing a raccoon ever before. Before we came to Jamay we lived in a real big town and the only animals we saw were dogs and cats. Big ones. I haven't seen any big dogs or cats in Jamay. I think things don't grow as fast here, or Alvin and Alicia's kitties would be bigger.

I'm worried about Mom. She isn't eating very much. Her face looks whitish.

I saw William, but he didn't say much to anybody. Then he went over and sat down next to a big girl and talked to her a long time. I wonder if she is his girl friend. She's really big, almost as big as a Mom, and even has boobies.

We had a lot of fun, but then it started to rain, and they had to turn the music off so everybody wouldn't get 'lectrocuted. That's when you get a big shock. I guess it can kill you.

After the rain wasn't so bad, we went back home. I wish the party was longer. I wanted more ice cream.

Alvin sure missed a good party.

Kevin:
Some party. This is for little kids. I don't care if I have a birthday party or not.

I saw William give old Lester the finger. I hate William, but I got to admit he's got some balls. Or maybe he's stupid and don't realize how Lester could beat him up if he wanted to.

I wonder if he got what he wanted from Lester. Maybe not, the way they was looking at each other.

Lester *is* a goddamn queer, but there's worse things. Me, I'd do about anything to get what I want. Lester ain't that bad. He don't really hurt you. Of course, what he wants is kind of creepy, and everything, but you just got to close your eyes.

I wonder what the doc would say if I told him about Lester?

192

No, I can't do that. Lester's the only guy who can get things for us, and Lester might get real mean if somebody told on him. He makes me mad sometimes, because he calls me "queer bait," which sounds pretty nasty to me. He says if I ever get in jail I'll probably be wearing diapers. I don't know what he means by that, and I won't ask him, because I ain't letting anybody shit on me just because I don't know something. Who says you have to be smart, anyhow.

William's smart, but he gets into trouble and nobody likes him. I guess he's not even good queer bait.

He sure gave me a good beating that one day. I didn't think he was that strong or that mean. I wonder how he learned to fight like that. If I ever want to get his ass, I'll have to get help from somebody. Or sneak up on him and coldcock him with a piece of two-by-four. Break his head. Break his balls. I'll get even with him some day.

Stupid party. At least there's a lot to eat.

But I guess I ate too much, because I had to throw up so bad it made me crap in my pants.

Mom was real upset.

She didn't ask how I felt about it.

Eddie:

The best part was the ice cream. I had some of each flavor. The best was the one with the nuts in it, butter pecan. I could eat a whole gallon of that stuff. I would've too, but there was too many other kids.

My Mom, she took a lot of pills before she came. She said she wanted to be real happy for the party. I don't know what that means, but Mom is hard to figure out sometimes. Somebody told me she has patrol men come to the house and she lets them touch her all over.

I think they rape her or something. Rape means when a man puts his thing inside a woman somehow. I don't know where he puts it. Kevin had a picture of a man doing that with a woman, but he wouldn't let me see it unless I did something for him. I said what, and he said to touch his butt. I said I ain't touching anybody's butt.

Kevin said I was a little wimp and to go away, so I didn't get to see the rape picture.

I don't know, Mom might do that rape stuff. I guess if a woman likes a man a lot then she lets him rape her. That's what I heard. Mom said she likes men a lot. I don't know why. Because she says she hates men too.

She hates them *and* likes them. I can't figure that out. If I hate somebody I don't mess with them except for hitting them or calling them names. That's what you're supposed to do when you hate somebody. I hate a lot of people. I don't hate Mom, but I don't like her sometimes, either. That ain't the same thing.

I guess she's not a real bad Mom. She lets me do what I want most of the time. I can run anywhere I want, just so I don't get in trouble with a patrol man.

She doesn't care. I could probably go and beat up a little kid and she wouldn't care. Or I could just set fire to something—like at the picnic. That was neat. I heard Kevin set the fire. Somebody else said it was William. Nobody knows for sure. If I find out, I'm going to ask him how he did it without getting caught.

Mom and another mom just went outside the tent. They must have a big secret to talk about they don't want anyone else to hear. I wish I knew what it was.

When the rain came, I just went home right away. There wasn't no use waiting around for Mom. She sometimes doesn't even come home and I have the whole house to myself to do what I want. Maybe that ain't a big deal to some kids, but sometimes it's a lot better when Mom ain't around.

Sometimes she hits me for no reason at all.

Alicia:
I miss Alvin. He's been in the clinic forever. I hate him not coming to the birthday party. At least Dawn is here so I don't have to be alone.

Mom won't even talk about Alvin when I ask her about him. Like he's dead or something. I know he's not dead, because Mom would tell me that.

194

Dawn and me ate lots of ice cream. We drunk a lot of red punch too. It's not like Kool-Aid like I thought it might be. It has soda in it, and something like wine, I think. When you get done drinking it, your tongue is red, and you look like you're wearing lipstick.

We burped a lot.

Dawn made me feel pretty good, and for a while I forgot about Alvin. Then it started raining and we had to go home and I was sad when I got there because my brother wasn't there.

I felt like crying, but I didn't want Mom to see so I went up to my room first and cried a whole lot.

Mandy:

William is very intense. He makes me nervous sometimes. I've heard he's a troublemaker, but he seems like at heart he's not really a bad person.

He does hate living here. Sometimes I can't blame him for that. I often feel like our life here is too confining. Our physical needs are met, but not our mental needs. I mean there doesn't seem to be a whole lot of concern about whether we are happy or not.

Most of the energy seems to go into making the mothers happy. But is it really happiness to be living without husbands or fathers in a little town in the middle of nowhere? If it is happiness, then why do all the women have to take tranquilizing drugs? It makes them into robots.

When I'm not taking care of Danny, or out looking for him—or now, talking with William—I like to write stories about Jamay Lake. I imagine it's a town of robots, controlled by an evil doctor, who is raising children to be fed to the devil. I've written several little stories like that in the notebook I keep under the bed. I write them to entertain myself, because the normal entertainment here is really for small children. I can no longer watch television at all, and the music we're allowed to hear is unexciting.

My mother is one of the most robot-like people. She

just goes through the motions of living here, doing as little as possible, like she's a kind of puppet controlled by invisible strings we can't see. She's not under the influence of drugs at all, not even the ones she's supposed to take. She seems to want something, but she won't tell anyone what it is. I've tried to talk to her, but she says I'm too young to understand a grown woman's problems. (I wonder how young I am.)

I think she needs psychiatric help. I've read all about psychology in the encyclopedia, and that's my judgment. I wonder if the doctor would do anything if I told him what I think about mother.

I think the doctor tries to be a good man, but I can't figure out what his purpose is. I mean, he's the doctor, of course, and gives us our shots, but what is his purpose after that? He tries to be a minister, but, honestly, I think my little brother could preach a better sermon. He tries to be the mayor and everything else, or maybe he's trying to be king of the robots here.

He's an odd man.

I helped William get a letter to the outside world. I wonder if his father will actually come and do anything. I also wonder what he *could* do. William thinks that getting a gate pass means he'll be able to get inside and save him. I don't really think it'll be that simple, but I don't want to hurt William's feelings or spoil his hopes about his plan. I like him a lot.

I wonder if his father would take me and Danny along? I wonder if Mother would want to come too.

I wonder what this strange birthday party is really about.

I wonder many things. I have many questions. I can't get any answers.

Maybe I'm a robot too.

William:
Mom won't tell me how old I am. I say I'm supposed to be fourteen, but she says I'm twelve. I remember being ten and eleven, and I know I was twelve, so I can't still be

twelve. Maybe Mom's been eating too much happy candy. She should still be able to count. The way she counts, I'll never grow up!

Maybe that's what she wants. All mothers seem to want their children not to grow up, so they can stay mothers. Mothers are like that, at least all the ones I've ever seen.

Kevin is over there. He's got that shifty look in his eyes, but you can tell he's afraid of me. He won't mess with me again. He looks half sick anyhow. Probably pigged out on ice cream. His face is broken out. It wasn't that way a couple of weeks ago when I was breaking it for him. Looks like measles. I thought we got shots to keep us from getting measles.

I ought to go over and pound on him for sending me to that Stultz guy. Stultz looked at me like he was going to jump on me or something. I wish I could tell the doctor about him, but then Stultz would say I wanted a gate pass, and the doctor would want to know what for, and I'd be in deep trouble, one way or another.

But I don't like the idea of Stultz getting away with the things he's getting away with. Maybe he's got all the kids doing gross stuff for him. Maybe some of the other patrol guys are like that too. Is the doctor stupid? Doesn't he know about all this stuff? Why doesn't he do something?

The doctor sure chose himself a bunch of great guys when he hired the patrol men! Like that Paul what's-his-name. I bet he's screwed Mrs. Henderson a dozen times in the last month or so. I've seen him go in her house at least that many times. He comes and goes as he pleases or he goes and comes. Whatever. Maybe he's screwing other women too. Maybe everybody's having a big orgy when we're not looking. Kevin had a picture of an orgy, which he let me see just to show off how he has things nobody else does. It was weird seeing people all over each other. I don't understand why anyone would do that.

Well, Mrs. Henderson and the patrol man can do that stuff if they want.

Why should I care?

I guess I don't.

I'm still worried about Alvin. He isn't here today. Some other kids and mothers aren't here either. I wonder where the hell they are? Does the doctor think we're so dumb we don't notice?

Maybe the mothers *don't*. They're so doped up, they probably don't know which end is up. They're all crazy. Anyone would have to be crazy to live in this crazy town.

I wonder if I could just run into the woods over there and keep on running and running and find another place?

Then what? I'm not old enough to get a job. Or I don't think I am. Mom's got me confused.

I don't know where any of my relatives live, or even if I have any. But if I could just get out of here, I'd find somebody.

Stultz, that son of a bitch. He's talking to one of the boys. I think he's giving him something. The boy's putting it in his pocket. Maybe a pack of cigarettes. Nobody's supposed to smoke at all, but people do it in secret. I wonder if the doctor knows about that. I wonder if the doctor is awake.

Maybe he gives himself dope. Maybe's he's as loony as all the women.

I'm twelve, Mommy, I'm twelve.

I'm *not* twelve. I know it. This whole party thing is a big lie, like the picnic was, like the Church, and school, and everything else that's going on around here. Lies and more lies. So many lies that nobody would know the truth if it bit them on the tit.

I'm twelve. My ass.

I don't want to be twelve. I'm too smart. I want to grow up, get away from here. Put my intelligence to use. Maybe tell the whole world about this weird place. If I was sixteen, I'd be big enough to kick some real ass. I could take on one of those patrol men, I'll bet, even if they do have guns. I think I might be a genius. A genius who's wasting his smarts in this wasted, wasteful little town—or whatever.

Like Stultz said, it's like a prison.

Stultz also said something else. About our shots. Like maybe they're not just to keep us from getting diseases or keep us healthy.

I don't notice anything weird about myself. Stultz was probably trying to scare me so I'd do that gross stuff he wanted. Or was he kidding me? He's so ugly. Maybe he does make kids do that stuff. I don't think many women would go for him.

Yeah, I'm smart, but I still haven't figured out that book I got out of the doctor's office. If I could take it to the library with me and look up some of the words— maybe I could figure out what the hell the doctor is talking about in that book. I'm certainly not going to ask him.

Maybe Mandy could figure it out. Mandy's the smartest girl I've ever known. She knows more big words than I do, anyhow. And she's not silly like the other girls, and not dumb like the little ones. She's got more brains than anyone else I know, except for me. She's more like a woman, really. She even has tits, except they're small. Sometimes I think about her and it gives me an erection. I wonder if any of the other boys my age—whatever the hell it is—get erections now. You can't ask much about sex of anyone around here. There aren't even any books about it in the library. I tried looking it up in one of the encyclopedias and the pages were missing.

The doctor doesn't want us to know anything about it. How dumb can he be? Does he think we won't find out on our own?

Maybe. He's got a lot of weird ideas.

Look at him. he's acting like everything's just fine, but I can tell from his eyes he's worried about something and trying to hide it. He's looking *all* of us over—looking for something, or looking just to be looking, maybe. It's like we're under this giant microscope that's Doctor Barry, and he's trying to figure us out, and when he does, he'll put us all in little jars like frogs, then take us out later and dissect us.

Mandy told me she's worried about her mother, because she doesn't watch her little brother much any more, and Mandy has to do it so nothing will happen to him. Her mother doesn't get doped up—she doesn't even

199

eat any of the candy any more, or take any of the yellow pills the mothers can get at the pharmacy. She told Mandy she's "getting straight," which I guess means getting off drugs. She sits around the house in just a robe most of the time, like she's never going out, but she's supposed to go to work in the doll place.

Maybe she's going crazy too. I won't say that to Mandy, but I know Mandy thinks it as well as I do. But you don't go around telling people you think your mom's getting screwy in the old head, even if you believe it yourself. Who wants to admit their mom's crazy?

I'm not totally sure about my mom any more. She just ignores everything—all the problems we have. She keeps saying everything is okay.

And we're all "special" in the eyes of the Lord. The doctor has her brainwashed, and I guess all the others too.

If I could, I'd take Mandy, and Dawn—because she's a good kid and deserves a better Mom than she has—and make a run through those woods. Even if we had to walk a couple of days, we'd run into somebody eventually.

But maybe I shouldn't think about that. I did send that letter to my father. It was nice of Mandy to help me with that. Maybe he'll come and rescue me and take Mandy, her little brother and Dawn too. We'll all get away from this place and go somewhere else, where Dad will take care of us.

I'm getting awfully tired of waiting, though. How long does it take for a letter to get somewhere?

Mandy says I don't have any patience. She's right about that. It's hard to have patience when things just never change.

They go on, and on, and on.

I wonder if this tent would burn.

The weather just changed. It's raining now, and people are going home.

I guess the doctor's big party is a washout.

Alvin:

200

I hear something.

It's the wind outside, shaking the windows. I wonder what it's like outside today.

They keep the blinds pulled shut so I can't see out. They say the sun would hurt my eyes. They keep the lights turned out most of the time too. Except they leave a night light on, so the nurse can find you in the dark and give you a shot. Or give you a pill. Or take out some of your blood.

They like to take out your blood. They test it. I'm not sure what that means. If your blood gets a bad grade, I guess you're in trouble. Or you're really sick.

I can't get out of bed at all any more, even to go to the bathroom. The nurse has to help me with that.

The nurse is a nice lady. She's a mommy too, she says. She says she has a little baby boy. I told her I'd like to see it some time. She said when I get out I can come to her house and she'll give me some cookies and I can visit her baby.

She reads to me when she can. Stories from books mostly. Like fairy tales. I heard most of them before, but it's nice to hear the nurse's voice read them. Her name's Sheila. And I can close my eyes and pretend I'm home and it's my mom reading to me.

I know there's other kids up here—other kids who have the same thing I have. It has a long name which I can't remember. I heard the doctor talking about it with Sheila. They try to whisper, but I can hear some of what they say. It doesn't make any sense to me, anyhow. It's doctor talk.

I think one of the kids up here died last week. I don't know for sure. Sheila won't tell me when somebody dies. She says it's too sad.

Today is the big birthday party. We got to celebrate too. We got a little cake. Sheila helped me eat mine, because when I try to hold on to something I start shaking, so I can't hold a fork and eat my own food by myself.

I wish I was at the big birthday party.

I don't know what I look like any more. Since I can't

get up, I don't get to the bathroom and don't see any mirrors. A couple of weeks ago, when I could get up, I looked in the mirror and I looked more like a gnome than ever.

All my hair's gone.

Sheila said it would grow back in if they cure me.

It's raining outside now. I wish I was out there. I like to run around in the rain and get real wet. It's lots of fun.

I like to have fun like that. But I don't get to do it any more. I wonder when I'm going to get well.

The doctor won't tell me.

Chapter Twenty

The Party's Over

The patrol man at the gate left his post and went to the body of Helen Snyder. He squatted down and felt her wrist for a pulse. He lifted her head gently and was lost in the cold depths of her dead eyes briefly. He shuddered. He returned to his post and called the clinic.

Warren was sitting in his office, watching the rain splash on his window then run down into the sill. Despite his natural inclination to melancholia when it rained, overall, he felt better about the state of things in Jamay Lake.

The party seemed to have been successful. He was sure it had renewed the spirit of the community, just as he himself felt somewhat rejuvenated. The rain had come too late to ruin things, and now it was slacking off. The evening would be cool, but comfortable. Good sleeping weather.

He wasn't fooling himself that he no longer had anything to worry about, of course. He just felt he could cope better. He had observed nothing particularly bothersome at the party to add to his problems. A couple of children had become sick from overeating, but that was to be expected. It was not a serious matter. He had not bothered even to interfere, allowing the mothers of the children to take charge. Nothing else had happened that he was aware of.

The only thing that disturbed him was the way some of the older children regarded him. There was criticism or censure in their eyes, and that made him wonder if they were having trouble in his society and he was not aware of it. Maybe it was only the normal fear and awe of authority he saw in their faces. He had done nothing to any child for which he should be hated.

He was taking very good care of them. All of them. No one could judge him for the way he was handling things. He was doing everything within his power to get the society back on track and running smoothly.

He was fairly convinced he was without blame or guilt of any kind, his mind accepting any inherent contradictions without questioning them.

Then the buzzer on the intercom broke the near silence.

Helen Snyder's flesh was very cold to the touch now, not only from death, but from having lain on the cold pavement while rain soaked her clothing. Warren and a nurse struggled to peel the wet garments from her body so that he might examine her.

There was a small bruise on her left cheek, probably caused by her fall. No bones were broken however. There were no outward signs of the cause of her death at all. The only peculiar thing he observed was that her mouth was smeared with lipstick. It was on her teeth and even her tongue, and he thought there were two different shades, not complimentary shades as women sometimes applied, but shades that were meant to achieve different effects as two different women would wear.

He would pursue that mystery later. For now, his intuition told him she was another victim of trauma-induced death, but he couldn't imagine what the trauma had been. Surely the rain hadn't provided any trauma; it was only an autumn shower, with no lightning or thunder.

He would perform an autopsy. But he didn't think he would find anything.

He draped a sheet over Helen's body and, his spirit laden anew with guilt and self-recrimination, walked home in the rain to be with Sondra.

The next morning, Warren arrived late at the clinic. The weather had cleared, but the temperature had dropped another ten degrees, making a heavy coat necessary. If the temperature went any lower, there would be a hard freeze.

Warren had barely slept the night before. He closed his eyes, and several times felt himself on the brink of slumber, but he would awaken with a jolt, then have to fight to get back to the brink again. He calculated he had actually slept only two or three hours, and that was mostly after the sun had risen.

As soon as he entered the clinic, he was confronted with the rather ugly visage of Kevin Hamilton, an older child who was known to be trouble; he was always starting fights, some of which he could not finish. He was a discipline problem to everyone, and Warren had not decided how to handle such children. They had not presented a problem until recently.

Warren recalled seeing Kevin throw up, but he had not wished to embarrass the child by calling attention to it. Now he wished he had done something; the boy's face was covered with brown spots. The diagnosis was obvious and disheartening.

"I think he's got food poisoning," the boy's mother, Harriet Hamilton, said, an accusation in her voice. "There must've been germs in the ice cream or something."

Harriet's presence was always a bit overwhelming. She was a big woman and used her size to intimidate anyone she could. Warren himself found it difficult to stand up to her, because she was not impressed by his authority, either as the town's leader or as a doctor.

"That's clearly not the case," he said, examining Kevin's eyes. He noticed a scar healing on the boy's lip and wondered if Harriet had perhaps been beating the child, though, knowing Kevin's reputation, it was more likely he was wounded fighting. "No one else became ill from the food. He probably just ate too much."

"What about those spots on his face?" she pressed.

"It is a virus," he said, using his standard line. "Perhaps contagious."

"A virus? What kind?"

"Nothing to be too concerned about. It's caused the outbreak, but he should be okay. Of course, we'll have to keep him here in the clinic . . ."

"I don't want to stay here," Kevin broke in. "I ain't no baby."

"Shush."

"I don't want needles stuck in me. I . . ."

"I said, 'shush.' We'll do what the doctor says. Do you want to die?"

"I never said he would . . ."

"Well, these things can get worse. My sister died from a virus!"

"I'm glad you see the necessity, Mrs. Hamilton. We'll put him in isolation first, to determine if he *is* contagious—then we'll let you know more in a couple of days."

"See?" She looked like she might slap the boy if the doctor was not watching. "You have to do what the doctor says. That's the only way you'll get better."

"Aw, Mom . . ."

"Shush."

Warren turned his face away and put a note on the chart he had prepared for Kevin: "Fourth floor." He was really worried about this case. Kevin was the first older child to come down with the disease.

That meant it could affect *any* of the children.

Before noon, another case presented itself, further eroding Warren's previous assumption that everything would be okay.

Sally Henderson, a pretty brunette, who he had always assumed was one of his most well-adjusted mothers, had come in to tell him she thought she might be pregnant.

He could tell her implied admission of having had sex was troubling her even more than the prospect of being pregnant.

She was, in fact, terrified that he would ask her about the father.

But he didn't.

He didn't want to know, not just yet, though part of him was outraged and indignant, and another part felt betrayed. He allowed none of his emotions to show before the woman. Her immediate welfare was more important than any of his personal feelings at the moment.

"You can't be pregnant," he said as calmly as possible. "You know that."

"But I missed two periods . . ."

"You can miss periods for a variety of reasons other than pregnancy. Stress. Dieting." Mentally he added "guilt." "Have you been taking your tranquilizers?"

"Yes, but they don't seem to do anything for me."

"Stress then. Stress in general—and stress from . . ."
He was growing angry with her. He wanted to shout at her for having sex, for breaking the rules. He wanted to demand who the man was—which patrol man, specifically—she had been giving herself to, so that he might punish him, and her too. He would cast them both out, as God had Adam and Eve from the Garden.

He caught himself. I'm God now, he thought sardonically. I'm judging people like I'm God. I'm the one who should be on tranquilizers. I'm having delusions of grandeur.

He turned away from Sally briefly to collect himself. He spied a bottle of yellow pills in the nearest cabinet. A few of those and he would no longer compete with God in judgment. He would no longer care; he could lift all his burdens. Hadn't that been what he had prescribed for his patients—for his congregation? For his sheep?

Physician, heal theyself, he thought mordantly.

He started to open the cabinet and reach for the bottle. "Doctor?"

He had forgotten he had a patient. Or was he merely

207

distracted? No, it wasn't a momentary lapse of attention. It was more; he had blanked her presence out of his mind. Deliberately. He closed the cabinet door. As he turned back to Sally, his eyes scanned a vial on another shelf.

As a doctor he had access to much stronger relief than any amount of yellow pills could provide.

His mind filed that thought away quickly, before it became an action, but like any Great Idea, it would not dissipate so easily; it would fester and gnaw in his awareness until he came to terms with it.

"Sorry, Mrs. . . ."

"Henderson."

"Sorry, I was looking for a medication which we seem not to have stocked here. Something that would calm you."

"I don't need calming. I've missed . . ."

". . . two periods, wasn't it? And your medication is in order. And you're not dieting." He had to repeat the conversation to remind himself what he was doing. He felt so disoriented, almost woozy. The vial seemed to loom in his vision, a latent image demanding attention.

"I know what it feels like to be pregnant. I had morning sickness today. That's why I came in."

"You may have only a mild case of stomach flu," Warren said. "I can give you something to take care of that."

Sally shot a look at him that could be fear or perhaps wish fulfillment. "Maybe the operation didn't take." She said quietly.

"Mrs. Henderson, your body is not going to replace two inches of tissue, which is what I removed. It's absolutely unheard of."

"Couldn't it happen? Couldn't I be an exception?"

"Do you want to be?"

"Please, just give me a pregnancy test."

"I will examine you and do a Pap smear, but I see no need . . ."

"I want a pregnancy test!"

"All right. That too."

He busied himself the next hour or so examining Sally,

taking urine and blood samples, and a Pap smear. Through it all he had fumbled and sweated. Once he pinched her with an instrument and had to apologize. Finally finished, he had her wait out in the hall for the results of the tests.

Alone in the room, he approached the cabinet and opened the door. His hand picked up the vial; it was like an involuntary reflex action. His other hand snatched up a hypodermic syringe.

He plunged the needle into the vial and filled the syringe.

Laying the syringe on the cabinet shelf temporarily, he rolled up his left sleeve.

He needed to find a vein.

Of course, the pregnancy test showed negative. Warren told Sally that, but she remained dubious.

"What about the other tests?"

"You're okay. No cancerous cells. No abnormal growths. You're a healthy woman."

"I'm pregnant. I just know it."

"Here," he said writing a prescription. "Go to the pharmacy and get some of these; they'll help alleviate your stress."

"But won't they hurt the baby?"

A few minutes before he would have lashed out at her for being such a stubborn woman. Now her manner barely ruffled him. The world had taken on a new hue.

And what he had done was not bad; he could function now. He *needed* to f-u-n-c-tion. How could he be expected to solve all the world's problems and be God, if he could not function on the simplest level?

"No," he assured her. "You're not pregnant. Do as I say. Take these pills, and everything will be better."

"Are you sure?"

"Absolutely."

"If I am pregnant, I don't want an abortion, Dr. Barry."

Warren smiled indulgently. "Of course not. I wouldn't

expect you to do that."

Sally sensed he was somehow different. Was he patronizing her? Was he lying about the pregnancy test?

"Promise me you'll take this medicine," he said. "That's all I ask. If you still feel 'pregnant' a week from now, you come back in and we'll see if we can determine what's happening."

"I—I promise."

"Good day, Mrs. Henderson," he said dismissing her.

She left reluctantly, regarding him with undisguised curiosity and perhaps a little hurt. He seemed to be pushing her away, as if he didn't want to be bothered by her.

Warren continued to smile as if his face were locked in position and he could do nothing about it.

He was still smiling after she shut the door.

Hours later, after it was dark outside, Warren awoke abruptly. He had fallen asleep in his chair, or rather he had left consciousness behind and attained a kind of liquid euphoria that was almost as refreshing as sleep.

Except now his arm ached where he had given himself the injection, and his facial muscles were tensed up as well. There was a brackish taste lingering on his tongue.

He tried to recall what had happened that day, and it was somewhat of a blur. Something about pregnancy, something about death and a woman's daughter, a bad cup of coffee. A weird pressure on his bladder. He arose from the chair and went to the bathroom to relieve himself.

Then he caught a glimpse of a stranger in the mirror over the sink, a stranger who had aged a decade in a month, a stranger whose chin was marred by an ugly black mole. Why had he not noticed this stranger before, he wondered. Could it be because the stranger he had become was no longer aware of the tedious details of maintaining oneself?

Could it be the stranger had forgotten he was a physician?

Perhaps.

The stranger's countenance nodded at him. You are old, Father Warren, the stranger said, and about to become feeble.

"I am no one's father," Warren replied irritably.

You are father to the town, the stranger said. You are everyone's father.

"I had forgotten," Warren answered.

Take care of business, the stranger went on. You have the responsibilities of God.

Warren smiled and the stranger smiled back. Delusions of grandeur were sometimes amusing. That this ugly-visaged thing in the mirror could consider itself a god of any substance was a humorous notion—an absurdity of the highest magnitude.

Warren abruptly halted his conversation with the stranger. He bent down, turned on the cold water tap and splashed water on his face several times, until some feeling returned to his flesh. He blotted his face dry with paper towels, then regarded the reflection again.

It was that of Warren Barry, not the elderly stranger, though Warren could see a resemblance between him and the other being who inhabited the mirror.

The mole on his chin seemed darker now.

Warren returned to his office. He took an alcohol swab and rubbed the mole. He opened the supply cabinet and withdrew a vial which contained a local anesthetic. He took this, a syringe, and a scalpel into the bathroom.

He filled the syringe, jabbed it around the mole a few times, flinching as the needle pinched his flesh, then waited a couple of minutes.

He picked up the scalpel and sliced off the mole. Blood ran down his chin and throat.

He had been trembling when he removed the mole. He was shaking more violently now. He cursed softly and pressed a wad of gauze on his chin. The mole was on the edge of the scalpel, resting there like a tiny snail. Clumsily, he slid the mole into a bottle for later lab analysis.

It was probably a melanoma, he realized, and, if so, he

211

had done nothing to help himself. It may have already spread into the flesh underneath its former place. In which case, Warren had much pain to look forward to, or, if he were too late in removing the thing, death in the near future.

His shaking approaching real tremors, Warren hastily made a bandage to cover his chin. He'd been a fool to do this on his own. He might bleed to death. It would serve him right for not thinking as a physician should. He would not treat any of his own patients in this casual fashion.

He passed back into his office. His recollection of the day's events was gradually becoming sharper. He had a woman on a metal table down the hall for whom he needed to determine the cause of death.

But he was too tremulous.

He needed to steady his nerves.

Fortunately, he recalled clearly how to do that.

By seven-thirty, Warren had finished his autopsy on Helen Snyder. He now read the results of preliminary tests on tissue samples he had one of the nurses do for him.

Traces of another person's saliva were in Helen's mouth and vagina. No semen, however, leading him to conclude she had been interrupted with a lover, perhaps by the rain. But at the time the rain had started, Warren had noted all the patrol men were in the tent. Was there a phantom man? Or was it, as he suspected, that Helen had been making love to another woman? That would explain the different shades of lipstick on her mouth.

That was two instances he had encountered in one day of the women's sexual activities. And if he had found two on his own—actually just stumbled upon them—there must be more. Perhaps when he was sleeping with his near-dead wife, the town of Jamay Lake indulged in all-night orgies. Perhaps people were fornicating and running naked in the streets.

It no longer mattered, of course. Helen was dead; that

212

was irrevocable. He had already told her daughter, and she was bravely going to relay the news to her brother.

He wondered what he should do with them. His mind was too foggy now to contemplate the problem. He needed rest badly.

He stitched the cavity in Helen's body together as best he could and covered her up.

Mandy was worried when her mother didn't come home soon after the picnic. She even stopped a patrol man in the street and told him about her mother being missing. The patrol man, a young man named Harold, said he would look into the matter. In the meantime, he advised her to stay inside with her brother and keep the lights on. The way he said that made Mandy think there was danger in being alone.

There had never been any danger before.

She did as she was told, however. The patrol man promised to tell her the minute he learned anything.

Mandy fell asleep in the living room awaiting news, but none came. The next morning, she packed Danny off to school and went out to scour the town for her mother on her own.

Eventually, she arrived at the inevitable place—the one place she hoped her mother was not—the clinic.

She stepped inside and went up to the nurse bravely. The nurse looked at her with pity, making Mandy very apprehensive, and told her to sit down.

Minutes later, the doctor came out and told her what had happened. He couldn't tell her what had killed her mother yet.

Warren arrived home around eight o'clock. He let himself in and entered the living room. He didn't wish to disturb Sondra tonight. She needed her rest more than he did. He would just flop on the couch.

He had left the light on in the hall, so the living room was not completely dark. He lay down on the couch, being careful not to crush the vial in his jacket pocket.

His eyes open wide, he watched the ceiling, as if it were a movie screen and he was waiting for the feature to begin.

He had read somewhere, a long time ago, in a book of oddball philosophy, that if a person stared at a wall in a room that was in semi-darkness, he could see movement—he could actually observe molecular activity taking place.

Warren stared, waiting for the molecules to dance for him.

Instead, floaters formed on his eyes. He tried to blink them away, but they resisted him.

He closed his lids over the floaters; they remained as latent images a few seconds, then a wonderful velvet blackness descended on his inner vision—a dense blackness into which he could crawl and be safe.

He wondered briefly if the orgy was beginning outside: patrol men running rampant, their members tumescent, mounting every mother in Jamay Lake; women pursuing women; children watching and learning. Perhaps even that old gnarled man in the sentry gate, Max the troll, got in on the action.

That image made Warren smile. Max was like Quasimodo in his mind—Quasimodo ringing the bell to alert the citizens the doctor was asleep, and it was time to play.

Who was his Esmeralda?

Warren chuckled. That seemed very funny to him for some reason. In fact, everything was amusing in its own twisted way. The world, the universe, whatever, was toying with him, having its little joke at his expense.

Abruptly, his humorous mood passed, and he concentrated on trying to go to sleep. Before his descent into the darkness, a wan smile curled his lips.

He was thinking of a wonderful subject for a sermon, maybe his last sermon before he closed the church:

Fornication.

Chapter Twenty-One

Death and Fornication

In a little under three weeks' time, several people died in Jamay Lake. None of their deaths was spectacular; none was surprising.

Four children, one of them Alvin Lawson, and all of them residents of the clinic's fourth floor, died of complications of their disease. Three women took the path Brenda and Helen had chosen and just stopped living. Oddly enough two of them were the mothers of children on the fourth floor who were still among the living. The third was Wanda McCoy, whose baby had come down only with a mild cold, but its condition traumatized her way beyond the actual threat presented to her child's health. She had a tendency to over-dramatize everything and, in this case, it was the end of her.

Another woman died of drug overdosing. Warren had ordered a one-third increase of the drug in the candy, and had enclosed explicit instructions with the packages that warned of consuming any more of the candy than was usual. This woman, however, had not paid any attention to the warning and ate twice as much as the rec-ommended amount.

Warren felt guilty about the candy death. His intention was to slow the women down, not kill them. Even though the increased dosage made the candy slightly more addictive, he didn't expect it to be a problem. He thought the women would be intelligent enough to comply with his instructions on dosage. Of course, they *were* intelligent enough; maybe they didn't care.

Warren had increased the dosage with the slim hope, which he now realized was of spurious origin to begin with, that he might control the mothers' sexual urges. He had decided sex was a big complication—which was why he had not allowed for it in his original plans for the foundation of the town and had come up with the use of tranquilizers.

Perhaps nothing could totally suppress the sexual urge—even neutered animals sometimes behaved as if they were in heat. If there were ever a society that used Warren's methods and his drug, it would have to account for that sexual factor. Warren's failure to do so was costing him dearly, seriously undermining the validity of the experiment.

In addition to those who had died, more people were now included among the dying. Three children were admitted to the clinic with the old-age disease. A woman was diagnosed to have advanced ovarian cancer, and, either most or least significantly, the doctor himself was likely to die from his own ill-considered removal of the mole, or to call it by its right name now, the melanoma. His face would be sore constantly were it not for his continuing to numb all his senses just enough that he could function. There was a only a very slight chance he would recover.

He didn't desire to pursue the cure.

Mandy grieved for her mother, yet she didn't miss her as she realized she should. Helen, before she died, had become so erratic in her behavior, so difficult to predict or to deal with, that it was tiresome to be around her. Her unwillingness to even participate in maintaining the family had caused some feelings of bitterness in Mandy, despite her outward signs of placid acceptance of the situation.

As a result of her ambivalence regarding her mother,

Mandy felt quite guilty, as if she had secretly wished for her mother's death, and the fulfillment of that wish was her fault.

Her little brother Danny took the news as expected; he cried and mourned for days. He assumed some guilt as well, thinking as most children do that everything that happens was partially his fault. In the child's self-centered universe, it made sense to interpret events that way; it gave the child an illusion of being in control.

Mandy found the doctor's explanation for her mother's death mystifying. He had said it was her heart, but that it was brought on by a trauma, and when pressed further, he would not explain what the trauma could have been. He merely remarked that trauma was not a quantifiable thing—some people could endure years in a concentration camp, for example; while others died if a loud noise occurred at the wrong moment. The condition and its response were completely unpredictable.

Mandy came away baffled. It seemed the doctor was unable to put anything into clear-cut, understandable terms. Mandy noted his glassy eyes when he was talking to her and wondered if he might be drinking, though his hands seemed steady and his speech, while ambiguous, was not slurred.

Because of the recent number of deaths in Jamay Lake, there was much shuffling of children. Motherless infants were placed with childless mothers whenever possible, to help ease the loss. Older children were asked to make decisions on their own.

Mandy, with a brother, didn't know where to turn. She had no idea who could want her and her brother. Yet she realized she couldn't stay alone, not with the implied dangers that awaited her according to Harold, the patrol man.

She could not face the world—especially the world Jamay Lake had become—on her own.

"You could move in with us," William suggested. "I'll talk my mother into letting you stay."

217

"I don't know. The doctor said he would take care of us." Her eyes were still red from crying, her face puffy. William felt compassion for her as he had never felt before.

"He's probably forgotten you already."

"Don't say that."

"That patrol man acted like it was dangerous for you to be alone. You know that's true too. You've heard of the stuff that's going on. You're the one who told me a patrol man tried to rape a girl. Maybe it was the one you were talking to!"

"William, you're scaring me."

"I hope so. I think we all have a lot to be scared about."

"What?"

"Lots of people are dying."

"Lots?"

"Well, people are missing anyhow. I've been noticing. I'm sorry about your mom, but she's not the first. I know Miss Stowe died—Pete's mother. I heard about it. She stole someone's baby, went into the clinic and never came out."

"How do you know that?"

"People talk—and I see things when I'm out at night. The mothers aren't paying much attention to anything. They're so wiped out from the candy and pills, if you ask them, they're liable to tell you anything—without even thinking about it."

"What are we going to do?"

"I don't know, but if you lived with us, maybe we could figure something out."

"All right—if your mother says it's okay."

Sharon Wesley didn't care. She said she felt sorry about Mandy's mother and that Mandy and her brother were welcome to stay as long as they liked—or until the doctor found a home for them.

Sharon was secretly relieved to have extra people in the house. It would take some of the wear and tear off her having to deal with William all the time. Maybe he

218

wouldn't be such a problem if he had other children to keep him company.

So she agreed without any argument on William's part. Then she went into the kitchen and indulged herself in more of that wonderful new candy.

The Nameless Church had been unofficially closed for six weeks. Now, with its doors open and the congregation settled, it was obvious it no longer had the spiritual ambience proper to preaching a good sermon, as if some of its status as a holy place had worn off from lack of use.

For one thing, there were very few people in attendance. Warren estimated they represented only about half the current population of Jamay Lake. He thought there should be many more. Perhaps he had not been keeping track very well. It was difficult for him to remember all the details as he used to.

Even some of his nurses were beginning to notice his inability to remember things from one day to the next, or from moment to moment. This morning, for example, he had to be reminded it was Sunday. He had almost gone into the clinic without even thinking about the church when Sister Bonita called to ask which hymns he would like to be played prior to his sermon.

He was prepared for that, at least. He'd had the presence of the mind the last few days to compose his sermon, making notes to prompt himself on three-by-five cards so he wouldn't forget the important points he thought it necessary to make.

Before taking the pulpit, Warren remained in the minister's study long enough to give himself an injection from the vial that was an ever-present fixture in his life now. He realized he didn't really need it, that he was indulging his desire to dodge reality, that he could just stop taking the drug any time, that he was merely taking the edge off things, actually—yet if he didn't have it, he almost immediately became an idiot and shook with paroxysms that made delirium tremens seem like nothing more than nervous tics.

219

He waited half a minute, giving the stuff time to creep up the vein and into his system.

Ironically, he realized, he would *have* to use this stuff when his cancer began painfully asserting itself—this or something stronger.

So what if he had started using it a little earlier than he needed to?

It helped him to *function*.

Warren straightened his tie, combed back a few stray hairs, and wet his lips. He stepped out into the church.

Sister Bonita, bless her heart, was playing the organ, while the congregation sang hymns. Their singing was ragged, uneven at best, a cacophony actually, but at least they *were* singing. As he faced them from the pulpit, he confirmed their number was way below what it should be. Now it occurred to him that many had chosen not to attend. That would never have happened before.

The "Rock of Ages" was over, and everyone settled down in the pews.

Warren looked out over them and was reflected in a sea of dazed eyes. The women were in their frilly blue dresses as they should be; their hair-dos seemed prim and proper; but their eyes were those of dazed automatons. Warren was almost intimidated. Could he preach to such zombies?

Why was he preaching at all?

Because, he reminded himself, it was a necessity. He had to exhibit strength to his people; he had to let them know he was still there for them, not only as their physician, but as their spiritual advisor.

He fumbled out his handful of three-by-five cards and glanced down at them, highly aware of the impatient shifting of weight and shuffling of feet among the congregation.

How odd, the thought, that each card had only a single word on it. He could have sworn he filled them with tiny, precisely printed letters. It had taken him hours to work on them. Even stranger was that the cards had only two words on them, one each appearing on alternate cards: Death. Fornication. Death. Fornication.

No textual references, nothing with which to under-score his spiritual message.

At that moment, something bit the base of his brain—it was the pleasant jolt of the drug flooding through his awareness—and suddenly the single words seem more than enough on which to sermonize.

Warren smiled, then frowned, then smiled again.

Death was serious. Fornication was not so serious. Both were solemn subjects. He needed to keep a straight face.

"Good morning to you all," he began. "I am glad to see there are still many left in this community who understand the importance of attending church on a regular basis. Unfortunately, due to certain problems that have arisen, it will become necessary to close the church down after this service—at least until these problems are cleared up."

He halted, expecting an outcry. The automatons stared back, some with frozen smiles, others with bemused expressons of total unawareness. The children among them seemed inattentive as well.

They didn't care about the church then. He'd have to make them care.

He cleared his throat and began anew. "Thus it is proper that this sermon be about the two singular most pressing problems we have in our beloved little community." Warren paused. "Two" and "singular" probably didn't go together like that, but maybe it made some kind of sense. Any kind of sense was okay. "The first of these is, I'm afraid, one that plagues all of us and begins the moment we are pulled screaming from the womb. That, beloved mothers and children, is the natural process known as *death*.

"We are dying from the time we're born to the time we actually die, so death comes to all of us. Sometimes it seeks us under the guise of something else—perhaps as a bad habit, or an addiction, say, to drugs. Other times it comes in the form of a senseless disease that renders us dead, just like that. Death, in essence, is the circle—I mean, the cycle—of life completed. We must all, therefore, die."

Two women looked at each other in disbelief. "What in the world is he talking about?" one whispered.

"I don't know. Maybe he'll explain it later."

". . . trees die, animals die, and ultimately human beings must die. Now, in a small community such as ours, a single death seems more tragic, because there are so few of us. Two deaths seems a calamity. Three or more deaths must seem like a catastrophe not less than the plagues of the Middle Ages. We have had more than our share of deaths recently, however, leading some to speculate that our community is on the brink of dissolution.

"This is not the case. Most of us remain healthy and strong. As the physician for this community I shall see to it that you are properly cared for. I have at my disposal . . ."

Warren continued preaching on the subject of death several more minutes, his pronouncements, arguments, counter-arguments, and explanations becoming more and more convoluted.

He was losing his audience, though many of his audience were not aware of it themselves.

William, sitting next to Mandy, whispered in her ear, "The doctor's flipped out." He had come not at his mother's insistence, but because Mandy wanted to come, perhaps because her mother had died and she sought spiritual comfort. "He's drunk or something."

"Maybe," Mandy said casually, "he's just confused."

Georgia Burrfield viewed Warren through eyes blurred with dope and alcohol, but her hearing was not affected. What he said was making her squirm. She was as fidgety as her nine-year-old, Eddie, who had become so bored he was down on the floor, carving his name in the polished wood with his pocket knife.

She didn't care to stop him.

Warren's talk about dying was making her queasy. She still had nightmares about Helen Snyder's death, about which, however much she denied it, she carried a great

222

deal of guilt. She had no doubt she was the last person to be with Helen before she died, and she tortured herself that she had somehow brought it about. She was also aware that children had died recently, and that was something she could barely endure; it was her one area of true sensibility.

Warren was making her suffer. She let her mind wander away from his words, blanking them out successfully until she heard the word "fornication" come from the pulpit.

"That," Warren intoned seriously, "is our second, very apt area of concern in this communication. Yes, I know there are children among this congregation. But I also know that many of them have been witness to the fornications taking place in our town, and they—these innocents—should not be exposed to such. You may have thought I was not aware of these things. You may have thought me a stupid old man who did not know fornication was infesting Jamay Lake like a cancer!"

Sally Henderson, her abdomen as swollen as if she were three months pregnant, gasped and turned red. She took Dawn by the hand, jerked her up and ran down the aisle.

"There goes a fornicator!"

Sally did not pause; she hurried out the door with her daughter.

The dazed eyes barely moved.

"Fornication takes many forms. It can be a fornication of the spirit as well as the flesh. It can be between man and woman, woman and woman, adult and child. I shall not stand for it! There shall be no fornication in my community!"

Georgia pulled herself and Eddie up. The two of them were out the door almost before Warren noticed. "Another fornicator leaves. Are there more? Will you stand up and be counted as a fornicator?"

Myrna Lawson stood up. "This is not a fit sermon with children in the room," she said.

"But it is. *They* must know as well."

"I'm not one of your damned fornicators!" She picked Alicia up in her arms and trotted down the aisle. She stopped at the door briefly. "This is not what we need from you! We need comfort, not brow-beating, damn you."

As the door shut again, Warren's voice fell. He was mumbling to himself and sifting through his note cards, putting one behind the other, over and over.

The dazed eyes waited.

"What's fornication?" William asked Mandy.

"I'll tell you later."

"Is it fun?"

"Shush."

"No, it's not fornication," Warren said, looking up again and trying to focus on those who remained in the church. "It's death. That's what I meant to talk about. Death and the dead. All the dead things. Dead ideals. Dead concepts. Dead souls. Dead . . ."

Sister Bonita pivoted on her stool. "Doctor?" she whispered.

"Let's say a eulogy for all the dead things," he continued.

"Doctor?"

"Dead things. Deadness. Decay. Fire—that's the only way to purge us of the dead. In the fiery furnace—or something."

Sister Bonita arose and went to Warren's side. "You're not making any sense," she said.

Several more people left.

"I'm not?"

"What's the matter?"

"I'm perfectly fine. Go back to your organ. Play a hymn. Play 'Jesus Loves me.' Anything."

She returned to the organ and poised her fingers above the keys.

"That, mothers and children, concludes my message for today. I shall not preach again for some time to come. I close this church until such time as a man fit to preach can . . ."

224

Sister Bonita started playing.

Warren appeared disoriented. He turned and walked back to the study, ducking inside without bothering to formally close the service.

Sharon Wesley, who had achieved a kind of perpetual nirvana recently, said to her newly-enlarged family, "What a wonderful sermon."

That evening, Mandy sat in the living room, watching television with her little brother. After Sharon was asleep, William came down, bringing with him the doctor's book.

He approached Mandy, carefully stepping over Danny who was sprawled out on the floor, and sat next to her.

"The doctor's nuts," he said.

"I know."

"That doesn't bother you?"

"I don't know what to do about it."

"Maybe this would give you some ideas." He placed the book in her lap.

Mandy leaned forward to examine the book in the glow of the TV. "*Children Who Grow Young* by Warren Barry, M.D. Where did you get this?"

"I swiped it from the doctor's office. I tried to read it, but it doesn't make any sense to me. I know you're smarter than I am, Mandy."

"And it kills you to say that," she pointed out, smiling.

"I guess so," he replied, his face flushing. "But if anybody can figure this out, you can."

"Why do you think it's so important?"

"Because this book is what we're living. I could figure that much out. We're part of a big experiment."

"That doesn't seem possible."

"Just tell me what you think."

"I'll do my best."

"And, by the way, what is fornication?"

Mandy cleared her throat nervously; a blush rose in her cheeks. "Well, it's like this. . . ."

Chapter Twenty-Two

The Empty Places

William no longer bothered going to school at all. Nor did Mandy. Nor did many of the other children. The teachers, whose ranks had been reduced by death and indifference, were not that concerned. There were no real rules any more, and only the smaller children were able to be disciplined.

The pall of discontent hung over the whole town, like a dense cloud, primarily felt by the children who were ten and over. Their group consciousness sensed something was about to happen, that the least little thing could set off a chain reaction of events that could result in calamity.

It was mid-December now, but the weather, as whimsical as ever in the state of Indiana, was almost balmy. The first snow had yet to fall. The only real indication that winter was approaching was the seemingly abrupt shortening of the daylight hours.

William wore a light jacket as he walked down the streets, aimlessly wandering. He was noticing how many empty houses there were. Mandy's was among them. She had left most of the furniture behind, a patrol man having helped with the beds needed to accommodate her and her brother at William's house, and anything that remained was of little value to them.

Some of the empty places had been vandalized. Eddie Burrfield, who had assumed the position of meanest kid in town with Kevin in the clinic, would throw rocks through windows in broad daylight. He and other kids also entered the empty houses and messed things up, or stole whatever they could carry out, unmindful of the consequences.

Of course, there were no consequences. The pall affected the adults by rendering them complacent. No one seemed to care about order in the community any more. The patrol men did their best, but there were not enough of them to be everywhere at once. They often just looked the other way, interfering only if they felt like it, or if there was a threat of potential harm to other people.

Growing bored, William went home to talk to Mandy. Being with her was the only comfort he had to look forward to. He had given up on his father ever coming. Maybe his father *was* dead, as his mother led him to believe.

The whole world outside Jamay Lake could be dead and they wouldn't know it.

Mandy was alone in the house. Danny still attended school at her insistence, and he still obeyed her as if she were his mother. Sharon still went to the doll store, playing at work, pretending to be functioning.

Despite his great fondness for her, William felt mildly uncomfortable when he was totally alone with Mandy, as if there was something wrong about it. She was a girl, after all, and he was a boy—who was beginning to feel sexual longings.

He couldn't tell Mandy how he felt, though. She was his *friend*; she was too good to be anything else.

He could not commit "fornication" with her. It was weird how, after she explained the term and pointed out how frequently it occurred in the Bible, William felt nasty about having asked her. But she had been very matter-of-fact in her explanation, like a school teacher or a mother. Her face had turned red a little, but it didn't seem to faze her to talk openly about sexual matters, as long as it remained on a clinical level.

Mandy had become much more than a friend. She was almost a mother to him as well—in many ways, the only real mother he knew. She certainly cared for her little brother better than their own mother had. And, since moving into their house, she had assumed many of Sharon's duties—naturally, without questioning—cooking and cleaning and making sure everyone had clean clothes to wear. Her sense of order, of maintaining a household, was almost inspiring. She was the ideal the real mothers were not.

Whatever she had to do, Mandy always had an even-going manner, and that brought a sense of well-being and solidity to the Wesley household. It made the fact of Williams' mother zonking out every night more tolerable.

But when William came in the front door and called out her name, Mandy didn't immediately answer. He called her name again.

"Back here," she replied from the kitchen.

Warren didn't like the look on her face when he found her sitting at the table, the doctor's book open in front of her. She appeared to be very worried and under a great strain.

"I think I figured it out," she said, her voice on the verge of either tears or terror.

William sat down across from her, afraid to ask her what he needed to know but even more afraid of not asking.

"Well?" he said tentatively, his voice cracking.

"It's like one of the little stories I wrote. You remember, I let you read one, and you thought it was funny, so I didn't let you see any of the others. You know, how like everyone is some kind of robot?"

"Yeah." Or "a toy," he added mentally. After having thought it over, he realized the story she'd written wasn't far from the reality they experienced; it was her view of it, anyhow. He had meant to apologize for making fun of her efforts; now it seemed awkward. The correct moment for that had passed.

She put her hands together, pausing to choose the right words. "You were right in a way. Doctor Barry *is* experimenting with us. If I understand what he's saying in this book, this town is a big experiment. It's sort of a

228

communist town, for one thing."

"Communist? Like with the Russians?"

"No, communist like some of the early settlements in America. Everyone pitches in and does according to his abilities. That's the idealism of it; it's socialistic. But that's only the structure of the society. It's what's behind the structure that has me worried. It's the experimental part."

"Well, what is it?"

"The doctor has a theory that effective population control could be achieved by limiting the age of children. He starts out with this argument that there are people who like kittens but hate cats—and then he says there are people who like babies but don't like older children."

William's expression was blank and uncomprehending. "I don't get it."

"You see, his theory is to stop the growth of children at the age the mother likes best. If she likes babies, then she should be able to have a baby—I guess, forever. If she likes ten-year-olds, or twelve-year-olds, she can have them—forever."

"You mean the kids wouldn't grow up. At all?"

"Right. And that supposedly keeps the mothers from having more babies. They're supposed to be content if they have what they think is the ideal child or children."

"That's what we are?"

"The book is just theory . . ."

"That's what we are, isn't it?"

"I think so."

William whispered, "You mean *we* won't grow up?"

"When the book was written, the doctor had not discovered a way to make it work. It was just theory then, an idea he was playing around with. He didn't talk about a way of making it happen. He was just saying in an *ideal* society it would help control population—especially with the lower class women—the dumber ones who had kids like dogs have puppies and saw them as pets until they started growing up. He even said such women should be sterilized when they had one or two children—so they could not have any more."

"Sterilized? Like how?"

"Like by an operation. They surgically remove a piece of the woman's Fallopian tubes on each side."

"You're losing me."

"The tubes let eggs go to the uterus. When the tubes are cut, the eggs can't get down. I guess it's basically a permanent thing. Once a woman has it done, she can't change her mind. They have a way of doing it so there aren't even any scars."

"How do you know so much about that?"

"Mom told me she had it done. If I'm right, and this town is an experiment, then all the women here had it done, because the doctor says his ideas wouldn't work if the women can still get pregnant."

"If he did that part, then he did the rest of it. He found a way to keep us from growing up."

Mandy's expression showed she agreed. "I think so. It fits in with everything in the book."

"That's what that bastard Stultz was talking about."

"Who?"

"Stultz the patrol man, you know, the ugly guy. He told me I was so dumb because I didn't know what was in the cookies, and the baby formula—and the shots we get."

Mandy's face paled. "You mean the shots we get—that's what keeps us from growing up?"

"What else can it mean? How long has it been since any of us has grown? The birthday parties—no one ever says what age you are. You're the same age over and over. So your mommy won't cry when you leave home, I guess."

"I could be wrong."

"I don't think so. It explains everything." He shifted in his seat. "Well, not everything. It doesn't explain why kids are getting sick, or why mothers just drop dead."

"Or why the doctor's on dope."

"Who told you that?"

"I overheard one of the mothers who knows a nurse saying she accidentally caught the doctor giving himself a shot—a pain killer, except he's using it like dope."

"That's great. The doctor's a dopehead, our mothers are wiped out on happy candy, and we're just sitting around waiting to get our shots, so we won't grow up. Who's in charge, then? Who's running things?"

"It's obvious, William."

"It is?"

"Nobody's running anything. Somewhere the experiment went wrong."

After talking with Mandy, William hit the streets again. He was too distraught to sit still, and he wanted to think things over. He felt empty inside, as if his soul had been cut out—and, in a way, that was true. He was no longer a human being. He was an experimental subject.

If Mandy was right, the book explained the Big Secret only the adults knew, that the children were trapped in children's bodies and would remain so, apparently indefinitely. They were less than robots or toys—they were mere pets—not much better than the kittens most of the little kids had.

Kittens who never grew up, either.

What if, William wondered, we refused to take our shots? What if we took away the drug-laced cookies and the baby formula? What if we said no to the doctor?

William realized he kept thinking "we," and stopped to ponder who that "we" consisted of.

The children of Jamay Lake.

As things were going, the children were becoming the only group that was able to do anything. They had to be told what the secret was, so they could all do something about it together. That way, maybe, they could get the mothers to realize this was all wrong, that their children didn't really want to live in Never-Never Land, that they wanted to grow up and become something other than children.

But could the children be convinced? How could you relate to a six-year-old child that he would never grow up and that it was a bad thing? How could you tell children their mothers were part of a conspiracy?

231

God, it was terrible. The experiment reduced all the children to lab animals with no rights at all. They were being manipulated and used.

The good doctor, William reflected bitterly, the man who took care of them, who provided them with food and shelter and millions of re-runs of *Bambi* was insane—a mad doctor who regarded them as mere guinea pigs.

And he had told them fornication was the problem with his failed society. Fornication! A fancy word for screwing! Fornication was the only interesting thing happening in this hellish place.

William felt like pounding somebody, like killing someone. All the adults in Jamay Lake were as guilty as the doctor. They all deserved an awful punishment in his view. He wished he was capable of inflicting it.

Perhaps he was.

There were a couple of things that remained unresolved in his mind, however. Given that they were part of an experiment, why were so many children disappearing? Was there yet another secret behind the Big Secret?

There had to be. He had seen the mothers' faces in church. They were as confused by the doctor's ravings as he and Mandy were. The doctor knew much more than he was letting anyone else know.

William had to discover what the doctor was hiding. Gaining all the knowledge he could was the only rational thing to do; with the proper knowledge he could decide what needed to be done and then he could help the other children, become their leader in effect.

The only place to gain the knowledge he sought had to be in the clinic.

William slipped out of the house without telling Mandy he was leaving. He didn't want to upset her unnecessarily.

There was a quarter moon that night. The temperature had dropped to below forty, but not quite to freezing, so William wore a sweater under his jacket. There was no wind.

He entered the clinic as he had in the past. This time he went directly to the roof and to the skylight. It was the only way he could get to the fourth floor.

After he had dropped through the skylight, landing in the unused lounge area, he peeked around the corner. The hall was empty. Even the nurse's station was unoccupied.

He had come to get answers—and to see Alvin.

He went to the room in which he thought he had discovered Alvin before, but there was an empty place where Alvin should have been. William backed out of the room and made his way down the hall, checking the name cards by the doors, only to find the names had been replaced with patient numbers.

The doctor had gotten cagey. Maybe William had unwittingly left evidence of his being there before, and the number system had been instigated to make it difficult for anyone to find a specific person without searching all the rooms.

William was too smart to do that.

He strode to the nurse's station, not paying that much attention to his steps sounding in the hall. He was seething with so much bitterness and pent-up anger he didn't care if he were caught.

What would they do to him, anyhow? Give him another shot?

Maybe he'd get a "happy shot," like the doctor was giving himself, and he wouldn't have to care about anything.

He went into the nurse's station and found a clipboard on which the patients were listed. He ran his finger down the numbers, and found "Hamilton, Kevin," by a number. That was interesting; old Kevin was up here in the weird place. He must have what Alvin had. Maybe he ought to pay Kevin a visit; he'd be the ideal person on whom to vent some of his wrath. Foremost in his mind, however, was visiting Alvin.

He continued down the list and found the entry he was looking for:

"Lawson, Alvin—Expired." The date by his name was

233

over a week ago.

Tears slid down William's cheek.

Alvin was dead.

Gone forever.

He never had the chance to say good-bye, or anything. There wasn't even a funeral.

A harmless little kid like that—dead for no reason William could see—except he had caught something the doctor could not cure.

As had many others according to the list he had in his hand.

William laid the clipboard back on the nurse's little desk, next to a glowing CRT.

It occurred to him that several people were known to have died—the doctor had admitted as much in his "sermon"—but there were never any services of any kind for them.

What happened to all the dead people? What did the insane doctor do with them? Dissect them as part of his experiment? As he would a rat or a frog?

"What the hell you doing in here?" a man's rough voice yelled, grating across William's spine.

He turned to confront Lester Stultz.

"Well, if it ain't the little queer bait! You gonna be a doctor? Or a patient?"

William looked around, considering his options for action. There was only one real exit—the space Lester blocked with his body.

"Still looking for a gate pass? Want some comic books? Want some smokes? Old Lester's got anything you need, sweet cakes."

"Go to hell," William retorted.

Lester laughed in response. "Come here, queer bait, and maybe you and me can be friends. I got a forgiving nature."

William sneered, saying nothing. He wondered if he could leap over the counter and get to the hallway door.

Maybe.

"What do they do with the dead people?" he asked, stalling.

234

"Curious sort, ain't you? You ask too many questions. That's why you get into trouble."

"Tell me."

"I don't have to tell you squat, kid. Now, come over here and make it easy on yourself. I won't take you to the doctor if you co-operate like a good little queer bait should."

William made his move. He jerked himself up on the counter opposite Stultz, and slid over, landing hard on the floor. Springing to his feet, he ran towards—

Stultz was a lot faster than he expected him to be. Darkness also descended on William with an equal measure of alacrity.

Kevin Hamilton was half-awake. He was kept sedated constantly, not because of his condition, but because he refused to stay in bed. He was not yet as feeble or fragile as the younger children.

He heard a tussle out in the hall, near his room. He pulled himself up on the bed's sidebar till he was in a sitting position and peered out.

He saw Stultz dragging a seemingly unconscious William down the hall, towards the elevator.

Kevin smiled.

He hoped William got what he deserved. It was too bad he wouldn't be there to see what happened to him.

Chapter Twenty-Three

Brian Wesley

William awoke in a hot place, his hands bound behind him with electrical wire. He was lying on his side in a dark corner, and he could hear flames roaring behind him.

He tried to maneuver his body around so he could see what was generating such heat, but his feet were bound too. He grunted, attempting to turn over.

He didn't have to waste such effort, because his curiosity was soon satisfied. Stultz flipped him over rudely with his foot. "So you wanted to know what happens to the dead guys. Well, I thought I'd show you." He pointed to the door of the crematorium which was wide open.

William could barely look at the intense flames coming from the gas jets.

"Ever wonder about that stink that gets in the air around here? Like burned meat? Well, it ain't your mama burning hot dogs, kid. It's the doc. When somebody croaks, he brings them down here and stuffs them in the furnace there. It's a crematorium for cremating stiffs. I guess you're smart enough to know what that means."

William gulped hard. So that's what had happened to Alvin—and any others who had died. The idea of it made him want to throw up.

"I think you'll get it better, if I stuff you in there. What do you think of that?"

William's mouth was dry. He could think of no suitable reply. Defiance wouldn't work; nor would acceptance. Lester Stultz was evidently crazier than William had imagined. Nothing would keep him from doing what he wanted.

"No answer? Cat got your tongue?" He squatted down in front of William, his ugly visage highlighted by the flames. His breath stank as if he hadn't brushed his teeth in years—if ever. "I got a little problem here, though. It's almost a moral issue. You see, I could just stuff you in there and let you burn alive—which I admit appeals to me, but it would be over so quick. You know?"

William grunted. Behind his back he struggled with his bonds, but the wire was unyielding.

"You see, I could kill you first too. That might make you happier, because I'd just snap your neck like a twig, and it'd be over pretty quick. You wouldn't feel a thing when I burned you up. You see, I got this little bit of the quality of mercy in me. It's one of my character flaws."

"Big problem," William replied weakly.

"No—that's the small problem. I'll figure that out. The big problem is your ass. I ain't had a little cherry boy like you in a long time, so I can't decide if I should rape your ass now, or do it after you're dead."

"You filthy queer!"

"No, you . . ."

"Stultz!"

Harold Thomas stood in the shadows near the crematorium. Something shone in his hand.

"You stay out of this, candy-ass," Stultz said, turning.

"Leave that boy alone."

"You can't do nothing to stop me."

The shiny thing in Harold's hand clicked.

William saw a flicker of fear in Stultz's eyes.

"You wouldn't shoot me, would you? I'm your partner. That ain't right. I was only going to scare the kid and let him go. See, it's that Wesley brat. He's a troublemaker. I caught him snooping around upstairs, and I knew he needed a lesson, so I thought I'd . . ."

"Shut up. Did you think no one would notice the crematorium being on? You can hear it up on the roof. And the doctor isn't in. You're a stupid man, Lester."

Lester dropped the lying and switched to audacity. "You won't shoot me. You're too chicken." Stultz stood erect and stepped hesitantly in Harold's direction. "What do you care what happens to a kid? They're all going to die anyhow. So this kid goes faster. I'm doing the little creep a favor, so he won't suffer."

"Don't take another step."

"You asshole!" Stultz ran towards Harold.

Harold pulled the trigger. A burst of concrete exploded out of the floor at Stultz's feet, stopping him.

"Want me to put one in your kneecap?"

Stultz backed away. Aggression wasn't going to work.

"That's the way you'd do it, eh? Me too. Make the guy suffer. The kneecaps, then the gut. Then maybe a shot in the balls. Guy takes hours to die, suffers like a motherfucker. I like the way you think. I thought you were a snot-nosed kid, but you . . ."

"Shut up."

Stultz spun around and headed in the other direction. Harold fired a shot after him, missing him. Stultz darted around a corner; his feet could be heard running up stairs.

"Shit." Harold holstered his pistol and approached William. Stooping, he untied William's hands and legs. "That better?"

"Thanks."

Harold stood up and went to the crematorium. He kicked the door shut and switched the burner off. "I don't know if he would've done it or not," he said, facing William again. "I know he's a lot of things, but I don't know if he's a killer. I'm sure anything he had planned for you wasn't going to be pleasant."

William was up on his feet, rubbing his wrists where the wire had abraded his skin. His head ached and his side was bruised as well, but it seemed nothing vital had been injured.

"I'll take you home, now."

"What about Stultz?"

"I'll keep an eye on your house tonight. I don't think he'd go there, but I can't be sure. Sometimes guys like

238

that are big cowards at heart. I'd guess he's going to hide out somewhere. He knows I'll turn him over to the doctor this time. I never caught him in the act before."

"He burned people before?"

"No, but I know he's done other things." He started walking down the basement corridor towards a door at the end. William kept pace beside him.

"Hey," William said, "what did he mean we were all going to die anyhow?"

Harold kept his eyes straight ahead. "Crazy talk. He doesn't know what he's saying half the time. He'll say anything to scare someone."

William took that as an answer for the moment, but it smelled like a lie.

Or was it another Big Secret?

Brian Wesley hadn't seen his son or ex-wife in over four years. Now he was on his way to find them, traveling in a plain white truck that was supposed to be a delivery van, and he had no idea if he was participating in an elaborate hoax or merely being drawn into another futile pursuit.

When he first discovered Sharon had run off with William, he had hired a detective. As a bank vice-president, he could afford to do that. He was determined Sharon would not keep his son from him. But the detective, who was noted for his ability to track down missing people, had come to many dead ends. The last lead he had provided had been an address in Fort Wayne, Indiana, which turned out to be nothing more than a mailing address for a drug company—from which mail was forwarded to an unknown place. He could find no direct connection between the company and Sharon Wesley, but he told Brian his instincts screamed there was one. He just couldn't prove it.

Brian paid the man and wrote a series of letters to the address. None was returned to him, so he assumed they were going somewhere. Apparently they were reaching Sharon—or somebody.

In any case, one had evidently gotten to his son, or William would have had no address to which to address the strange letter Brian had received a month and a half before.

He had waited before acting on the letter, thinking perhaps it was some kind of prank. He wasn't certain if it was written in his son's handwriting or not, since he had nothing with the boy's writing on it. Sharon had taken everything with her when she disappeared with the boy.

He toyed with the idea of turning the whole matter over to the police and letting them take care of it as they should. But this was not exactly an abduction. Sharon had legal custody of William, according to the courts. If he went to the authorities—through the so-called proper channels—she might be alerted and move to yet another obscure place, the whereabouts of which he might waste another few years finding.

He finally decided to pursue this on his own. It was his son who was sending out the cry for help. If the letter was falsified or a cruel joke, he'd only be out a little time. He would do what the letter told him, taking it at face value. It seemed to be the most practical resolution, and it might really lead him to his son.

Brian was thirty-eight, six-foot-one, with light brown hair and blue-gray eyes. His frame was not muscular, but not mushy either. He took walks in the morning to exercise, but he didn't work out or follow any special diets. He was naturally trim and generally fit, a person of average build and habits. His face was basically oval and nondescript. He had the perfect overall look of the executive—a person who could blend into the background when necessary, or assert his presence, whichever the occasion called for.

He did not consider himself a brave man. He believed in duty, however, and if duty—such as his paternal duty—took him into a perilous situation, then he would deal with it.

He wished his son—or whoever had sent him the letter—had given him a map of the surrounding area where he was supposedly being kept. All he had was a map

240

of the town. As a result he had spent the last three days driving around northeastern Indiana, asking directions at every filling station, roadside restaurant, or truck stop he saw.

No one he questioned had heard of Jamay Lake, of course, but a few remembered the old Cummins Military Academy. Remembered was all, though; none could place where it was, except it was in this general area of the state—which, unfortunately, was about thirty-five-hundred square miles. He even asked a state trooper about the whereabouts of the academy and was told it had been closed for years. It was no longer on any map. If he really wanted to find it, he would have to go to one of the state offices in the capital and search back through old land records.

Brian knew that could take days, or weeks. Sometimes too, records going back more than ten years were on microfiche, requiring hours of intense study to search. Sometimes they were destroyed or lost over the years.

This morning, however, he had come across an old mom 'n' pop grocery store off the main highway on a state road, which had been there for years. Its proprietor, a man of at least seventy, wearing glasses with one black lens, had said, "Cummins? Yeah, I know where that is. I used to deliver things there, back maybe twenty years ago or so. It's been closed down that long at least. I thought they razed it."

"I don't think so," Brian said.

"What you want to find it for?"

"I'm thinking of buying the land it's on."

The old man blinked at him. "It's way the hell out in nowhere now. Used to be a good highway going back that way, but they cut it off when they built the bypass. If you buy land back there, you'll have hell getting back and forth."

"I just want to look it over," Brian said.

"Well, I'd recommend not buying."

"I'll judge when I see it—if I can find it."

The old man obviously considered Brian slightly deranged, but roughed out a map on a pad and gave it to him. "This is as close as I can remember. The tricky part is this turn here. If you're going too fast, you'll miss it, because it goes off at an odd angle to this road. See? Be sure you make a hard left there—slow down, or you'll go in a ditch. You understand?"

Brian glanced at the map, noting the sharp curve and the square which indicated the location of the school in relation to the store. "I understand. How many miles is it?"

"I expect it's about twenty to thirty miles or so, but the road is so jagged, it'll seem like fifty . . ."

Actually, Brian thought, as he took yet another sharp curve, it seemed like a hundred. He was sure he had missed the turn the old man had said was so important, and was about to head back in the opposite direction when he saw something that resembled a fortress up ahead.

He slowed down, approaching cautiously, remembering the paranoid tone of the letter that had brought him here. He had to be prepared for anything.

The place seemed deserted until he was right up on it. Then he saw smoke rising from chimneys inside the wall around the place. He saw the weathered "Cummins Military Academy" sign above the gate.

His adrenaline started pumping. He was in the right place; now he had to make the right moves.

He glanced at himself in the mirror. He had a day's growth of beard, but he figured that would help contribute to the working-class image he was trying to project. He was dressed in gray coveralls—as he thought a delivery man should wear—and he had the van full of paint.

Everybody needs paint, he figured.

He stopped, let the engine idle, and stuck his head out the window of the van.

"Delivery," he yelled.

A misshapen, ugly old man hobbled out and came around to the driver's side of the van. He was dressed in a uniform and wore a sidearm, which Brian eyed nervously. Suddenly he felt like a spy in an old World War II

242

movie, trying to sneak across enemy lines.

"What ya carrying?" Max the troll asked.

"Paint."

"Who ordered it?"

"You did. I'm just bringing it where I was told."

"Have a hard time finding the place?"

"Yeah, it was a bitch. I've never been out this way before."

"I thought you were a stranger. Where you taking it?"

"What?"

"The paint?"

Brian hadn't thought of that. Taking a chance, he said, "It's for the school." Every school needed paint.

The wheels were turning inside Max's trollish head. Brian thought there were probably a few teeth missing in the cogwheels. Finally, Max said, "You got a gate pass?"

"Sure." Brian handed Max the gate pass William had sent him. Max put it close to his eyes and examined it for what seemed like much longer than necessary.

"Looks okay to me. Who cares anyhow? I just wish they'd let *me* know what's going on sometimes."

"I just deliver," Brian said. "I don't ask questions or think about it."

"That's the way to cut it nowadays," Max said. "That's the only way to survive."

Max pocketed the pass. "I'll go open the gate. The school's to the left a block down, two blocks south of that. I guess you can find it okay."

"Thanks," Brian said.

Max entered the gate house and fiddled with the remote control buttons. The gate swung inward.

Brian drove through, took a left as he was told, then made his way to the school. He parked out front and took a deep breath. He was inside. But where the hell was he exactly? It was a town, yet it wasn't. The streets seemed unnaturally bare. He hadn't seen anyone out at all on his way to the school. There was a slight stench in the crisp December air that irritated his nose too, like burned meat.

He didn't like this place at all.

He pulled William's map out of one of his breast pockets. The school, clinic, church, and other buildings were well-marked as reference points. From the school he needed to head east about two blocks.

He decided to take a chance and walk the distance. A van sitting in front of the school would probably not draw undue attention, but a van sitting in front of a house would. If he encountered anyone, he would say he was lost. So far, he had been lucky.

He climbed out of the van, locked it, and walked down the street, counting houses. None of them had numbers. None had mailboxes, either.

There were undoubtedly many other odd details about this psuedo-town he was missing as well, things on the subliminal level.

He came to the house where his son might or might not be.

He went up the walk to the front door.

He hesitated, then knocked.

William almost fell out of his bed when he finally awoke. He had slept very late, but then it had been after four a.m. before he was returned home safely by Harold Thomas. He had crept to his room, fallen on the bed, and slept in his clothes. His ordeal had exhausted him.

Now, in the bright of day, it seemed like a dim nightmare, except for that crematorium and the monstrous face of Stultz leering at him while he taunted and threatened him.

He recalled with a shiver that Stultz had escaped. He could be anywhere in town. A guy like him probably must have a lot of hide-outs.

William realized he was hungry and went to the kitchen to make himself a snack. On his way there he discovered he was alone in the house. And there were no notes posted anywhere, such as Mandy might usually leave, to tell him where anyone was.

A horrifying thought occurred to him. Maybe Stultz had sneaked in and taken Mandy!

Or did he like little girls?

That didn't matter; he'd take her just for the sheer hell of it, to torture her, maybe use her to get at him.

But Harold had promised to watch the house.

Maybe Stultz had sneaked up on him. Maybe he had killed him. Maybe . . .

William drank a glass of milk. This was ridiculous. If anything had happened during the night, he would have heard it. He was letting his imagination get the best of him.

But imagination hadn't taken him to the brink of death in the crematorium.

Stultz's words echoed in his mind again—"They're all going to die anyhow."

The other man had said it was nothing, but William sensed some truth in it. Stultz had no reason to make up a lie like that; in fact, he probably wasn't clever enough to manufacture such falsehoods. He used brute force and intimidation to get what he wanted. He didn't have to lie.

The scariest part about it was that Stultz had not specified *how* they were going to die. For all William knew, the doctor intended to line the residents of Jamay Lake up against one of the walls and order the patrol men to shoot them down.

Or maybe he'd poison them. The doctor had access to the entire food supply. He probably knew all sorts of undetectable ways to poison people.

William set his glass down. Suddenly the milk tasted a bit tainted—or was it only his imagination?

There was a loud knock at the front door.

William threw himself to the floor without thinking about it, expecting a volley of bullets to burst through the house.

There was a second knock.

William felt foolish. Stultz wouldn't knock.

It was probably a neighbor or a kid.

He got up from the floor, dusted himself off and went towards the door. Opening it slowly, he saw a familiar-looking man in coveralls.

"William Wesley?" Brian asked.

The man's face became clearer. "Dad?"

"I think so. It's been so long . . ."

William almost swooned. He had totally given up hope and wasn't sure how to act. This man was his father, yet he was a stranger.

In any case, their meeting out in the open presented a potentially dangerous situation.

"Come in quick," William said.

Brian stepped inside and William closed the door behind him immediately, latching it. He turned and regarded his father. "I've got a lot to tell you," he said.

"Why don't you come with me right now? We can talk later."

"I want to. But it's not going to be that easy. Even if we get through the gate, they might follow us."

"Who's 'they'?"

"Lots of people. There are only two people I trust in this whole town—and they're kids."

"What is this place anyhow?"

"I don't know myself. But I can tell you what's been happening to me."

"I'm listening," Brian said.

William sat down with his father and started talking. Before he was through, he didn't know if he had persuaded him he was telling the truth or convinced him he was as crazy as everyone else.

But he had someone to whom he could tell all of it—at last.

Chapter Twenty-Four

Brian Surprised

Brian was truly astounded. "That's the weirdest story I ever heard," he told his son. "It seems so absurd I don't know if I can believe it."

"It's true. All of it."

"I'm not doubting you, William. It's obvious there's something odd about this place. It's almost impossible to find, and the streets—it's like a ghost town. But why in the world would anyone want to keep you from growing up? It's like science fiction, or a warped fairy tale."

"Why would I make it up?"

"I'm not saying you are. I just find it hard to believe. If you were an average person coming in off the street and somebody told you they were part of a mad doctor's experiment—well, you'd be a little skeptical."

William weighed his father's words and knew he was right. The situation had become so complicated and outlandish that it was very difficult to believe. But he didn't care whether his father believed it; it was beside the point, after all. "Does that mean you're not going to take me away?"

"Of course not. Something's going on here, for sure. But I'm not a police officer, so I don't have the resources to do much—but I promise you after we leave I'm going to inform the authorities. Okay?"

"Yeah."

"I *want* to believe you. I know *you* believe what you're saying, but you don't have much hard proof. That's why I think the best thing to do is just get the hell out. Do you have anything you want to bring with you?"

"Not really." He paused. "Except my friend Mandy and her brother. Can you take them?"

"You like this Mandy, don't you?"

"Yes," William admitted. "She's like a sister—or even a mother. Her mother died. The doctor burned her up like the others."

Brian was having trouble accepting that horror too. But, as William had rightly pointed out, why should he make it up? "I'll take them too, if that's what you want. We should be able to find a home for them, and they can stay with us until we do. When will they be back?"

"Soon. School's out in about ten minutes. Mandy's probably waiting over there to bring Danny home."

"All right. Ten minutes. But not much longer than that. If you friends don't show up, we'll try to find them on the way out, but I can't afford for us to hang around. Every minute increases the chance I'll be found—and I don't have any weapons other than my fists."

"I understand."

"In the meantime, I'm going to have a quick cup of coffee."

"I'll go wait out front for Mandy."

"Sounds like a good plan to me."

William went outside, walked down to the corner and watched for Mandy. He hoped she didn't linger on the way home; he could hardly wait to tell her his father was going to take them away from Jamay Lake.

Sharon Wesley took off early from her job at the doll store. She had been highstrung all morning, and could barely focus on what she was doing. There had been no customers, and there were few orders to fill, so she left. Besides, she didn't care to work that much any more. She'd rather lie around the house, eat candy, and pretend she was a human vegetable.

No one she knew had much ambition. No one seemed to care, either. It was as if all the pressure was gone from

248

life in Jamay Lake. To be feckless and self-indulgent was now the norm.

Lost in her fuzzy thoughts, Sharon found herself going in the wrong direction, so she had to double back and approach her house from the east.

As she came in the door, she sensed a strange presence in the house. It was almost a smell—a masculine odor, accompanied by the aroma of fresh coffee.

"William? Are you back already?"

Sharon was startled by the deep male voice. Then she realized it sounded vaguely familiar.

But it couldn't be.

She went into the kitchen and found her ex-husband casually sipping a cup of *her* coffee.

"It's been a long time, Sharon," he said calmly. "You look the same, except you've gained some weight."

"What in hell are you doing here? How did you get here?" She did a take at his coveralls. "And what's that weird outfit for?"

"A disguise, Sharon. I've become a spy for the Allied Forces. But the real question is, what the hell are *you* doing here? William's my son. I have a right to see him. That was established in court."

"No one can come here."

"I did."

"Well, you can get the hell out."

"You've kept my son from me for four years, and you think you can just throw me out like that?"

"Why not? I don't owe you anything." She reached for the candy jar, taking it down from top of the refrigerator. She started nibbling a piece immediately.

"Still got that sweet tooth, I see."

"And you're still as cocky as ever."

"Look, Sharon, what was between us doesn't mean anything any more. I accepted that long before our divorce was finalized."

He examined her more critically with his eyes. She hadn't really gained any weight. He had said that merely to rile her; if anything she was slimmer than she had been. She was, in a way Brian could never quite

249

indentify, a sexy woman. Unfortunately, she did not bring any sexuality to the bedroom; she was frigid and unadventurous in bed. That had been one of the main points of contention in the divorce. The other was her unwillingness to allow William to be enrolled in the gifted program at school. She insisted she wanted William to be a "normal" child, not one of the "nerds," buttressing her argument with her assertion that developing social skills were more important than advanced studies for a child. Social skills would make him more successful than overdeveloped intelligence. It was the typical middleclass cop-out, usually made by people who were too ignorant or stupid themselves to let their children become "smarter" than they were. Brian had, of course, disagreed totally. He wanted William to realize his full potential.

At one point in their extended arguments, Sharon had called him a "nerd," as if that were the worst epithet in the world, and she vowed she would *not* allow her son to become a nerd too.

Brian watched Sharon eating candy. According to William the candy was loaded with drugs, so Sharon was getting high right now. He considered stopping her, but maybe she would be easier to control if he just let her eat the "happy candy" till she passed out—as she apparently often did. If he kept talking to her as she mindlessly consumed the candy, it might be a lot easier to take William away. Otherwise, he knew Sharon would call the local "patrol men" on him the minute he, William, and the other children left the house. They probably wouldn't even make it to his van.

"I guess you consider this a 'normal' upbringing for our son. Is he learning a lot of social skills in this little berg? Are you keeping him from becoming a nerd?"

"That's right! Taunt me. You don't even have the right to be here."

"But I do."

"I'm saving William from you. Here he's around very *normal* children who make him behave as a normal child should."

250

"He says none of the children grow. Is that normal?"

"William is full of imagination. He'll say anything."

"He also says they give all the children weird drugs in this place. In shots and in their food."

"Vitamins, yes. Vitamin shots." She munched another piece of candy. "That's all. The doctor is very health-conscious."

"I don't think so. William's growth looks stunted to me. I can take him away from you, anyhow, because he's old enough to choose me now."

"He's only twelve. He isn't old enough to think on his own."

"He's fifteen, Sharon." He gave her a sharp look. "Why would you say he's twelve?"

Sharon appeared confused, or guilty. "Just a slip of the tongue. I think of him as twelve, that's all. Mothers don't like to see their children grow up and go away from them . . ."

"William's telling the truth, then. You *don't* want him to grow up."

"Not the way you mean it." She dipped her hand into the jar and started on her fourth piece of candy.

"What *is* going on here?" he demanded.

"Nothing. This is a refuge for women whose husbands battered them."

"I never hit you in my life . . ."

"You abused me sexually."

Brian almost laughed. "By expecting sex on a semi-regular basis? That wasn't abuse."

"I never liked it. It was . . ."

There was a loud noise near the front of the house. Two men stormed into the kitchen—patrol men, Paul Daniels and Harold Thomas.

Paul pointed his pistol at Brian. "All right, bud, who the hell are you?"

"I'm William's father. I've come to take him out of here."

"No, mister. You're a trespasser, and you're coming with us."

"You can't do this."

251

"Better do as he says," Harold warned. "We could shoot you and be within our legal rights."

"This is outrageous!"

"Stand up!" Paul ordered. "Frisk him, Harold."

Harold quickly searched Brian for hidden weapons. "He's clean."

"This way," Paul said, gesturing with the gun. "We're taking you to the doctor."

"Bye, Sharon," Brian said. "I'll be back."

"That's what you think, buddy."

William was so excited he could barely control himself when he met Mandy and Danny at the corner.

"He's here. He's here! Dad came to rescue us."

"Really?" Mandy said, her eyes wide with wonder at the idea. "Today?"

"Right now. We have to get going right away."

He started running back towards the house. Mandy and Danny had trouble keeping up with him.

He arrived just in time to see the patrol car drive away with his father in the back seat.

Brian had been locked in a small room at the clinic for about two hours. The blinds were drawn, sunlight coming in through the slits. He checked his watch, and it was quarter till five. It would soon be dark.

He lay on the bed, waiting.

A few more minutes passed, and he heard a key inserted in the door lock. An old man with shaggy eyebrows, a badly bent nose, and livid scar on his chin entered, followed by one of the patrol men who had brought Brian there.

"Congratulations," Warren said, "you are the first man to have penetrated our security. I think you probably would have gotten away, except Max took a closer look at that gate pass and discovered it had not been validated. After we found your van and broke into it, it was a simple matter to deduce where you'd gone.

You shouldn't have left anything with your name on it in the truck, or we'd still be looking for you. Or you'd be on your way to wherever you were going. Overall, though, it was a fairly good plan for an amateur. A little more luck and it would have worked out for you."

Brian sat up and glared at the two men.

"Who are you?"

"Warren Barry. I'm the doctor here."

"I should've have recognized you. William told me about you—and the shots, and a lot of other things too. I thought he was making some of it up. Now I think he was understating the situation around here, if anything."

"William is a boy. He's capable of outlandish tales."

"Sure. I guess he made up how one of your rent-a-cops tried to molest him too."

Warren's eyes, though slightly glassy, showed some concern. "I hadn't heard about that."

"It was Stultz," Harold said. "I was going to make a full report. I was watching the Wesley kid's house, hoping I'd catch Stultz—he's the type who'd go after him for revenge."

"Goddamn it," Warren muttered. "Isn't anything going right? Why didn't you tell me before?"

"Sounds like all's not well in paradise, doctor," Brian said. "What's going on in this place, anyhow? I mean what's your version of it?"

Warren was so upset he had almost forgotten about Brian's presence. "I owe no explanation to a man like you. Did you come to beat your wife?"

"I never hit Sharon."

"According to her, you hit her and molested the boy."

Brian was genuinely shocked. "That's a pack of lies. Sharon said that to keep me away from my son—for spite."

"I have her signed deposition stating you battered her several times and tried to molest your son, but she stopped you."

It seemed Sharon had some imagination after all, Brian reflected. She had manufactured the perfect lie to get into this place, and it seemed the bigger the lie, the more inclined people were to believe it.

"Do I look like that kind of person?"

"There is no particular look. Wife beaters, child molesters—they come in all shapes and sizes, from educated to ignorant. I learned that many years ago. That's why we founded this town . . . it's a sanctuary—a place where women are safe from brutes like you."

"I'm not a goddamn wife beater. Sharon took William away from me. I had visitation rights. She had no right to . . ."

Warren came closer. He was having trouble following everything Brian said. "In any case, you will have to leave."

"I'm not leaving without William." Brian noted the sheen in Warren's eyes, remembering how William said the doctor was doped up too. Arguing with him was probably futile, but Brian had to express his indignation, even if there was a rent-a-cop with the doctor. If Warren had any shred of reason left in him, perhaps Brian could appeal to it.

"That's out of the question. William is safe here."

"He says you give him shots—to keep him from growing up. He says you're using him in an experiment."

Warren seemed slightly taken aback by these accusations, but he recovered quickly. "The boy might say anything to leave. You see, he's one of our problem children. He makes a lot of trouble. He's too smart for his own good, as we used to say."

"He couldn't make it all up. Why would he? Why wouldn't he just write and ask for my help? He didn't need any kind of story. I'm his father. Sharon is the nut case . . ."

"Oh, come, Mr. Wesley. Children love to imagine themselves in all sorts of adventures. A boy his age—a twelve-year-old—"

"Goddamn it, he's fifteen."

"No, I'm sure he's only twelve." Warren was uneasy; his mind was drifting off to another place, where troublesome fathers did not exist, where things were easy, as they had been only a few short months before.

"I'm his father, I should know how old he is. Maybe he looks twelve—because you've given him something that affects his growth. You're looking at a big malpractice suit here. . . ."

"What else did William tell you?"

Brian's expression was stony; his voice unwavering. "That all the children are going to die."

Warren's mind looped back to the primary concerns of the moment; he was unaware any of the children had such knowledge, and it shook him. How would he deal with the children if they knew what was happening? What would he tell their mothers? How could he maintain order?

But there was no order to maintain. He could see that now; his ideals were all crumbling around him.

He regarded Brian wearily. "Nonsense," he said. "All nonsense. The product of a child's mind and nothing more."

"Why does William think that then?" Brian demanded. "Where would he get such an idea?"

"I don't have to explain anything to you, Mr. Wesley. You have trespassed on private property. If you have a problem with your wife and the custody of your child, you should go through the proper legal channels. Harold, we'll leave him locked in here for the time being."

Brian was on his feet. "It's all true, isn't it? That's why you can't let me go. You know I'll tell the world what's going on in this place!"

Warren looked back once more. Emotion was absent from his face. "We shall see what is true and what isn't, won't we? In the meantime, have a good stay in the clinic."

Chapter Twenty-Five

Sexual Awareness

Lester Stultz lounged on the couch in the living room, his feet propped up on a table, lazily drinking coffee and eating a doughnut. There was nothing in his manner to suggest he was a fugitive hiding out in Georgia's home. He seemed to be the man of the house, and he felt like he belonged.

He'd been there often enough.

Georgia's craving for drugs and even greater highs had made her a steady sex partner for Lester, who was not, in his own estimation, really a child molester or rapist or anything even close to being that nasty. He was simply a man who chose a variety of ways to satisfy his sexual urges. He had never seen anything wrong in that, even the times he had been caught and prosecuted. The rest of the world didn't understand him very well; that was the problem, and he had learned how to deal with it.

Georgia herself was of like mind to an extent, except she would never abuse children in any way. A tenet of her strict upbringing drew the line for her there, and she possessed maternal instincts too, though they were not so highly attuned as other mothers' were.

She liked sex.

She didn't like Lester that much.

But since all he required of her was a trifling bout of bestiality every now and then in exchange for extra drugs, she forced herself not to be repulsed by him. Besides, by the time she got around to giving him the sex, she was usually high enough to imagine Lester was much better-looking than he actually was and not as repugnant as he normally appeared.

At present, however, she was not particularly pleased he was hanging around so long. She didn't mind screwing him, but she didn't want him as a house guest. She had decided he should be on his way; she wasn't in the mood for him or his perversions, and, besides, he had brought her no drugs to compensate for his odious presence.

She worked up her nerve and asked him to leave.

Lester swatted her hard, knocking her to the floor, where she lay and whimpered.

Dawn was curled up on the floor much like a kitten, with her doll Shirley to comfort her. Shirley was her only real companion nowadays.

She was watching something hideously dull on the TV, because she was too listless to do anything else.

Her own world was in turmoil. Alicia had not been allowed to play with her for a few days, because her mother had learned Alvin had died, and they were in "mourning," a process which apparently consisted of sitting around and crying constantly.

Dawn had cried for Alvin. A lot. But she couldn't do it indefinitely. Maybe his mother should cry longer, and Alicia too, but they couldn't do it forever, either. Though it seemed like they were trying.

No one would talk about how Alvin had died. Alicia didn't know, and Mrs. Lawson wouldn't even discuss the matter.

Dawn's own mother was being difficult too. Sally had acquired a paunch that made her look fat and ugly, and she told Dawn she had a baby growing inside her.

Dawn didn't know how to react. She had a good idea where babies came from—out of moms somehow—but she wasn't certain how the babies got in there in the first place. She'd heard rumors, of course, but they were too silly to believe. But she had never seen a pregnant woman in Jamay Lake since they'd been there and wondered why

257

her mother decided to get that way.

A baby sister or brother might not be that bad, because Dawn was very lonely sometimes. But the way her mom acted made her think getting a baby might not be worth all the trouble.

For one thing, Sally refused to leave the house. She made Dawn go get groceries or things from the free pharmacy for her. Sometimes Dawn had to get help from someone to carry all the stuff home.

And she wouldn't talk much. She stayed in bed most of the time, threw up a couple of times a day, and ignored Dawn as much as possible, unless she needed something.

Her mom was getting crazy.

It seemed like everyone was getting crazy. The doctor, when he acted like a minister, got so crazy her mom had to take her out of the church. William was acting strange too—not crazy, but not like the William she knew. He didn't even take time to tease her when he saw her outside. Since he had that big girl Mandy living in his house, he didn't seem to care about anyone else. He liked her better than anyone else now.

Big girls had boobies. That's why boys liked them—for some reason. Dawn didn't understand it totally.

Maybe when she had boobies, she would understand. She pulled down the front of her top and peered inside. She was surprised to discover that she *was* getting boobies. Her nipples were swollen and protruded from her chest about an inch. She hadn't noticed that before; it must have just happened.

She was growing up!

She ran upstairs to tell Sally. Her mom couldn't ignore her now.

William was disconsolate and depressed—so much so that he set on the floor in his room in darkness, where he wouldn't have to be confronted with his mother's smugness over his father being taken away. He had never known his mother hated his father that much.

He didn't think things could ever change now, not for

the better anyhow. Whatever the children's destiny was, it was apparently preordained. He felt powerless to do anything to change his fate or that of the others.

The door to his room opened slightly, allowing a triangle of light to spill in from the hall.

"Go away," he said.

"It's me," Mandy said, "but I'll go away if you want me to."

"No. You can come in. I thought you were Mom."

Mandy closed the door behind her. Moonlight guided her to William, once her eyes adjusted to the gloom. She sat down on the floor beside him, sliding her body within an inch of his.

"Are you going to stay up here forever?"

"Maybe."

"Won't you rot and die?"

"It's the other way around."

"Oh. I'm sorry."

"What do you have to be sorry about? It's my father they took away. Like he was a criminal or something."

"William," she replied, placing her hand on his knee, "I had a lot of hope too. I wanted to get away as much as you. You know that."

"I guess so," he replied grudgingly. He was aware of her hand on his knee now. Her warmth radiated through the fabric of his jeans, and her breath was warm on his neck.

"At least we're not alone."

"I guess not."

She stroked his hair with her other hand. William's body tingled at her touch.

"Don't . . ." he said.

"Why not?"

"Because."

She kissed him on the cheek. "I want to make you feel better," she whispered.

"You're—it's not right—you're like my sister."

"No, I'm not."

She pressed against him, kissing him on the lips. William returned the kiss clumsily, then quickly got the hang of it.

"I hope I do this right," Mandy said presently.

Within a few minutes, she had made him feel much better.

"Son of a bitch," Georgia moaned, as Lester raped her. "You bastard. Get off me!"

"Keep talking, honey. It only makes me get harder." He had her arms pinned down, and was doing her on the couch.

"I hate your stinking guts. I always hated you. I only screwed you to get what I wanted."

"Oh, you're hurting my feelings now," he mocked her. Grunting, he caught his second wind, then started over again. "Hell, I never asked you to like me. I don't need anybody to like me."

"You're hurting me, goddamn it!"

"Too bad. Need some Vaseline?"

Georgia let go of a guttural scream.

"Mom, what's wrong?" Eddie stood in the doorway. He was supposed to be asleep, but his mother's cries had awakened him.

Lester was undisturbed by the interruption. "Hey, kid, come on over—join the fun."

Temporarily distracted, Lester let go of Georgia's right arm. She reached up and raked her long fingernails across his face. "Don't you talk to my kid like that!"

"You bitch!" Lester slapped her hard, then disengaged himself from her. He laid his hand on his cheek and pulled back a palm full of blood.

Georgia pulled herself up and slashed his back. "Pervert." Lester elbowed her face, breaking her nose. She yelped and blood poured down her face.

Eddie ran out to the hall.

Lester grabbed the boy before he could get through the front door. "Let go of me, you big queer."

"I ain't a queer," Lester said. "Your nasty old mommy is a queer, though. She's a whore too. What do you think about that?"

260

Eddie thought to kick Lester in the stomach, but he couldn't reach it the way Lester was holding him.

"Feisty little creep, ain't you? Well, uncle Lester can take care of that."

Georgia had staggered out to the hall. "Let him go."

"So he can run out and get help? You think I'm stupid?"

Georgia threw herself at Lester, landing on his back. She pummeled his head, pulled his hair and scratched at his eyes.

Lester merely shrugged the woman off, sending her flying half way down the hall, and carried Eddie into the living room. He set the boy down and slapped him hard—just enough to knock him unconscious.

Georgia came running into the room. She had a kitchen knife in her right hand, raised to strike.

"I'll fix you, you son of a bitch!"

Lester caught her arm and twisted it violently behind her back. She dropped the knife.

"God, you're a nervy bitch. I never knew you was so full of piss and vinegar. You're making me tired." He made a fist and punched her as hard as he could on the jaw; he heard bone cracking.

Georgia went limp.

Lester placed her on the couch.

He went to the bathroom and found some adhesive tape. He returned to the living room and jerked the wires from two lamps. He tied mother and son up, covered their mouths with tape, set them up on the couch, and stood back to survey his work.

"You guys ain't going anywhere."

He dressed hurriedly and went out into the night in search of more satisfaction.

Georgia hadn't let him finish.

Later that evening, Paul Daniels stopped by Sally Henderson's house.

He knocked and waited a few minutes. Finally Sally came to the door, opening it only part way, hiding her

261

protruding stomach behind it.

"What do you want?"

"I thought maybe you and me could get together tonight. It's been a while."

"I don't ever want to see you again."

"Let me in. Let's talk it over."

"No. Go away. Get somebody else pregnant."

"What the hell are you talking about, Sally?"

She opened the door. Her body was wrapped in a robe, but it did not disguise her prominent abdomen. "See what you did?"

Paul's expression was one of profound amazement. "I thought that was impossible."

"I guess not. Now, go away."

"Just let me talk to you. Maybe I could do something for you. I'm not a bad guy."

"You can't do anything but leave me alone."

Paul withdrew quietly and returned to his car. He drove away, still shaking his head in wonder.

Sally slammed the door shut and went to see if Dawn was asleep yet.

She was worried about her daughter. Dawn was not only growing breasts, but as a further examination revealed, she also had sprouted three pubic hairs.

Something was wrong.

William and Mandy were curled together, now on William's bed. Mandy's head lay on William's chest and she was slumbering peacefully.

William was staring into the darkness.

Part of him felt wonderful; part of him felt guilty.

Yet he had no regrets. Their love-making had been a bout of numb fumbling, punctuated by clumsiness, and lack of co-ordinated movement, but they had somehow managed to consummate what had been only hinted at before in their relationship.

After thinking it over a while, William realized it did not make that much difference. If they were all going to die, they might as well do what they pleased.

Everyone else did.

Elsewhere in the town, others were indulging themselves in sexual fantasies or realities.

Every patrol man was occupied with a woman, including Paul, who had found solace only a couple of blocks away after his rejection by Sally.

Lester had moved into another woman's house—Carla Schuell's. Carla helped tend to his wounds, which he told her Georgia had inflicted on him for no particular reason—except that she was crazy for dope.

"She's a nasty woman," Carla averred, and said it was fine with her if Lester stayed the night. She understood how he needed comforting.

She had unspoken yearnings too.

Women without men found other women. Those who could not bring themselves to participate in homosexual encounters, did what they could on their own, allowing their fantasies to bring them a kind of satisfaction.

The town of Jamay Lake was engaged in an orgy, as Warren had only imagined before.

He didn't know this was his own doing. His increasing the drug dosage in the candy had produced the opposite effect he had desired. Women were more aroused than ever.

Except for a few—such as Sally.

And Sharon Wesley.

They liked being alone and within themselves.

Chapter Twenty-Six

William's Voice

Every day there are more empty houses. And empty places, and empty spaces. I got one inside me.

There are empty times too, when you expect something and it doesn't go the way it's supposed to. Like with Dad today. I thought for sure everything was going to be okay, and I was just gone a few minutes to get Mandy and when I got back, nothing was okay.

Things were worse.

I saw them take Dad away, and I don't know where. Mom said she doesn't know and doesn't care. She said she wouldn't tell me if she did know. She hates Dad.

I'm really worried for Dad now. I don't know if the doctor would kill my father or not. I know he's let people die, and maybe he had something to do with it, but it's not the same as killing, like with a gun. He can't be that crazy. Or can he?

When I saw Dad in the back of that patrol car, I just about jumped in front of it, like that would stop them. Mandy pulled me back, and I realized how stupid I was being. But if she had let me do it, I wouldn't be hurting so much right now.

I should be heading away from Jamay, with Mandy and Danny and Dad, not still stuck here, waiting for—I don't know what. Everything should have been okay.

I should've known it wouldn't be that easy.

If I knew where Dad was, I could go try to get him out. Except they probably have him guarded. I'd need a gun or something like that. I wish I was bigger and knew some moves. I can beat up a kid all right, but I can't go against someone with a gun like a patrol guy.

That reminds me—I still don't know what's happened with old Lester, either. I probably ought to check with that other guy—the one who rescued me, Harold, but that would mean going out after dark, and I don't dare do that if there's any chance Lester is around. He might cut my throat—or worse.

Maybe he left. I'd feel a lot better if I knew he was gone for sure.

A lot of people ought to be leaving. But we can't. We're just stuck here, not only me, but a lot of other people. I bet I'm not the only one who wants out. If I had a car, I'd get out. Except I don't know how to drive a car, and if I could, I couldn't get past the guy at the gate. Old Max probably would throw a bomb at me. He's crazy just like everyone else.

I can't think of anything I can do right now. My brain is all screwed up, like I was on happy candy or something. Maybe I ought to get me some of that and not have to worry about anything until I die. I'll watch *Bambi* over and over on TV, and it'll seem like it's really good. Except I'll be happy when Bambi's mother gets shot. It'll seem really funny.

I think I had sex with Mandy tonight. No, I don't think, I *know* we did it. Mandy said it hurt her, but she wanted to anyhow, and I couldn't stop, either. I thought if we ever did anything like that we wouldn't be friends any more, but I was wrong and Mandy is still my friend. She told me so before she went to sleep. She's not mad at me at all. She says we're better friends now than ever before, only it's in a different way. I have to think about that. I wonder if that means we have to have sex all the time. I think I could if that's what Mandy likes, but I'm still not sure it's right. It's like sort of a nasty thing.

No, it's like this—when Lester talks about it, it sounds like a real nasty thing, but when you actually do it with someone you think you like, it's different. It's something I can't really describe. It's more like an experience that

265

way, like something new and different, which is something I haven't had in this town in a long time.

When Mandy and I were doing it, I thought I should be thinking about Dad instead, but I coulnd't. It was like my whole brain was locked on this sex stuff, and it wouldn't let me think about anything else until we were done.

It's a crazy feeling.

Maybe tomorrow I can go out and find out where Dad is. I mean knowing that might help me figure a way to help him escape. There aren't that many places they could keep him.

Maybe I'm being a chicken by not going out right now to look for him. But there are too many things that can happen in the dark. I used not to be so afraid of it, but after waking up by that crematorium thing with Lester, I know the dark has a lot of mean, bad things in it, just waiting to happen to people—things like Lester Stultz.

It's probably like death.

I've been thinking about it, and it makes sense that dying is going into a big dark place. Only you don't ever come back.

That's where Alvin is now. And Mandy's mother. In the big dark place.

I wonder what it was like when the doctor burned them up. I know Stultz didn't make that part up. I can almost see the doctor—all doped up—putting people in that fire and letting them burn until they're just ashes. What does the doctor do with the ashes? There must be a lot of them by now.

It makes me sick to think about it. I mean what if they put you in that fire and you weren't really completely dead yet? You'd feel the flames.

That's what Hell is supposed to be like. When the doctor was doing his minister act one day, he talked about Hell. He didn't scream about it or anything, but he just kind of said it's a hot place, and that's where you went if you didn't do what was expected of you by God.

What I want to know is how you get God to talk to you so you know what He expects in the first place. In the old days, I guess, God was talking to everybody, like he'd

266

come down and go to lunch with them and tell them what he expected. Well, the answer to that is supposed to be the Ten Commandments. That's what the doctor said. I looked those up in one of the toy bibles—because I couldn't remember them all after the doctor recited them—and I read them two or three times and a lot of them didn't make much sense to me. Like—*Don't covet things.* That means you shouldn't want something somebody else has. You can go get something like they have and that's okay, but you can't want what they *have.* I think that's a tricky thing God invented, so you'd get your head all messed up thinking about it, and then before you know it you're burning in Hell because you went and coveted somebody's ice cream.

All that religious stuff is hard to figure out.

I'm getting really tired.

This has been a weird day. I think I've felt everything there is to feel in one day: scared, happy when my dad came, sad when he was taken away, sick at heart, warm when Mandy and I had sex, and now I feel like the inside of me is burned out and there's a big empty space inside me. Like I can't feel anything really, but even that is a feeling.

You can't get away from feelings.

Not even my mom when she eats the happy candy. She still could feel hate for my dad, and I think maybe she hates me too now, because I brought him here.

I should've known this day would be weird because it started out that way. When that patrol man was bringing me home, I saw a dead kitten lying in the gutter. It wasn't hit or mashed or anything. I stopped and picked it up, and its face was lumpy looking, and its whiskers were grayish. I never saw anything like it before. I asked the patrol guy about it and he said it probably was killed by a little kid who didn't know any better.

But the kitten didn't have any blood on it. I put it back down, because it felt creepy to hold it, and I went on home with the patrol man. Finding that dead kitten should've warned me.

Dead things always mean trouble, one way or another.

PART THREE

THE DOCTOR WHO CAME DOWN TO EARTH

"To die will be an awful big adventure."

—Sir James Matthew Barrie
Peter Pan, Act III

Chapter Twenty-Seven

Birth And Death

Warren and Sondra had decided before they ever married they would not attempt to have children. Sondra was almost past child-bearing age by then, anyhow, but she agreed that his work and the proving of it was more important than their having a family. Since they were both physicians, they would have little time to care for children properly. And they had seen so much suffering by children in their work at the center that they couldn't bear to bring a child into a world that did not regard its children very highly.

In later years, Warren secretly regretted not having tried while they had the time, even if the worst happened and Sondra gave birth to a mongoloid child. It would be a part of her that would live on.

Now she was dead and none of her would live on, except in Warren's memory, which itself was now a limited quantity.

She had passed silently in the night, as if she did not wish to disturb her troubled husband with her dying. Warren, who had not slept in the bed with her, found her the next morning, as he was getting ready to go to the clinic.

He wept for some time. Sondra had been his only respite from the growing horrors of his ideal society, the only person to whom he could tell all his troubles.

Perhaps he should pick this time to join her. He had, perhaps, a year to live if he didn't treat the cancer that was consuming him, and even if it were treated, he would not live much beyond that. What was the use in living without her?

Of course, he had known she had little time left. Each day she continued to live was a gift. Now the gift had been withdrawn.

Her passing made it clear at last what he must do. There were other people still dependent on him. He had to determine how he could dissolve the society without hurting any of those people. But how could he shield them from the pain that was inevitable and unavoidable?

Could he tell the remaining mothers that their children—probably all of them—were going to die from the old age disease? Should he direct them to hospitals where perhaps the children's lives might be prolonged? He couldn't decide what was right and what was wrong anymore.

But he had finally come to realize his dream was a moribund thing. It was in its last throes, awaiting the coup de grace that would extinguish it forever.

His anguish at Sondra's death temporarily abated, he lingered by her side only a few more moments. Sondra would have wanted him to take care of things as she would have if the situation were reversed.

He left her lying in her bed for now. He didn't think he could dispose of her as he had the others. He didn't think he could even have someone else do it. From now on, he had to own up to his responsibilities.

Warren knew the problems in his society were multiplying daily. He had heard the rumors of sex and rape. He knew people had died and their deaths had not been properly reported. He knew all these things, but the fact remained he could not easily give up his ideal.

But he had made his decision. There was no use putting it off any longer. He would call the proper authorities as soon as he put together the necessary papers for each family.

He would let William's father go too. Let him take William with him if he wished. Why keep him? Let him live his few paltry months or weeks of life out with his father who he obviously preferred to his mother.

Thus resolved, Warren walked to the clinic through the fresh snow that had fallen in the night to start the agonizing process of dismantling Jamay Lake.

While Warren was mourning the loss of his wife, Brian Wesley had broken the window in his room and planned to drop from the second-story ledge. If he landed just right, he would only sprain his body a little. If he landed wrong, if he miscalculated, he would break his leg.

Either way, he had little to lose. He blew the snow from the window ledge, climbed out on it, and let himself down slowly until he was hanging by his fingers, dangling above the sidewalk, building up the courage to let go. He glanced up at the window and heard someone entering the room. There was no more time to deliberate. He let go.

He hit the sidewalk at an odd angle, sliding in the snow, and twisting his left ankle badly. But nothing was broken. He limped towards the school, hoping his van might still be there. If it wasn't he would go to the house, take William and the other children, and find another means of escape.

A shout came from the window.

Brian kept moving. He heard a gun fired.

"Stop, goddamn it!"

He didn't look back; he kept moving onward. The corner of the school was only a couple of feet away. But his injured ankle and the snow on the street were impeding his progress.

Another warning shot rang out.

Brian ignored it. He was several yards from the clinic now; only a damn good marksman could hit him with a pistol at this distance.

Paul Daniels was a damn good marksman.

After leaving Carla's house, thanking her for her "hospitality," and promising to give her a little

273

something extra later, Lester stopped in front of William's house.

He considered terrorizing William once more before departing, perhaps popping his cherry ass, but the kid was surrounded by too many people. His mother was home, as were that big girl—a juicy-looky piece too—and the girl's little brother. The mother would be easy to get rid of, but William was strong enough to put up a nasty fight, and Lester was not sure all the roughhousing necessary to subdue the mother, the girl, and William would be worth the fleeting revenge he would gain.

Lester figured the kid would probably worry himself to death just wondering if he was around. That would have to be revenge enough for the moment. The kid was going to die, probably, anyhow.

Besides, it was daylight, and he had other things to do. He planned to leave this berg forever. It was turning into a bad scene. You didn't have all these people dying and some crazy son of a bitch like the old doctor all doped up and stuff like that without it eventually leaking to the outside world.

Lester couldn't afford to be around when the authorities came busting through that gate. He'd helped to drag in the trooper Max had shot, and he and Paul Daniels had disposed of the car. That, added in with his previous transgressions, would send Lester up for life in Michigan City. He didn't want to spend the next twenty or thirty years in prison.

"Why in God's name did you shoot him?" Warren asked Paul Daniels.

"He was getting away."

"He couldn't get far. All you had to do was pursue him. You and another man could have caught him." Warren turned away from Brian's body. One bullet had exited over his right eye; the other through his stomach. There was a lot of blood.

"I guess I panicked."

"I was going to let him go today. Let him take his son

274

with him and leave, as he had every right to do."

"Wouldn't that breach our security?"

Warren licked his lips. He was feeling the need for a session with the little vial. "Our security doesn't mean anything any more, Paul. My experiment is a failure. I'm going to let everyone go free."

"Where does that leave me?"

"You're free to go too."

"And what about this stiff? How do I know you're not going to turn me into the authorities?"

"You know I won't."

"What about the stiff?"

"I'll—I'll dispose of him. There'll be no evidence."

Paul leaned on Warren's desk, his expression threatening. "There better not be. Remember, I know about the state trooper. Old feeble Max may have pulled the trigger but, in court, your ass would be on the line."

"Are you trying to blackmail me? You want money?" Warren was not upset; he expected this sort of thing from the caliber of men he had hired. He had not researched their backgrounds thoroughly enough, looking only for dependability and loyalty in their psychological profiles. He had overlooked the criminal possibilities inherent in their positions.

"I wouldn't mind some 'severance pay,'" Paul said.

Warren cared little for money now; he wouldn't need that much for the time he had left. "Will twenty-five thousand do?"

"I guess. I'm not a hard guy to get along with."

Warren could see that Paul would no doubt tap him again and again, until he was drained dry, not knowing Warren would not be around much longer.

"You're a very admirable fellow, aren't you?"

"Be sarcastic if you want. I don't want to be around when it hits the fan anyhow."

"What do you mean by that?"

"The feds are going to have you up on so many charges, you'll be serving time the rest of your life. When those women find out what you've *really* done to their children . . ."

"That's none of your concern, Mr. Daniels," Warren replied coldly. "Now, if I were you, I'd leave as soon as possible and cash that check while it's still good."

"I think I'll take that advice."

Paul closed the door. Warren chuckled. He imagined himself in prison. That wouldn't happen. He'd be dead before the case came to court.

One way or another.

Sally admitted herself to the clinic that afternoon, complaining of stabbing pains in her abdomen.

"I'm going into labor," she told the nurse at the front desk. "I'm going to lose the baby!"

The nurse hustled Sally into a treatment room and up onto an examining table, helping her undress, then draping a sheet over her, which immediately slid to the floor.

"Breathe in and out slowly," she said, darting out. She returned momentarily with Warren. He stopped abruptly in the entrance, dumbfounded by the sight of Sally's swollen abdomen and breasts; she was dilating too, as if she really was about to give birth.

Her features were twisted in agony. "Do something! The contractions—are—a minute apart."

Warren brought himself to attention and rushed to her side. He busied himself examining her, checking her heartbeat—which was erratic—and her breathing.

She moaned.

He laid his hand on her abdomen; it seemed to be churning inside, building up pressure as if it might explode.

"Mrs. Henderson, this is just impossible."

"I told you!" she said. "I told you. You wouldn't—" another shriek of agony "—listen to me. Now I'm going—to—have a miscarriage."

"Nurse, get my instruments. Quickly, now!" Warren positioned Sally's feet in the stirrups at the bottom edge of the table. He gave her a shot to ease the pain.

She groaned. The flesh of her abdomen rippled. She

clenched her fists and began pummeling herself.

"Stop that!" Warren shouted. "You'll hurt yourself."

"I can't take it! I'm . . ."

The nurse returned with a tray of instruments.

Sally's uterus contracted; her vagina was at full dilation; something came sliding down through the birth canal, expelled by great effort.

It was a mass of blood. No fetus. No placenta. Nothing more than blood.

The nurse gasped and turned away.

"It's over," Warren said, covering the mass with a towel. "Relax."

"Is it dead?" Sally inquired weakly.

Warren's mind raced for an answer that both would please her and lessen the shock of her having given birth to blood.

"I'm afraid so," he said.

"Was it a boy or a girl?"

"I couldn't tell. It wasn't—it wasn't developed enough."

"I want to see!"

"No, Mrs. Henderson. You don't want to see it. It's a very unpleasant sight. It will only make it harder on you. Please trust my judgment in this . . ."

Sally emitted another piercing scream and another mass of blood was expelled. She let out a deep breath, her legs slumped, her eyes stared at nothing.

"Another casualty," Warren murmured.

The happy candy, anti-growth drugs and tranquilizers were made in a small facility two blocks south of the clinic. Under the name "Natind," a contraction of "National, Indiana," the facility also manufactured a number of generic drugs for export to the outside world, which were another source of income for the community. Included among the generics were many mind-altering medications, not only mild tranquilizers, but strong pain killers, and even stronger tranquilizers. Among these were pills and capsules that would have good street value: uppers, downers, inside-outers. And Lester Stultz had the right contracts—in Chicago, Indianapolis, Detroit—to sell them. It was merely a matter of deciding in which city he would peddle the drugs.

He figured he could steal enough drugs from the facility to let him live in style for a year, maybe two, depending on the current market values.

He parked a patrol car he had decided to steal in back of the facility and let himself in the rear entrance with his pass key. Now he was loading every space in the car with cartons of drugs. He packed the trunk, the back seat, and the passenger side of the front seat with the cartons.

"This stuff is as good as gold," he muttered to himself. "I'll be living like a goddamn king."

When the car would hold no more, Lester got in to drive away. He honked at the gate and Max activated the controls to open it, not paying any attention to who it was in the car.

"Wait, Stultz—take me with you!" Paul yelled.

"Bug off." The gate swung open, Lester put the car in drive.

Paul grabbed onto the window. "I got money from the old man—twenty-five grand—all we have to do is cash the check."

"A goddamn check." Lester accelerated through the gate, with Paul still clinging to the window.

"Let me in, damn it. Stop the car."

"I don't need any partners," Lester said. He brought up his pistol cocked and fired, blowing off the back of Paul's head. His hands clung to the window briefly by reflex, then he dropped off.

Max ran out of the gatehouse, aimed his rifle and fired at Lester's car, missing widely.

Lester merely laughed as he headed towards the open countryside, weaving his way along the snow-covered, twisted roads to freedom.

Around ten o'clock Kevin Hamilton struggled to get

out of bed. He had only pretended to swallow his last two doses of sedative, spitting the pills out after the nurse left.

Now he was alert enough to do what he had been planning for the last few days.

He was going to escape.

Movement was difficult. But by concentrating on his leg muscles, he could force them to propel him along at a halting pace. After a few steps, walking became easier.

There was no real pain. He felt drained and tired, but not much else.

He went to a closet, pried it open with trembling hands, and took out his clothing. He spent fifteen minutes dressing himself, laboriously pulling his jeans up over his legs, twisting his arms into a shirt, forcing his feet into socks and shoes.

He had to go to the bathroom. He trod softly to the facility in his room and closed the door behind him, so no one passing by would hear the noise.

He turned on the light.

Staring back at him from the mirror was the *new* old Kevin, his face mottled with brown spots, his features lined by creases and wrinkles in his skin. He looked like a bad caricature of himself, rendered by a little child.

He looked like a monster-Kevin.

So that's what was happening to him. He was turning into an old man.

He didn't give a damn. He had heard the doctor and the nurses whispering when they thought he was asleep. He had heard them saying all of them were going to die.

So he had determined he would not die in a hospital bed—not when he knew he could move if he put his will power into it. He channeled every ounce of residual meanness into energizing his body, driving it by a locomotive force exceeding adrenaline.

He had a score to settle, and he would not allow himself to die without having evened things up between him and William.

He peed, turned the light off, and left the bathroom. He made his way into the hall, gaining strength and

279

confidence with each step. He rode down on the elevator.

He went out the back way.

Cold wind, accompanied by whirling wisps of snow, stung his skin. He had no jacket or sweater.

He continued to move at a grim pace, heading towards William's house. He could barely see through the snow. His nose started running, and he kept licking his lips. His eyes burned.

His ears began to sting from frostbite. Every minute was an hour of torture. But he had to keep moving even though it hurt.

The thought of getting to William kept him going. If he had to die, he would take William with him. He lost his way momentarily, became disoriented and panicked. He could scarcely see three feet in front of him.

Then, as if guided by an invisible agency, he found himself at William's house.

He trudged towards the door.

The knob was only inches away. Within reach. Now the imperative of getting warm was almost as intense as his hatred for William. He *had* to get inside.

The wind and the snow played tricks with his vision. His hand seemed to extend into infinity. The doorknob receded, as if it had been whisked back.

He was only halfway up the walk.

His hand stretched out, he lost his balance and fell forward into the snow.

He decided to rest a few seconds. All he needed was a little sleep . . . just a little . . . and he could . . .

That night, sitting in a chair in the basement, Warren dozed. He was barely aware of the muffled roar of the crematorium wherein the remains of Brian Wesley and Paul Daniels were being incinerated.

He was hardly aware of anything. He had given himself an extra dose from the vial before coming down.

He heard a rustling noise that gnawed at the edge of his consciousness, intruding on his drug-induced slumber. He shifted in the chair, trying to ignore the sound.

More rustling. Louder now.

Warren's eyes popped open.

Approaching him were Brenda Stowe, Wanda McCoy, Helen Snyder, other women, the state trooper, and Alvin, and other children. They were advancing slowly, dragging their feet. Their eyes were blank with only tiny black dots for pupils, like cartoon eyes. Their faces were yellowish green. Their mouths were frozen in a rictus of agony.

As they passed by the crematorium, the red glow shone through their bodies, illuminating the skeletons beneath.

They gathered around Warren. He was unable to move. They extended their arms towards him. A cold finger touched his face.

They descended on him, pulling at his arms and legs, scratching his torso, jerking things loose.

Warren felt his own hot blood gush into his face.

He awoke. He was alone.

Shivering, he arose and went nearer to the crematorium for its warmth, backing up against it.

In front of him was another table, the one on which lay the covered form of Sally Henderson.

She bolted erect. Her cover fell forward, revealing her dead, slack breasts. Her eyes were blank with tiny dots in them. She climbed down from the table, her blood-stained thighs shining in the semi-darkness.

Warren opened his mouth to scream.

Sally stumbled towards him.

He awoke.

He heard the shuffling of feet.

They came again.

Sondra was among them this time.

Chapter Twenty-Eight

Winter Traumas

The snow was not deep. Less than an inch had accumulated during the night, and much of that was swept into shallow drifts along the roads and sidewalks. The temperature, however, had plunged to well below freezing overnight and remained there most of the following morning.

William awoke abruptly from the chill of being alone. Mandy was no longer in the bed with him, as she had been the last two nights. She had either gone to her own bed, or was already downstairs, possibly fixing breakfast.

He got out of bed, dressed and came down the stairs. Mandy, wearing only a flannel nightgown, was standing in the front door, which was open, staring outside.

"What's going on?" William asked.

Mandy covered her mouth with one hand and pointed towards the front yard with the other.

William joined her and sighted along her arm.

"It's . . ."

". . . Kevin," William finished for her. "I wonder how he got out of the clinic."

"It's awful. Freezing to death, like that. Can't we do something?"

William was inclined to say Kevin deserved his fate, that in fact freezing was too easy a way for him to go, but he knew Mandy had compassion for any living thing, even a thing like Kevin. Instead, he said, "I'll take care of him. You better go get dressed, or you'll freeze yourself."

Mandy faced him; her cheeks were rosy from the cold. "I just had this feeling," she said, "that I should look outside, almost like he was calling to me."

"That's weird."

"It's spooky," she said, her eyes wide. "William, I think something bad has happened. Everywhere. I can feel it inside me. It's not just Kevin. I feel . . ."

"Say it!"

". . . like lots of people are dead. All of a sudden. Like in a plague."

William closed the door gently and pulled her to him. "You're cold. You're imagining things."

"I don't think so."

"Go on and get dressed." He kissed her lightly on the lips. "I'll take care of Kevin. Then we better think of how we're going to take care of ourselves."

She nodded mutely and returned his kiss. "I'm not taking Danny to school today."

"That's fine."

"I'll go get dressed."

She went up the stairs slowly, as if in a trance. Watching her, William felt an awesome cold descend on himself, penetrating to his soul.

He could feel it too—what Mandy had said—something happening in the night: a great passing.

But what did it mean?

He glanced out the door glass at the frozen form of Kevin. He couldn't abide having *that* in the front yard.

He bundled up in a thick coat, put on a muffler, knit cap and heavy gloves, and went outside to drag the corpse away.

He would discover the corpse wasn't ready to leave.

Eddie Burrfield had awakened twice in the night. Each time he struggled in the darkness with the bonds Lester had used to tie him and his mother up, but he couldn't get any slack. After several futile moments, he would fall back asleep.

Now, with the morning sun on his face and the

283

dawning of a new day, he felt he had gained strength and put all his energy into pressing his fists outward against the wire wrapped around them.

Something gave. His hands came free and he brought them around from his back. He looked at the wire, hoping to see a break in them, but was he disappointed. The knot had merely come undone, so he wasn't that strong, after all.

He pulled the adhesive tape from his mouth as slowly as he could, but it still seemed it was ripping his lips off. He yelped a little as the last of the tape peeled off. With his mouth uncovered, he turned around to his mother, who was propped next to him on the couch. The blood around her nose had dried, making her face a contrast of white and reddish-brown.

"Mom, I got myself untied!"

He leaned closer to Georgia. She smelled strange. He shook her. "Mom?"

Georgia's head dropped forward, her dead eyes staring down at nothing.

Eddie started crying.

The second William stepped outside his teeth started chattering. He trudged towards Kevin's inert form, his eyes stinging with cold, then stopped at the point where Kevin's hand stretched out towards the house.

Kevin's flesh was blue-white. Frost had formed on his eyelids and lashes; his nose was pink. He was like a human icicle.

William could still see all those nasty-looking spots on Kevin's face, and he was startled by the gray thinness of his hair. He knew it was Kevin, but he had deteriorated even more than Alvin had the last time William had seen him alive. He was repulsively ancient-looking, worse than a mere corpse.

William squatted down, kneeling closer to the other boy's body, thinking about where he should drag him.

Kevin's left hand shot up, snatched William by the collar and jerked his head down.

"You . . ."

William tried to pull away, but Kevin's grip was like cold-hammered iron.

A noise like churning phlegm issued from Kevin's cracked lips, followed by scarcely intelligible words. ". . . you're going to . . . die . . . too . . . sumbitch. . . ."

His mouth crinkled and became a crooked smile. The eyes no longer moved. The hand clutching William stiffened.

William grabbed Kevin's dead arm and wrenched it from his collar. "Bastard!" He stood erect and kicked Kevin's body hard; his foot felt like it was pounding a rag doll. He kicked it again and again. When he grew tired of kicking his body, he started on his head, driving his foot into the glacial dead face over and over until it was a bloody pulp.

Despite William's savage blows, somehow the death smile remained on Kevin's countenance.

William could endure it no longer. He wrapped his muffler around Kevin's head, tying it in a knot, so he wouldn't have to view Kevin's last laugh as he dragged the body off the walk and into the back yard.

He left Kevin out there, face down. Later, he would figure out a way to dispose of him entirely. At least he wouldn't have to look at him out here.

He returned to the house through the back door.

Mandy was dressed. Danny was standing behind her. They stared at him oddly, and he thought it was because of the way he had treated Kevin's body.

That wasn't it at all.

"Your mom's dead," Mandy said.

Dawn rapped on the front door of Alicia's house. After several minutes, her friend came to the door and let her in out of the cold.

"Is my mom here?" she asked.

"No," Alicia said.

"I wish I knew what happened to her. I think she went to the clinic, but she never came back home. I had to

285

sleep in the house all by myself, except for Shirley. It was scary."

"My mom's gone too," Alicia said. "I looked all over the house for her, and I didn't find her. And my kitty's gone. I can't find anybody."

William regarded his mother's body with great ambivalence. He searched through his feelings for her, seeking the one he might call love, but it just wasn't there. In the last few months, she had not been there for him in any way, and, looking back, he couldn't recall when she had ever been a true mother to him. Her only assertion of maternal feeling was to exert as much control as possible over his actions, and when that proved impossible, she had just given up on him, providing him with nothing but food, shelter and criticism.

William was finding it extremely difficult to cry. He stood by his mother's bed, looking down on her, expecting her perhaps to move, but it was as Mandy said—she had passed with the night.

There were no signs of pain or struggle. Were it not for her open eyes and the dullness of them, she would seem to be merely sleeping. Perhaps she had taken too many drugs.

William realized the cause of her death had no real significance.

He left his mother lying there and closed the door on her room. Forever.

William said nothing when he rejoined Mandy and Danny in the kitchen. His expression confirmed what Mandy had told him.

She handed him a cup of hot cocoa, and he sat down mechanically to drink it. Mandy sat next to him.

There was a long silence among the three children. None of them knew what to say.

Presently, the silence was broken by someone at the

front door.

"I'll get it," Mandy said.

William started to warn her it might be Lester Stultz, but he didn't care. What could Lester do to him that would be any worse than what he already felt inside?

You're going to die too sumbitch.

Kevin had affirmed Stultz' prediction.

That was Kevin's parting gift to William, the worst thing he could do to him—give him the truth only the dead or dying dared to speak.

Mandy came in the kitchen with Alicia on one side of her and Dawn on the other.

"We can't find anybody," Dawn said.

William focused on Dawn. He had been so enmeshed in his own problems and concerns he had almost forgotten the little girl who used to look up to him and let him tease her. Under any other circumstances, he would smile.

"What do you mean?" William asked with concern.

"My mom went to the clinic and didn't come back."

"Where's your mom, Alicia?"

"I don't know. I looked all over the house."

"Did you look outside?"

"No."

"I'll go look for her."

"William," Mandy said, "are you sure?"

"I can't just sit here anymore."

Eddie tried to use the telephone to call the clinic, but the line was dead. He cussed at it and hung it up, then went to his mother's side again.

She still was unmoving.

He knew in his heart she was dead, but he thought maybe somebody at the clinic could fix her. They had shots they could give people there.

He put on his winter coat and left the house, headed to the clinic to seek help for his mother.

*   *   *

287

William circled the Lawson house three times, looking for footprints in the snow that might indicate where Alicia's mother had gone, but any such evidence had been obscured by drifting during the night.

He went inside the house and searched every room, thinking perhaps a little girl like Alicia might have overlooked an obvious place. Myrna Lawson was not anywhere.

Stymied, William returned to his own house and delivered his disappointing report to Alicia and Dawn.

"I'm going to the clinic," William announced. "My dad's probably there, and all the answers are there too. I'm sick of sitting around doing nothing."

"I'm coming too," Mandy said.

"What about the kids?"

"We'll all come. If anything's going to happen, it'll happen to all of us."

For a moment, William considered telling them to stay put, that he needed no help, but he wasn't feeling particularly brave. He needed moral support, and he needed company. There was also a somewhat better chance—a slim one, to be sure—that there was protection in numbers, even if they were all children.

Besides, what if he went there and didn't come back? He'd never see any of them again.

Mandy was right. If anything happened, it should happen to all of them.

Warren hadn't gone home at all. After awakening several times during the night, caught in spectacularly vivid nightmares within more nightmares, he could not bear to be alone. He had gone up to his office and lay on the couch with the door open, hoping the noise of the nurse going up and down the hall occasionally would help keep him sane until daybreak.

Warren finally slept when the sun rose.

He was sleeping when the children came in the front door.

On the way to the clinic, William had spotted a strange man parked by the school. He and the children went to it and found one of his father's business cards on the floor. That's how he had been tracked down to his house.

William cursed bitterly, and they all continued on to the clinic.

Now they stood in the reception area.

It was very quiet.

"Where's the nurse?" Mandy whispered.

"Where's my mom?" Dawn asked.

"Hold on, everybody," William said. "We'll go to the doctor. We'll make *him* tell us what's going on." As they walked down the hall, William thought involuntarily, *You're going to die too sumbitch.*

When they reached the door to Warren's office, William told them to wait outside.

"I want to ask some things too," Mandy said.

"No, you stay out here and watch the kids. If I need you, you'll know it."

"All right," she replied reluctantly.

William pushed the door open all the way, then let it fall almost closed behind him, leaving a crack for Mandy and the others to be able to hear.

Warren stirred on the couch, his movements catching William's eyes.

"Doctor?"

Warren responded from a deep well of unconsciousness. "I'm not here," he said. "I'm not here."

William approached the doctor. His face seemed extremely ugly in repose, even worse than when he was awake. William fought back violent impulses and shook the doctor until he opened his eyes.

William took two steps back.

Warren sat up, bleary-eyed, and seemed unsurprised at William's presence.

"So," he said thickly, as if his tongue were covered with scum, "I see you've come for your shot."

289

"No, I haven't," William answered.

Warren stood, turned on the overhead light and wen to the supply cabinet. William didn't move an inch, bt his eyes followed Warren's every action.

"But you have to have your shot, son. Everyone mu: have a shot." Warren sounded like he was distracted an disoriented.

"I don't want any damn shot."

"What *do* you want?"

"I want to know where my father is and where Dawn' mother is, and everything else."

"Everything else?"

"You know what I mean. I want to know what's goin; to happen to us. Stultz said we were going to die. Kevir said it too, this morning. Well?"

Warren stood still. William backed further away, unti he hit the edge of the desk. He remained there, watchin; as Warren took a hypo and a vial from the cabinet. He stuck the needle in the vial and filled the syringe. William recognized the green fluid with which he had been injected so many times before.

"You ask a lot of questions," Warren stated evenly, "but getting your shot is the most important thing."

"What's in that shot?"

"Vitamins. Isn't that what your mother told you?"

"My mother is dead."

Warren's eyes barely moved. "How . . . ?"

"I don't know. She just died."

Warren shifted his gaze to the window; the glass was covered with frost. "Winter is finally here. Real winter, when the old, the weak, and the tired often decide to die. Did you know that, William?"

"Know what?"

"That old people—especially—die most often at the onset of winter? Because, apparently, they cannot take another season of the unrelenting cold. I think it shows good sense on their part. Suffering is hardest in the winter."

"My mother wasn't old."

"No . . ." Warren faced the boy again. ". . . none of

them was. But they were weak, and bored, and perhaps ready to die. I made them that way. The trauma of winter is daunting to us all."

"You're crazy."

"I probably am by now. Insanity is the body's last defense mechanism before giving up."

"Answer my questions!"

"You need your shot, William. All the children need their medicine. How is our society to succeed if we don't maintain the health of our children—our precious children? Don't you see? A child is always loved. An adult—an adult has to find love, and it isn't the same. Isn't it nicer to be a child, then?"

"No!"

"This may pinch a little." The doctor held the needle ready, approaching the boy.

But William was determined not to take any more shots. He waited until the doctor was just about to prick his skin with the hypodermic and snatched it from his hand.

He jammed it into the doctor's shoulder, hitting bone, then drove the plunger home with his fist.

Warren screamed and fell back, clutching at the protruding syringe as he stumbled around the room in agony. He finally slumped to the floor, his features contorting as his body shuddered. He closed his eyes, almost losing consciousness.

William saw something gleaming on a tray in the cabinet the doctor had left open. He went over and picked up the shiny thing, the scalpel.

He knelt by the doctor, intense hatred for the man twisting his features into a scowl. He placed the edge of the scalpel at Warren's throat.

Warren's eyes opened as the cold steel grazed his skin. "I thought you were a nightmare . . ."

"Where's my father?"

"Dead."

"Where's Dawn's mother?"

"Dead."

"What's going to happen to us?"

291

"I'm sorry about your father—it was a mistake . . ."

"What's going to happen to *us?*" William repeated, pressing the scalpel's edge down, piercing the skin of Warren's throat. A single drop of scarlet rode the edge of the blade briefly, then slid down over William's thumb.

"I did it all for your own good. For the good of the people. I didn't mean for anyone to die . . ."

"Are we going to die?"

Warren's lips trembled, but no words came forth.

"Answer me!"

You're going to die too sumbitch. For a moment it seemed Warren's face had become Kevin's—with that same frozen nasty smile on it as he had died.

William jammed the scalpel into the doctor's throat.

"You have to keep taking your shots . . ." Warren gurgled. Blood trickled from the corner of his mouth. More blood splashed down his chest, leaking on William's arm.

He never thought there would be so much blood. He threw the scalpel down and stood back, not really accepting what he had done. He'd never realized killing would be so easy.

"William!"

Mandy and the others were standing in the door. Eddie Burrfield came up behind them and pushed his way through.

"Look at that," the boy said, "you killed the doctor!"

Dawn had been crying for several minutes.

"We heard everything," Mandy explained. "I'm sorry about your father."

"You better be sorry for us all."

"But the doctor never said . . ."

"He didn't have to. Eddie, what are you doing here?"

"I came for help. My mom won't move."

"Another one," Mandy whispered.

William bent down and patted Dawn on the back. "Don't worry. We'll take care of you."

"All I have is Shirley now." She held the one-eyed doll

292

o. "Shirley won't die, because she's a pirate."

"No, you have us too," William said with tenderness.
We're your new family."

"What are we going to do, William?" Mandy asked
gently.

"We're going upstairs. I want you to see what's up
here."

"What good will it do?"

"Maybe we can free them, or help them or something.
The doctor's been out of his mind for days. We don't
now what's going on. They may be dying."

William returned to the doctor's office. By now the
doctor's blood had stopped flowing so copiously. William
almost vomited, but swallowed it back, as he searched
Warren for his keys. He found a keyring in the dead
man's pocket on which about thirty or so keys were
attached.

He came back into the hall.

"I got his keys. Now we can go anywhere we want."

They went to the elevator first. William fiddled with
the keys for several minutes, trying to find the one that
fit the locked access button to the fourth floor. When he
found the right key, he inserted and turned it. The
elevator doors shut and the car ascended to the fourth
floor.

They all got off.

"This place is scary," Dawn said. "Is my mom up
here?"

"No," William said. "She's gone." He remembered
the crematorium. He thought he had detected traces of
its odor in the morning air but wasn't sure. Maybe he
ought to be looking around down there too.

They approached the nurse's station.

William looked over the counter and saw the prone
body of Sheila Pate. Her mouth was agape, her eyes
unmoving. Shifting his line of vision away from her, he
scanned the monitoring equipment. There were several
red lights on, each indicating a room.

"We're too late," William said, "I think."

They went from one room to another, hanging

together as a group, finding one corpse after anothe
After a few minutes, Mandy started crying.

"They all . . . look . . . so . . . old," she stammere
between sobs. "Why, William? Why did they die?"

"Winter," he said, recalling the doctor's words. "The
died because they couldn't go on."

Mandy gradually gained control of herself. The smalle
children were clinging to her, looking up for guidance

"Why are you crying, Mandy?" Dawn asked.

"I can't help it. A lot of innocent children—an
adults—have died. It makes me feel bad."

"I feel bad too," Dawn admitted. "I feel bad fo
everybody."

A tear streamed down William's cheek too as he stare
at a shrivelled little girl in the nearest room. "There," h
said to himself, "is our future."

They could do nothing for anyone on the fourth floor,
so the children went to the third and second floors. No
one occupied any of those rooms, not even a flu patient.

The first floor was still tenanted only by the body of
the doctor.

An eerie malaise was descending on William's
perception of things. He viewed himself in a nightmare
that was becoming more prolonged as he continued, as if
it could never end.

But everything was too real. Beyond real. Traumati-
cally surreal.

He had Mandy watch over the others, while he went to
search the basement. Perhaps he would find answers
there. Mandy didn't want him to go alone.

"I don't think the little kids should see what I might
find down there," he whispered to Mandy.

"You won't have us to help—if you need it."

"I've been down there before. I know how to get out.
Give me half an hour. If I don't come back, then come
looking for me."

"All right."

William suddenly realized he had naturally assumed a

aternal role in the new family that had formed only that
morning. Mandy was the mother. The responsibility was
awesome, yet somehow fulfilling. Maybe, William
reflected, he was meant to be a leader. Maybe that's why
he seemed to know what to do next with each situation—
instinctively, without pausing to think much about it.

This was a hell of a time to find out he had such sterling
qualities. For all he knew, he and the other children were
all that remained alive. What could a mere handful of
children do, after all?

He might be a leader, but his troops were a little
ragged.

He entered the elevator and rode down to the
basement. When the doors slid open he was struck by the
overwhelming smell of charred flesh; he was right, the
crematorium had been in operation.

That goddamn doctor had burned his father!

He took a step down the corridor that led to the
furnace that consumed bodies and a creepy thought
entered his mind. What if Lester was down here, waiting?

It was a good place to hide.

He should have thought to bring a weapon with him. A
scalpel, or anything else.

He didn't encounter Lester.

But he found Lester's stash. It was inside a room the
door to which had been left open by somebody. William
peeked in and saw somebody on the floor—another
nurse, the one usually at the front desk. An empty
syringe hung out of her arm. Nearby lay an empty,
unmarked vial. William could only guess what might
have been in it.

He wondered why she would have chosen to kill
herself that way. Or had she overdosed on something
without realizing it? Whatever it was, it had been potent.

William stepped over her and surveyed the contents of
the room, which held rows of shelves of contraband:
cartons of cigarettes, bottles of liquor, stacks of new
comic books and men's magazines, x-rated videos, x-rated
cartoon books, and just about everything else that could
not be obtained "legally" in Jamay Lake.

Lester must have had many customers, and he was operating right under the doctor's office!

William was tempted to go through the banned goods but he didn't have the time. Maybe later, he thought.

He continued towards the crematorium. A few feet from its door, he found the table on which Sally Henderson still lay. A pool of blood had coagulated between her legs.

William had already seen a lot that day, but this was too much. He turned and emptied his stomach, heaving up half of his dinner from the night before.

Maybe Sally's corpse had driven the nurse to take the drugs. Or, looking past Sally, maybe it was the man's blackened foot hanging from the door of the crematorium.

William rushed back to the elevator.

Harold Thomas and Max Karp were the only two patrolmen in their quarters that morning when they awakened. They both knew what had happened to Paul Daniels and Lester Stultz, but the absence of the other three men was a mystery.

"They ran out," Max remarked gruffly as he mixed himself a cup of instant coffee. "All of them, like rats."

"Why?" Harold asked.

"I overheard them. They thought I was asleep, but I wasn't. They were spooked by what happened to Paul—and everything else that's going on in this goddamned place."

"That means there's no one out there to protect the town, and the gate is unguarded."

"Hell, boy, are you as dumb as you sound? There ain't that much left to protect. Why do you think the other guys left? They could see the handwriting on the wall. Deserters, that's what they are. Ought to be tracked down and shot." He gulped half his coffee down and shuddered, his face contracting in a grimace. "Worst damn coffee I ever tasted."

"What are you going to do?"

296

"I'm a soldier; I do what I'm told. I'm not a chickenhearted deserter."

"I'm going outside to see what's going on."

"I'll be out at the gate directly." Max squinted at Harold with scorn. "If I see *you* trying to leave, I'll shoot your ass."

Harold noted the warning with a nod and exited. he had no intention of deserting Jamay Lake—not yet, anyhow.

As he walked down the first floor towards Mandy, William took an abrupt detour into the doctor's office. He had all the keys now; he could get into the files.

He avoided looking at Warren's body and searched through the keys until he found the one that opened the metal file cabinet. He went through every drawer, until he found a section marked, "Special Cases."

He grabbed a couple of files at random, then flicked through the rest until he discovered those of Alvin and Kevin. He kicked the file drawer shut, pivoted and returned to the hall.

Now, he had something to study. He would find the answers he sought on his own.

"What did you find, William?" Mandy asked when he had rejoined her and the children. "I was worried about you."

William's face was pale. "I'll tell you later. I don't want to talk about it in front of the little kids."

"What are those files for?"

"I hope they have some answers. I have to know what's going to happen to us—for sure."

"Do you really need to know? Wouldn't it be better to just live as well as we can, until we're rescued?"

"If ever."

Mandy tried to look hopeful, but she herself had discovered yet another problem. "Did you know none of the phones works? I tried to call the patrol men, but all I got was static."

"It doesn't surprise me. Nothing will surprise me for

the rest of my life after what I've seen."

"You know, you shouldn't have killed the doctor."

"I couldn't help myself. I just hated him so much—it was like that was killing him, not me."

"I think I understand."

"Didn't you hate him?"

"I don't know. Maybe I should, but then I think what good is that going to do for us? We need help—from the outside world. There must be a place somewhere that has a way to get messages to some nearby city. They had to communicate—to get supplies, for one thing."

"There's probably enough food in the store to keep us going for a while," William said. "Since there's not so many of us."

"Then what?"

"I don't know. Let's just go home. Everybody's probably getting hungry. We'll figure it all out later."

The children went to the front door. William glanced outside. It was afternoon now, and the sun was shining brightly. The snow was melting in the street.

They stepped out and started heading east.

Coming towards them were all the other children. There were no mothers among them, and some of them were carrying babies.

Chapter Twenty-Nine

Voices

Part One, The Dead:

Alvin:
I hear something like people talking. They're not mad or anything, just talking.

I don't hurt any more. I'm not cold, either.

I'm in a dark place at first, then I see a light that's far away, so I walk that way, to the light. The light is closer than I think.

There's a nice lady waiting there for me. She looks like Sheila, my nurse. She takes me to another place, where everything is green.

My kitten's there.

Mom's there. So are some of the kids I know.

Best of all, I'm not a gnome any more.

Sally Henderson:
I'm alone right now. Except for the baby I had. It must have been stillborn.

I worry about Dawn. I guess someone will take care of her. She's a loving child. I never had the chance to give her the love she deserved, but she loved me anyhow. Anyone would want to love her.

I miss her. I even miss her silly little one-eyed doll. I miss other people too.

I miss life.

My new baby is a boy. I press him to my breast and nurse him and I feel renewed. I wonder if he will grow up here.

There's a delightful melody in the air.

Helen Snyder:
Because of disgust for myself I have been cast into limbo.

Because of disgust for myself I have no moorings here. I drift in a meaningless sea of nothingness, like in a vacuum.

Amanda, my darling daughter—she was the mother in the family and I let her be, because I no longer possessed the strength of character, because I allowed the trivial concerns of sex to distract me from living a full life with my daughter.

She will care for people and fall in love and I will never see any of it, and then she will grow old before her time, from too much loving and caring as sometimes happens to people whose innate nature is to love.

Because of disgust for myself, I will accept this fate, this nothingness.

Even if I'm given another chance.

Warren Barry:
All the endless sorrow, all the guilt, the self-recrimination, all the soul-rending does not end. With the end, these sins are only the beginning. I suppose there's a cosmic sense of judgment at work here, in this continued sense of self-blame.

It will never end.

Never.

When you make your choices, you must choose well. You have to realize that everything you do *is* your choice, that no one else, ultimately—no matter how much you may wish to fool yourself otherwise—made your choices.

I chose to play God on a small scale. Perhaps that is an

insane notion. Insanity is a defense mechanism, but when you scrutinize your own inner being, you discover you are not really insane, but only hiding from the real world in a fanciful ideal that insanity is an excuse for anything.

We are taught from the beginning that we are responsible for our actions, but we never really accept that idea. Because we are also taught that we can always find someone else to blame for our transgressions.

These truths are embedded in the very structure of our earthly society, yet we choose to ignore them. We say we are insane, that we are religious, that we are leaders of the people—anything to justify our self-chosen actions.

The choice now is to determine how much suffering I will endure. Yes, *I* must choose that as well. I have to look into my own soul and ask, what measure of suffering will equal that which I have inflicted on others?

Thus, I suspect I will be alone for a long time, and time here bears as heavily on the soul as it does in life.

There is no turning back. How absurd that we should ever think there is!

Now I dwell in the winter of my own soul, cold forever, because I did not recognize the warmth of human feeling as I should have.

Winter is daunting to us all.

Kevin:
William!
William, I'm waiting.
You're going to die too, sumbitch!

Part Two, The Living:

Alicia:
We hunted and hunted and never found Mom anywhere. The only grown-up we found was the doctor. He was in the clinic, of course, where he usually is.

301

William asked the doctor some questions and found out some people were dead. Like William's father. And Dawn's mom. I feel real sorry for Dawn. Now I have to be her sister.

William got real mad at the doctor and stuck some kind of knife in him. I wasn't supposed to see that, but I did. When people get a knife in them in real life, a lot of blood comes out. It can make you sick to see it. I closed my eyes.

The doctor died. Now there are no grown-ups at all, and we found the other kids.

William and Mandy are going to take care of us.

Mecca:

This morning I woke up and my mama was talking to herself about the evil of "forncashun." I could hear her, because it was more like yelling than talking.

She was in the bathroom. I opened the door, and she was in the tub. The water was real hot, because I could see the steam. It was making Mama sweat.

Most of the time, when I come in the bathroom and Mama's in the tub, she lets me get in with her. Unless she feels funny about me seeing her titties. Then she covers them up and makes me go away. I thought that was what she was going to do, because she looked at me, and said, "Shoo."

I didn't want to go away, because I could tell Mama was sick or something because of the look on her face.

I asked her what she was doing, and she said, she was punishing herself for fornicating with a bad man. She said that I should go next door and live with that family because she wasn't going to be my mama any more. She said she wasn't good enough to be my mama, so I needed to be with better people.

I started crying and said she was the best Mama, and I didn't care about forncashun, because I don't even know what it is, so it doesn't matter.

I got closer to the tub so I could tell Mama I wanted her

302

to be my mama and nobody else.

The water in the tub was all red, and the red stuff was coming from Mama's arms where she cut herself. She kept her arms in the hot water.

She closed her eyes and started going down in the water.

"I love you, Mecca," she said.

Her head went under the water and bubbles came out and I tried to pull her out, but I wasn't strong enough.

So I did like she said and took my new doll Tammy with me and went next door.

They didn't have any mama over there, either.

Eddie:

This day has been gross. First, I get loose from where that Lester guy tied me up, and I go to untie Mom, and she's acting like she's dead.

Later, I find out she *is* dead. But I didn't know that yet, so I went down to the clinic because the phones didn't work to see if maybe they could give Mom a shot to fix her up.

When I got to the clinic, I saw William cut the doctor's throat with a little knife.

Pretty gross.

That's not all.

We found out there were lots of dead moms and dead kittens and puppies and even some dead babies. Dead babies are gross. So are dead puppies.

I don't care about kittens that much.

Just about everybody is dead, except for us, I guess. I keep thinking I might wake up and be dead myself.

That'd be kind of gross too.

Mandy:

William is, as always, very intense. I don't think he even realizes how wrought-up he is about everything. He's not intense about the same things, though. He's changed a lot in the last couple of days.

I haven't written any stories in my notebook in a long time. Ever since I met William and we became friends—I guess more than friends now—it's like I don't have to write the stories.

The stories were about how Jamay Lake is a town of robots. Now the robots are gone. Overnight. Maybe I should write a story about that.

I don't think William understood what the doctor meant by the winter. But I do. Winter is the hardest time of year, and it was something the robot mothers could not face, and it all came to a head, somehow, last night, as if the mothers' minds or souls were all connected and their deaths were a chain reaction.

Some of the women, such as the nurse on the fourth floor of the clinic, seemed to have died of shock—if I understand that correctly. The doctor would call it trauma. I don't know what happened last night to make all the children in the clinic die at once—unless it was because they were not children any longer and winter was too much for them to bear as well. Maybe I could talk to William about that, but I'm not sure it matters. We have ourselves to worry about now.

I was shocked, of course, when William killed the doctor, but I also felt his rage and knew he was not guiding his own hand so much as all the hatred in him and in the rest of us was. How could we be blamed for our hatred considering what the doctor has done to us?

After William came up from the basement was the worst moment in my life, even worse than when I learned mother had died. His face was like that of a person who had brushed with death. He still won't tell me everything he saw down there. Whatever it was confirmed something hideous for William which he won't share with anyone, not even me.

William is carrying all the burden for us—not just me—but the other children as well. He has become very careful all of a sudden, and very protective, and I feel such a warmth towards him because of that.

It's not just sex, either. That was just something we

id, and it is something we will do again, but I don't think
t means that much by itself to either of us. It's part of us
eing together now, just as eating and sleeping together
re.

All that means anything now is being together until
ome part of this world, this way of living, is resolved.

We live for the moment.

Dawn:

Shirley has seen some bad things. It's a good thing
she's a pirate or she would get sick and throw up. She saw
William kill a man, but I had to tell her the man was a bad
doctor, who was going to give William a shot, and shots
hurt.

I know, because when I showed Mom my boobies, she
made me get a shot. A nurse came to the house and gave it
to me. She said I was too young to get boobies. The shot
didn't make them go away, though, and now they kind of
hurt. I guess they will stop hurting some day.

Shirley understands now why William had to kill the
doctor. She says pirates have to kill a lot of bad people.
Sometimes they cut their heads off with their swords. Or
make them walk the plank. That's a big board on a pirate
ship—and they tie your hands together and make you
walk off the end and a shark gets you.

Shirley made lots of bad people walk off the plank.

Shirley heard that Mom died and she cried so much it
made me cry too. Shirley liked Mom, even though Mom
didn't like to look at her because she's only got one eye.

I liked Mom a lot too, even when she used to act funny
at night, and when she got fat with a baby in her belly and
even when she yelled at me. Moms do things like that, but
that doesn't mean they're bad moms. The bad moms hit
you real hard.

I don't know what happened to the baby in her belly. I
guess the doctor hid it or maybe it died too. I don't
know if it was a little boy or a little girl.

Now, Alicia—who lost her mom—and me get to live
with William and Mandy and we pretend it's like a family.

Shirley likes that idea.

Pirates know what's best.

William:

Like the mothers say, "You're too smart for your ow
good."

I have finally reached that plateau. Before, when
only suspected the Big Secret, I didn't have to worry
because I didn't know. I could always tell myself thi
person or that person was lying or didn't know what he o
she was talking about. Or that they were trying to fool m
or mess with my mind in some way. I could hope the Big
Secret was a Big Lie that would go away.

It didn't go away.

Now I know just about everything.

I gained my knowledge of exercising my hatred, by
killing an old man who was probably already dying.
should feel sorry, I guess, but I cannot find it in myself to
feel anything for the doctor except hatred.

Even now, long after what I did, the hatred simmers in
me, just below the surface. I keep it in check by making
myself busy, by being close with Mandy, by helping the
other children. I have to be their leader.

I suspect what we are doing is pretty much useless, but
it's better than sitting around waiting to die. If it wasn't
winter, we might attempt to find the nearest city, but,
even then, what could be done? We would be separated
and put in foster homes and probably never see each
other again, and we would have to suffer the effects of the
Big Secret without help from people we know and love. It
would be especially hard without Mandy.

The Big Secret is not something that can be changed.

The doctor didn't really say exactly what would
happen to us, but I could read it in his eyes.

What I saw on the fourth floor and in the basement
made me realize the truth was almost certainly as I
thought.

Then I read the medical files.

And I *knew*.

Chapter Thirty

You Are Old, Father William ...

Lester Stultz had arrived in Indianapolis in the middle of the night. He parked his car in the far corner of the lot at a Lee's Inn just off Interstate 65 and locked all four doors.

He took a single room and paid cash up front. He signed the register with a phony name, got his key and went back out to the car to unload all the cartons of drugs that were visible from the windows.

The next day, he planned to make a few phone calls. By this time tomorrow, he would possibly have several thousand dollars in his hands. Then he could set out for points west, far away from Jamay Lake, where he could buy a new identity and start a different life.

He envisioned himself driving up Sunset Strip in an Excalibur, jewel-festooned whores at his side, while he made the scene big time.

The West Coast was just the place for a man with his talents and ambitions.

William laid the last folder aside. After reading the doctor's reports on Alvin, Kevin, and the other children who had occupied the fourth floor, he realized what his fate probably was—what the probable fate of every child left was.

He was angry.

He had been cheated of life. Cheated of childhood too,

for what he had endured was a forced, unnatural childhood that had provided little joy.

All he had left was the present moment, and the few precious instants he might enjoy with Mandy and the other children.

They looked to him even now for decisions. They couldn't all stay in his house. It was way too small. The clinic was too scary, and no one wanted to stay in the school.

He came down from his room and announced to Mandy they were all going to take up residence in the Nameless Church. It had the room they needed, there was a kitchen in the basement, and beds could be brought in. They would stay there until word could be gotten to the outside world.

Or they would remain until they died, William added mentally.

Harold did not get much further than the clinic. When he found the doctor's body there, he began to search the rest of the building and encountered the numerous other corpses. He tried to call Max at the sentry station and discovered the phones were down. He would have to tell him in person what he had found.

Yet something told him not to go to Max just yet.

He went back to his quarters, taking the one remaining car, and started cruising the streets, rolling along slowly as snow crunched under his tires.

Within the next half hour, he found the bodies of several women, a boy whose face had been badly pulped, a frozen infant, and several dead kittens and puppies. It was almost dark by the time he finished cataloguing the dead.

He wondered where the other children were. It was as if they had become invisible, or had disappeared.

By nightfall, William and the new order of Jamay Lake, the order of the children, had settled into the Name-

ss Church. One of the first things they did was to rip
p a section of pews for their makeshift dormitory
hich consisted of mattresses and basinettes for the in-
ants.

William would sleep with Mandy in what had been the
octor's office.

The children were energetic and had made good prog-
ess carrying things to the church, especially as the sun
rought the temperature up over 35° and the danger
f slipping and falling on ice was minimized.

The children were also good at taking care of each
ther. The eight-to-ten-year-olds fed the babies and
hanged them. The younger children were occupied
vith games. Dawn was telling a group of children
anciful pirate stories.

Mandy made a big supper for them, helped by
Alicia and her brother Danny. They had chicken and
mashed potatoes and a giant pot of mixed vegetables,
all of which had been found in the church's pantry.
With the food there and the food that was in the
general store, clinic and school cafeteria, they could
hold out for quite some time.

Later that evening, the smaller children played together, while William and Mandy rested in the office
that had been converted to their general headquarters
and bedroom. They lay together on a large mattress.

"What did you find out?" Mandy asked.

Her face was drawn, she was sweaty and tired, but
her presence still made William feel stronger somehow.

"About what?" he said, rolling over on his stomach.

"The files you took. I know you've read them."

"You don't want to know," he said simply, "and
neither do I."

By ten o'clock, Harold and Max had collected most
of the bodies they had discovered, and had stacked
them in the clinic. They had covered two-thirds of
the town before tiring out. Harold had become ex-

hausted before Max, even though the older man was hampered by a bad leg and a worse disposition. They agreed they'd find the rest of the bodies tomorrow when the sun was out. Then they'd hit the church, and the houses in the last third of the town. There had to be more of them, living or dead.

Now, they were discussing their next move. Max was telling Harold that the right thing, the soldierly thing to do, was to cremate the bodies.

Harold could hardly believe what Max was proposing. "But why?"

"Are you thick in the head? They're evidence. We got to get rid of them to save the town."

"I don't follow you."

"These corpses—you get a bunch of doctors looking them over—they'll find *us* to blame, somehow. I been to 'Nam, and I know how the system works. Whoever's in the driver's seat when the smoke clears is *it*."

Harold stared at an infant who had frozen to death. He'd wrapped it up himself.

"It was the doctor, not us . . . and he's dead. Someone murdered him."

"You want to be blamed for that murder?"

"Of course, but I'm not up to burning bodies, either. I knew all these people. So did you. Burning them would be like Auschwitz or . . ."

"We burned them in 'Nam. Stacks of them. Like logs."

"This isn't Vietnam."

Max's features contracted into a fierce grimace. "Goddamn it to hell. I'm giving you an order. You and me are carting these stiffs downstairs and burning them." His eyes glistened with madness.

"You can't give me orders," Harold said. "I've had it. I'm getting out of here. That's the sensible thing to do. I'll get to the nearest phone and call the State Police. . . ."

Max unholstered his Smith & Wesson .357 Magnum, pulling it up quickly and smoothly, as if he were a

310

"We was both working as rent-a-cops for this place up around Fort Wayne. It's like a—you won't believe it—it's run by this crazy old doctor, and the other guy—Max is the name—he popped your boy because he didn't have a gate pass."

"Why would he need a gate pass?"

"To get in the place. It's like a concentration camp or something—worse. All the kids got a disease. The doctor gives them shots . . ." Lester stopped. All the explanation in the world wouldn't convince a normal person that such a place as Jamay Lake existed.

"So Max killed Dietrich?" Castle asked.

"The doctor as much as gave him the orders, though."

"What happened to Dietrich's body?"

"They burned it. They burned all the bodies."

"Bodies?"

"Lots of people dying up there. Women and kids too. The doc cremates them."

"What do you think, Rick?" the trooper said to the detective.

"To tell the truth, Mort, I think old Lester's been taking some of his own dope."

"It's the truth, goddamn it. I can prove it all."

"How would you do that?" Castle asked pointedly.

"I'll take you there. It's way out in the middle of nowhere . . . but I can help you find it, and you'll see it, all right. You'll see the craziest place you ever seen."

The two officers left Stultz alone in the room. After an hour or so of deliberation, they returned.

They agreed to let Lester show them the way to Jamay Lake.

In the morning, William was up before Mandy. He was outside the church, burning the medical files he had read in an old oil drum. If Mandy saw them, she'd figure it out even quicker than he did. There was no use in them both having to know.

As he watched the flames spill over the edge of the

313

drum, he felt as if he were also being consumed by the fire. It reminded him how Lester had threatened to put him in the crematorium.

Maybe it would have been a merciful way to go.

What would they do today? he wondered. Look for the bodies of other women and children? Play games all day?

What could they do? How long would they last? How would they care for the children when they started showing symptoms of the disease?

William didn't have all the answers. No one did. The rest of their lives would be unpredictable.

Shivering, William returned to the church. As he entered, the children were stirring about, and he sniffed the aroma of eggs, sausage and biscuits coming from the basement kitchen. He realized he was very hungry.

They ate breakfast, sitting as they had the night before in the remaining pews. The little kids joked and played games, except for Dawn, who sat next to William and Mandy, her doll Shirley propped up next to her.

While they were eating, Dawn tugged at Mandy's sleeve and said, "Shirley has a question."

"All right," Mandy replied. "What does Shirley want to know?"

"She wants to know if we're still 'special.'"

Mandy patted Dawn's hand. "Yes. You're more special than ever. We're all special."

"Shirley too?"

"Of course."

William was listening and he realized that they were, indeed, special—as they had never been before. The idea of it made William want to address the children, to tell them that things were okay and they needed to stay together, so they wouldn't wander off or become too unruly. He also had to affirm he was their leader. Not only to them, but to himself as well.

After the group finished with breakfast, William ascended to the pulpit as if he were the minister.

He felt very out-of-place, yet the leader that he had

314

found within himself yearned to speak to them, to show them he was strong.

"We are all alone here, now," he began. "Jamay is our town. Something terrible happened to our mothers, and the doctor, and we've been abandoned by everyone else. We have plenty of food, though, so we can survive a long time. For now, all we can do is wait and hope someone will come along and find us."

The children started whispering among themselves—about silly things like puppies, kittens, and dolls, and how they could play all day, and how no one would tell them what to do or what not to do, and what it was going to be like to be all on their own. Someone giggled; someone threw a wadded-up napkin. Only Dawn, of the little children, was paying attention. She was holding Shirley up to listen as well.

William was about to reprimand them, when he realized how absurd it was to chastise them for acting their ages. They were children, after all, not his troops, not his congregation. They were his family and they asked nothing more from him than care and love. He could provide those things to them—with Mandy's help.

He managed a thin smile. He couldn't expect them to take his posturing as a public speaker very seriously. As long as their stomachs were full and no one was chiding them, they would be happy.

Even if they missed their mothers and their friends and the other people who used to be part of their lives.

Yet William felt compelled to leave them with a message, something vital and important, even if they didn't listen that hard.

But the only vital and important thing he knew was that their happiness at being "free" would be cut short.

William held out his hand, waving it to get their attention, not entirely certain what he wished to say, except that they had more work to do, but after that,

315

there would be plenty of extra time for play and . . .

Whatever great statement William intended to make, it never left his lips.

His eyes had focused on the skin of his outstretched arm. It was dotted with tiny brown flecks.

Epilogue

Troopers In Never-Never Land

There are many ways to look at a town, each way revealing something different according to the observer.

The act of observation, as it has been established in every imagination of every thinking being, alters what is being observed. Observation is influenced by the personality of the observer, and that often determines whether a thing exists *per se*, or is only the product of the imagination.

That is, it can affect whether the thing observed exists at all.

As two Indiana State Police vehicles completed the tortured drive to the place where Lester Stultz said Jamay Lake was, it did, in fact, seem to exist—after a fashion—as yet unperceived.

There was a wall. There was, as Lester had described, a gate, though there was no sentry guarding it. The gate was open.

The two cars drove through the gates and parked. Four state troopers emerged, one of them pulling Lester out of the car, his hands still cuffed.

The subatomic particles of which it may be supposed Jamay Lake existed danced, awaiting recognition by the troopers so that they might come into existence by being observed.

Skepticism lurked in the hearts of the troopers.

This, they said, was a deserted military academy, nothing more. It belonged to no one.

317

Lester pointed out the clinic where he said all th
evidence was.

Of course there would be a clinic, Sergeant Castl
remarked, or a health center. Every school campus ha
one. It proved nothing.

Lester asked them to enter the clinic. After all, his lif
was at stake here.

The troopers entered reluctantly, stomping snow of
their boots in the reception area.

The subatomic particles shifted warily, screaming to
be observed.

Sergeant Castle dispatched two troopers to search the
clinic. They returned in a few moments. They found
nothing, they said, except evidence of a facility that had
long fallen into disuse. The two troopers were then
ordered to search the rest of the town.

Lester felt a part of reality starting to recede, retreating
into the corners of his mind. He was trying very hard to
see what he had seen before, to re-create the reality, but it
was dimming on him with every second. His faith,
apparently, was not strong enough, and the troopers were
not doing anything to buttress that faith.

He remembered the basement.

Starting to feel they had been run on a fruitless chase
and becoming irritable, the troopers nevertheless agreed
to search the basement, taking Lester with them.

The subatomic particles, formerly vying for attention,
started to flicker. Lester could feel them dying, even
though he had no idea what they were.

In the basement, after they were directed to the
crematorium, or what Lester identified as the crematorium, the troopers grew very impatient indeed.

This was a very ordinary furnace, not an oven for
cremating bodies.

Lester told them to open the door.

Inside was a half-burnt body.

Lester began to feel more confident regarding his
version of reality. So it was an ordinary furnace, was it?
Then why was there a body in there?

Sergeant Castle peered into the firebox, remarking

318

that the body was not wholly consumed. As he aimed his flashlight at the partial corpse, he illuminated a fused chunk of metal on its chest that could be a badge. He also saw remnants of cloth clinging to the blackened flesh. A lab analysis, he speculated, would identify that as the uniform of officer Dietrich. Dental records would confirm his identity.

Sergeant Castle marvelled at Lester's stupidity. why had he made up such an outlandish story? Why not admit the truth—that he had murdered the officer—perhaps to avoid being taken in for an old warrant—and had tried to dispose of the body?

Why this elaborate, stupid, meaningless charade?

Lester denied he had killed the officer. Everything he had said before was true. Wait until the others get back, he said. You'll see. They'll tell you about the kids, and that'll prove I'm not making this all up.

The two troopers exchanged skeptical glances. Was Lester trying to build up a case for insanity? Did he think this myth would save him from the supreme penalty he deserved?

Apparently so.

Lester hung on to his story, with almost admiral tenacity and not a little desperation, as the troopers took him back upstairs and out of the clinic.

They waited a few minutes for the other men to return.

They had found no signs of life, they reported. Only empty houses, and a burned-out church.

So your story was a big fairy tale, Sergeant Castle said. What did you hope to gain?

The sub-atomic particles whisked away, spinning into the nothingness from which they had come. No one would observe them.

Lester bowed his head. He had been beaten somehow, by some agency he didn't know existed, by some fluke of the machineries of the universe. He had been bested by something no one could expect to conquer.

Crestfallen, Lester fell silent. The troopers loaded him back into the first car and drove back through the gate.

Before the second car left, one of the troopers spied

something a few yards away on the street. He asked his partner to wait a minute.

He walked down the center of the street and bent over to pick up the object he had seen.

Brushing off the snow, he saw it was a doll for a small child. It bore a patch over one eye and was slightly scorched.

The trooper held the doll a few seconds, thinking maybe its meaning might somehow become apparent.

The trooper in the car yelled at him to hurry up.

He dropped the doll on the street and joined his partner. They drove away, hurrying to catch up with the other vehicle so they would not get lost in this uncharted area of the state.

The great question, of course—whether the universe has already been created or is continuing to be created, from nanosecond to nanosecond, by the people who live in it and reshape it with their constantly-shifting perceptions as to what the universe should or should not be—was not resolved that day.

Or perhaps it was resolved once and for all. It's all in the way you look at things.

The troll standing on a hill half a mile away, who had reached the summit only by great effort, dragging his bad leg like a dead weight, looked out over the vastness of the Indiana countryside and wondered what the troopers had been doing down there.

He blinked, and the old military academy blurred in his vision momentarily.

He turned around quickly and hobbled south where he knew there was a city. He dared not look back.

If he did, he knew Jamay Lake would no longer be there.